KISS AT MIDNIGHT

A Town Called
Forgotten

BOOKS BY RACHEL BRANTON

Lily's House Series
House Without Lies
Tell Me No Lies
Hearts Never Lie
Your Eyes Don't Lie
Broken Lies
No Secrets or Lies
Cowboys Can't Lie

Finding Home Series
Take Me Home
All That I Love
Then I Found You

A Town Called Forgotten
Kiss at Midnight
This Feeling for You
Reason to Breathe
Everything About You
Never Letting Go

Other
How Far
Royal Quest

Picture Books
I Don't Want To Eat Bugs
I Don't Want to Have Hot
    Toes

UNDER THE NAME TEYLA BRANTON

Unbounded Series
The Change
The Cure
Protectors
    Ava's Revenge
    Mortal Brother
    Set Ablaze
The Escape
The Reckoning
Lethal Engagement
The Takeover
The Avowed

Other
Times Nine

Imprints Series
First Touch (prequel)
Touch of Rain
On The Hunt
Upstaged
Under Fire
Blinded
Street Smart
Hidden Intent
Checked In

Colony Six Series
Insight (prequel)
Sketches
Visions
Travels

KISS AT MIDNIGHT

A Town Called Forgotten

#1 INTERNATIONAL BESTSELLING AUTHOR

RACHEL BRANTON

WHITE
STAR
PRESS

This is a work of fiction, and the views expressed herein are the sole responsibility of the author. Likewise, certain characters, places, and incidents are the product of the author's imagination, and any resemblance to actual persons, living or dead, or actual events or locales, is entirely coincidental.

Kiss at Midnight (A Town Called Forgotten, Book 1)

Published by White Star Press
P.O. Box 353
American Fork, Utah 84003

Printed in the United States of America
ISBN: 978-1-948982-18-4
Year of first printing: 2020

To my family with love.

CHAPTER 1

The bus shook as it clattered over a rusty bridge that spanned a dry stream. A green and white sign rose up, clearly visible through the left window: *Forgotten 30 miles*. There were other cities on the sign as well, but she ignored them. She'd loved the name Forgotten from the moment she'd heard it, and seeing the destination on her ticket this morning at the bus station had made her feel safe. The small town was in Kansas, some few miles over the Nebraska border, far away from her old life. Forgotten sounded like a good place to start over, a place where she could leave behind the person she had been and become the woman she knew inside, the one who spoke her mind, wasn't afraid, and would never stay in an unhealthy situation because of that negligible thing called fear.

She'd cried for nearly the entire ride so far. Mostly because she knew that if she had found her courage earlier, her entire future would be different than it could ever be now. But there was no going back, only forward. That was what she was doing. She'd go to Forgotten and remake her life.

Maybe then she could forgive herself.

Pain washed over her at the thought, fresh and raw, biting deep like a wound that would never, ever heal.

And it wouldn't, of course. She knew that. But she had to survive . . . somehow. Happiness was optional. When her old life caught up to her—and of course it eventually would—she would be in control.

Or could she hide forever? It might be possible in a town called Forgotten.

She gently rubbed at her right wrist, which ached badly, the skin tender and bruised. One more scar that would hopefully fade into the past, along with the bigger one cracking her heart. Her despair was enough—almost—to wish the fogginess she'd briefly found comfort in hadn't lifted. But the awareness had gotten her this far, and she was grateful. Soon she'd be able to rest. Maybe in Forgotten she could forget, if only for a while.

Her head pounded, which was partly because of the accident, and her aching body screamed for relief. *So dizzy,* she thought, gripping the armrests. She leaned back in the comfortable, high-backed seat and shut her eyes . . . and let it all go—the past, the betrayals, and most of all the heartache.

"Miss?" came the voice of the bus driver sometime later. "This is your stop."

She blinked her eyes open. "My stop?" She felt confused as she looked around. What was she doing on a bus?

"Forgotten," he clarified. "I'm sure that's what your ticket said. The stop is on the outskirts of the city, and it's not much of a station, but there's a bathroom and a place to sit. You can wait out of the sun until your ride comes to take you into town."

She had no idea what he was talking about, but she did remember she had been heading to Forgotten. From where she'd come, she didn't know. She rose, clutching the backpack on the seat beside her that seemed to be her only luggage. She was sitting near the front of the bus, so she walked toward that exit.

She could see herself in the huge mirror over the driver's head that allowed him to observe the passengers at will, though there were only a handful of people still on the bus. Her long blond hair, pulled up in a messy ponytail, looked odd somehow, not from the escaping hairs but by the fact that she didn't recognize the hair style . . . or really her entire person, yet she knew it was her. She had blue eyes with deep shadows under them and a slender figure except for her middle where her yellow summer dress seemed to hide a few extra pounds. The long, flowy, shapeless dress didn't stir a single memory, but she liked it.

The grizzled bus driver cleared his throat. "Someone's coming to pick you up, ain't they?"

Did she look so helpless that he had to ask? She didn't feel helpless. She was strong and ready to face the world. She tossed her head as if her hair were loose and flowing around her. "How far is the town?"

"Sixteen or so miles straight ahead. Shorter if you cut across the fields." He eyed her sandals doubtfully, as if implying they were impractical for cross country, though they barely had two-inch heels.

"I'll be fine. Thank you."

He shrugged. "Don't have much call for people going to Forgotten. That's why we don't drive all the way into town."

She nodded as if she knew what he was talking about and exited the bus. The late-morning sun shone brightly down on her, but it was May and not that hot. The air smelled fresh and new. She glanced back to find the bus driver staring at her uncertainly, as if afraid to leave her here alone. She waved at him and turned her back to the bus. The door squeaked shut, and the engine sounded loud as it pulled away. Turning right on the adjoining road, the bus soon disappeared from sight.

She studied the ribbon of road stretching out before her as far as she could see. It appeared a lot longer than sixteen miles. Better to face that after a bathroom break.

The man hadn't been joking about the station being small. It was little more than a wooden hut with a big gap where a window might have once been. A short bench took up the back wall, and there was a heater, which seemed to be broken. The bathroom connected to the other side of the structure but had only one stall and no soap in the sink. At least the water worked. Searching her backpack, she found an empty plastic bottle wedged next to a box of feminine hygiene pads. Too bad there wasn't an extra pair of shoes.

After filling the water bottle at the bathroom sink, she started down the road.

A sweet smell pierced her unconscious dream. She wanted to lie in the sweetness forever, her body cradled in warmth. But the *clump-clump* of footsteps dragged her closer to consciousness. With that awareness came the sensation of itching—her arms and legs, mostly—and an odd dryness caught at her throat. She moved slightly, and something sharp poked her back.

"What are you doing here?" demanded a voice she didn't recognize. Definitely a man. She felt more than saw him bend over, sweeping off her covering.

An unreasoning fear rose in her chest, threatening to choke

her. She opened her eyes and saw the man's face above her, peering down curiously. The fear receded, as if belonging to another life. Above the man, bare rafters crisscrossed the ceiling. She appeared to be lying in a pile of hay.

Hay?

"It's okay." His voice was softer now, less demanding. He brushed more of the hay away and extended a hand to help her up.

Ignoring the hand, she pushed herself to a seated position, away from the offensive object poking her in the back—a pitchfork apparently. More hay streamed from her body.

With a calculated move, she reached for the pitchfork under the hay. Aiming it at the man, she jabbed it once in his direction. "Back off," she warned, pleased to see him back up a couple steps.

"What? Are you kidding?" he demanded, his face more puzzled than angry. "I'm not here to hurt you. I was offering you a hand." He had a nice face with a clean-shaven, square jaw that spoke of strength, and brown eyes that didn't make her feel like running. He was lean and handsome, though, and this she didn't quite trust.

"But I do need to know what you're doing here," he added.

"Here" was in a barn or a loft of sorts. Bright sunlight streamed through slats at the far end of the loft that covered a large window but still let in enough light to illuminate the area. Behind her rose a tall pile of hay—a veritable mountain of it. All in neatly stacked bales, except the mound that made up her bed. A vague memory of tugging hay from the bales danced in the back of her mind. With the memory came an ache from her finger.

She brought the hurt finger to her lips, sucking gently. Her lip was cracked, and the motion hurt more than soothed her finger, so she drew it away.

The man's gaze didn't leave her face. "You're not from around here, are you? Did your car break down or something? Are you hurt?" He spoke as if talking to a frightened animal. She didn't know whether to applaud his efforts or feel offended.

When she didn't answer, he asked, "Where are your shoes?"

She looked down to see that she wore only a yellow summer dress. Her bare feet were swollen and itchy like her arms where the hay had rubbed against her skin.

"They got wet," she said, her throat hurting from dryness as she spoke. They'd also been muddy and completely useless, but he didn't have to know about that. Trying to get to town, especially after she'd cut across a field and attempted to wade through a river, hadn't worked out as well as she'd thought.

She kept her hands firmly on the pitchfork and tried to stand. Now that the sweet-smelling hay was off her body, she was cold.

"Can you please put that thing down?" he asked in the same steady voice. "I'm not going to hurt you. And if I were, I'd use this." He opened his denim jacket, revealing a handgun in a shoulder holster.

In her mind she envisioned pinning him against the wall with the pitchfork and taking his gun, but her limbs wouldn't obey her. She couldn't remember the last time she'd eaten. With an internal sigh, she carefully laid the pitchfork to the side, still within reach.

The man took two steps toward her and squatted down, studying her. He wore khaki pants, work boots, and a snug green T-shirt under his jacket, which he filled out nicely. That made sense if this was his barn, though he didn't seem like a cowboy. His brown hair was short in the back and sides but longer in front, looping over a bit messily to one side. If they'd met under different circumstances, she might have tried flirting with him.

"I'm Dylan Morgan," he said. "What's your name?"

She'd opened her mouth to respond when she realized she didn't know. But how could anyone not know their name? She remembered nothing except stepping off the bus, walking for miles, and a swift-moving river.

He smiled now, rocking back on his heels. "You do have a name, don't you?"

"Hay," she said, her voice coming louder, sounding hoarse. She'd meant to ask him why she was in the hay, but that was stupid. She already knew he didn't know.

"Hay?" Dylan asked doubtfully.

"Hailey," she improvised. It felt right.

"Hi, Hailey. Can you tell me what you're doing here?" His eyes never left her face. They felt warm, and she was so very cold.

"I don't remember." She couldn't hold back the shiver now.

He shrugged off his jacket, moving forward to drape it around her shoulders. *So warm,* she thought. *Like his eyes.* She wanted to trust him, but that was probably a terrible idea, and she'd go with her feelings over a handsome face any day.

"What's your last name?"

She shook her head and didn't respond.

His brow furrowed as his eyes searched the hay around her, his eyes landing on her backpack. "You might have hit your head," he said, more to himself than to her. "Or maybe you were wandering in the sun too long. Forgotten's weather has been hotter this May than most other parts of the Midwest."

For a moment, she felt adrift, as if even the words eluded her comprehension. She shook her head to throw off the sensation.

"I'm fine." She pulled her backpack over one shoulder. It felt heavier than she remembered.

Dylan offered her his hand again, and this time she accepted it. He tugged her up gently, and a rush of something dribbled down the back of her left calf. He let her go as soon as she was on her feet, and her legs nearly collapsed.

"Woah," he said, grabbing her elbow. "Easy now. Are you dizzy? We'd better get you into town. You probably need something to eat and drink."

She wanted water more than anything, but she simply nodded. "Thank you. I'd appreciate it."

He led her to an opening tucked in between the hay mountain and the wall. She was relieved to see it was a real staircase leading down from the loft and not a ladder. She wouldn't be able to manage one of those now with the dizziness. She swallowed hard, and it felt like she'd gulped a mouthful of glass.

"If you want, go on down," he said. "Or you can wait if you need help. I have to throw down some hay while I'm here. I won't have time to come back until evening, and the horses can't wait that long."

She watched him open a trap door on the floor, grab the pitchfork, and start throwing the hay she'd slept in down through the opening. Taking an awkward step, she clung to the single banister near the wall. Something more dribbled down her leg. She was dizzy, her cheeks felt hot, and her stomach ached. The backpack seemed to weigh a hundred pounds. No way was she going to make it down those stairs by herself. What was wrong with her? She was sure she hadn't felt this way yesterday. Maybe.

Dylan repeated the hay throwing twice more through other trapdoors. He didn't take long, but by the time he finished, her legs were threatening collapse. She wanted nothing more than to curl back up in the hay and return to her dream.

Somehow, he made it to her side before she toppled over. "I've got you," he murmured as his strong arms went around her. She had no choice but to lean on him as he half dragged, half carried her down the stairs.

Stalls made up the bulk of the lower portion of the barn, only three of which were currently occupied, and these held beautiful horses, whose coats shone as if they'd recently been combed. One whinnied as she and Dylan moved over the concrete floor, but Dylan only called, "You're welcome, Lady," and didn't pause.

They did stop at the door of the barn, where, besides a short farmhouse situated across a large back yard, a whole lot of nothing met her gaze. She saw only acres of land, growing green stalks about a foot above the ground, and the ribbon of road winding through them. No wonder she'd stopped here. In fact, if Dylan hadn't come along, she might not have found her way into town at all today.

The sun wasn't directly overhead, but she could feel its warmth on her face. She didn't know if it was morning or afternoon but guessed it was morning if he was feeding the animals.

"It's only a little further." He motioned to a dark gray vehicle that seemed vaguely familiar. Not a truck but an SUV.

Instant terror rolled through her at the sight of the vehicle, but with the nearly the same speed, the emotion was gone. She didn't know this vehicle. It wasn't after her.

After her? The thought didn't make sense. Even so, she was relieved that no one was inside.

"You're hurt," Dylan said, his stare directed toward the ground near her foot where a few drops of blood had pooled.

She followed his gaze as he looked back into the barn where more blood spotted the concrete.

That's when she remembered the stick from the river. "Oh, yeah. It's a cut." She lifted her dress a little to examine the cut on the back of her left calf. It looked worse than she remembered, covered in both dried and fresh blood. Blood caked on the back of her dress as well. "If you have a little tissue, that might help."

He bent over to take a brief look. "That's a nasty cut. Needs more than tissue. There's a first aid kit up at the house." His gaze flicked in the direction of the farmhouse. "Can you walk that far on it?"

She wanted to say no way, but if she did, he'd probably carry her—or take her in the SUV, where she'd leave even more blood. She let her dress fall back into place.

"Sure." The word came out as strongly as she'd intended, and it irritated her that his left brow crooked doubtfully. That brow was missing a slash of hair at an angle near the end, she noticed, as if a scar prevented growth, though from this far away, she couldn't be sure that was the reason.

They started for the house, with her wobbling more than she could prevent until he steadied her again with his arm. The hard-packed dirt path wasn't too hard on her feet, for which she was grateful.

"I can take your backpack," he offered.

She shook her head, unwilling to let it go from her hands. As far as she knew, it was all she owned.

"Let me know if you change your mind."

She peeked at his profile. He didn't look angry, only intent on the house. Better yet, he hadn't repeated his question about where she was from, for which she was grateful. She didn't have an answer, not yet. But she would, because until she remembered exactly why she was here, she didn't want to appear like someone who should be in a mental hospital.

They hadn't gone far when a dog came running to meet them, not from the house but from the fields, where it had likely been chasing a rabbit or a field mouse, or whatever they had in this town. What had the man called the town? She couldn't remember, though she was quite sure she'd known yesterday. She couldn't remember the man's name either.

The dog was a large gold one with furry ears, a Golden Retriever, she guessed, and though its face was sleek, its belly was hugely distended, as if it had eaten far too many fat-laden dinners. It gave a low woof and sniffed at her with great interest.

"No." The man leaned over to shoo the dog away. "Leave her alone. And if you're looking for petting, you should have thought of that when I tried to feed you instead of running off after some jackrabbit."

Dylan, she remembered. The man's name was Dylan. It was a nice, strong name. But why couldn't she remember hers? Maybe she really had hit her head yesterday. Or maybe her name really was Hailey.

Yes, she decided. It was as good a name as any until she searched her backpack for ID.

The dog barked again and angled around to the man's side. Or waddled because of its ungainly weight. Hailey found herself smiling.

The house was old but well-kept, from the short and very green grass in the back yard to the fresh paint on the clapboards. Not a weed dared to grow in the modest flowerbed next to the cement patio, where a wooden picnic table beckoned to them. She wanted nothing more than to lie down on one of the benches and fall asleep in the sun.

A disoriented flash came to her of lying down in a field. *Yesterday,* she thought. *Must have been before the barn.* Nothing more came to mind, though.

Dylan let go of her to open the door with a key. No one else must be home, so maybe he'd been heading out to his fields or something. The dog, growing impatient, pushed past Dylan as the door opened and was waiting for them when they entered into a short hallway instead of the kitchen she'd been expecting.

"Go get your food," Dylan told the dog, who remained standing near him, wagging its tail and staring up with eager eyes. Dylan sighed and moved onward.

Hailey walked carefully over the vinyl flooring that was cool on her feet. The hallway was lined with photos, and she scanned them as they passed. One of the larger photos, a vintage black and white, featured an old man with white hair and old-fashioned clothes standing by a street sign that read *Forgotten, population 1400.*

Forgotten. She remembered the name of the town now. The knowledge brought her relief, even though she couldn't remember anything before the bus. Whatever had happened to make her forget her own life, she'd meant to come to this town.

Ridiculous laughter bubbled up inside her. She'd forgotten coming to the town called Forgotten. The word seemed to describe everything about her. Maybe the town was where she finally belonged.

Finally? She had no idea what that might mean.

Dylan stopped at the end of the hallway and bent over, petting the dog despite his earlier comment about the animal losing out. He appeared to be enjoying it as much as the animal, and a strange longing crept up inside her. For a stark instant, she wished this was her house and her dog and her man. Her life.

Was Dylan wearing a wedding ring? She strained to see and found him watching her. Her stomach at once felt fluttery inside.

He thumbed over his shoulder. "The first aid kit is this way, in the kitchen." He must think her a complete idiot.

"I'd like to use the bathroom first, if that's okay." She lifted her chin a little, getting ready to insist if he protested about the dribbles of blood she was leaving on the cheap flooring, never mind that sections of it seemed to be missing or peeling up.

"Sure. Bathroom's that way, first door on the right." He pointed down the intersecting hallway. "Let me know if you need anything else. I'll be in the kitchen so this picky dog will eat."

Hailey didn't know what to make of that. Dogs ate when they were hungry, didn't they? It wasn't as if they were children who sometimes needed coaxing. Warmth filled her chest at the thought, but no accompanying memories hinted at why she might feel that way.

She edged slowly over the few steps to the bathroom, determined to make it without any more help from this stranger. As she stepped inside, she caught sight of Dylan still standing in the hallway, his eyes locked on her. He tipped his head, and she felt a rush of gratitude that he hadn't pushed her for answers she didn't know. She nodded back and shut the door.

Inside the bathroom, she let his jacket slip to the floor and practically collapsed on the sink, pushing her mouth close to the tap and sucking eagerly at the water. It tasted warm at first but cooled quickly. Her throat burned and she choked a little, but the coolness was a balm to the dryness. It tasted wonderful, so definitely not the softened water many people had in their bathrooms these days. Or at least she thought they did. Maybe she didn't know anything anymore.

She didn't stop drinking until her stomach felt full and a bit nauseated. Even then, she stood there, hunched over the still-running water. When her stomach calmed, she let another mouthful ooze down her throat before splashing water over her face. It wasn't to hide the tears because she wouldn't admit to crying. For long moments she stayed that way, splashing her face and drinking again when she could.

Between sips, she examined the small bathroom. Next to the single sink was a holder with a blue toothbrush and a tube of toothpaste. Below the sink was a cabinet with a main cupboard and three drawers running down the right side. After briefly eyeing the clean but age-yellowed bathtub, she rejected the idea of filling it with delicious hot water to soak her scratched limbs and dirty feet. This wasn't her house, and she wasn't an invited guest. Besides, now that she was feeling stronger, she needed to get into town and learn why she was here.

She met her own gaze in the mirror. Her face was bare of makeup and reddened from the sun. More hair had escaped the messy ponytail than remained in it, and pieces of hay still clung to the strands. By any standards, even her forgetful ones, she looked a mess.

Another urge reminded her to use the toilet. She did so, retrieving one of the pads from her backpack. Just her rotten luck that it was her time of the month. Her body aches apparently weren't only from walking and falling into the river.

As she stood to flush, she noticed the thick bulge of something that sat at her belly under her dress. She'd assumed the pressure there had been from the ruched part of her dress's waistline, but now she wasn't so sure. Tucking her dress up under her chin, she discovered a tan money belt. Gingerly, she unzipped the main pocket to find that the thickness of the belt had nothing to do with the material, which was so thin as to be almost nonexistent. Instead, it was the contents that made the bulge—a stack of hundred-dollar bills. She counted one hundred of them, which meant she had ten thousand dollars.

For a moment, she stared at the money, a sick feeling growing in the pit of her stomach. Maybe she didn't belong in the psych ward of a hospital but in a prison. Who walked around with that kind of money? She'd certainly have to keep her memory loss a secret now, at least until she figured out what was going on.

Why couldn't she remember?

Replacing the money and letting the dress cover the belt once more, she methodically explored her skull, finding no telling lumps. Her body ached all over, but that wouldn't make her memory vanish. Unless maybe the cut on her leg had become infected to the point where it was affecting her brain. But she remembered getting off the bus, the river, and pulling hay from the bales in the barn, so that didn't make sense.

Enough, she thought. This wasn't getting her anywhere. She'd meant to come here, and she had to trust that knowledge. Maybe this was her life's savings, not something she'd stolen. At least she'd be able to pay for new shoes and a place to stay in town until she found a job. Though without ID, a job might not be possible.

Shutting the toilet lid, she sat on it and delved into her backpack to search for ID. If she'd hit her head, knowing her name might jog her memories. She found three hundred and twelve more dollars in the small pocket, plus a bit of change. There was no wallet, no ID, no cell phone, and no used bus ticket, either, though she vaguely remembered having one.

Next, she pulled out an empty plastic water bottle, a pair of shiny red gym shorts, and a black, impossibly large T-shirt with a lion on the front. A little plastic holder contained a hairbrush, a tube of lip balm, a tiny bottle of lotion, a toothbrush, and trial-sized toothpaste. She felt no connection to any of the items.

She returned everything to the backpack. Then, on second thought, she pulled out the personal supplies and set them on the sink counter. She brushed her hair and put it back up in a ponytail, looping the hair through again halfway to keep it off her neck. Then she brushed her teeth, spread balm over her cracked lip, and patted lotion on her burned face. Her arms were also burned, and she used the edge of the hand towel she found hanging on a hook to dab cold water on her arms and neck before spreading on more lotion. Her skin felt much better already, though she'd be peeling soon.

She cleaned up the stray pieces of hay and put them in the garbage next to the toilet. Grabbing Dylan's jacket, she pulled it on again, relishing its warmth. Finally, she hefted her backpack, which felt lighter now that she knew its contents.

So little to start a new life. But she was going to do just that.

CHAPTER 2

Dylan Morgan pulled down the first aid kit he knew the chief's wife kept in the cupboard above the refrigerator exactly like her mother-in-law had when Dylan had come here with his father as a child. Then he focused on the dog, Sable, who had finally eaten her food. Sable had grown ungainly the past few months during her pregnancy, but she would have the pups soon.

Hailey was taking longer in the bathroom than he expected, which gave him plenty of time to go over their strange meeting. When he'd found her in the loft of the barn, she'd been almost completely buried under the hay, with only her bare toes poking out. Lying so utterly still, curled on her side in a ball like a sleeping child, her arms wrapped protectively around her middle, he'd feared she was dead. To his great relief, closer examination revealed light breathing.

At first he'd thought she was one of the town's teenagers, who was perhaps having problems at home and had known Chief

Caleb McColl was out of town this week and so she'd hidden in his barn. But one glimpse of the woman's face told him that wasn't the case. He knew almost everyone living nearby, and he'd have remembered her if he'd seen her even once. He doubted she was even from Forgotten.

Why had she been in that barn?

The McColls lived within the town limits, but near the edge, and nothing else was out this way for miles around. Well, he'd help her bandage her leg and give her a ride into town, and his part in her story would be over.

At last, Hailey limped into the kitchen. Her hair was still messy but artfully so, restrained now in an elastic, and the bits of hay were gone. The change was curiously disappointing, though her beauty was more apparent now. She had high, prominent cheekbones and an oddly perfect nose. A hint of the exotic that flared in the angles of her face and eyes made her stand out even more. Blue eyes, he noted, emphasized by dark circles that hinted at fragility. She was still wearing his denim jacket.

He stopped petting the dog. "If you'll sit here." He indicated the chair nearest his and opened the first aid kit on the table.

Apparently not hearing his words, Hailey examined the pictures on the shelf above the small, square table. His eyes ran over her profile, feeling a stirring inside him that he almost didn't recognize because it had been so long. Since Bristol.

Hailey turned to him, her gaze meeting his. "This isn't your house, is it?" Her voice was slightly husky, and he didn't know if that was because of exposure or her natural tone. It was decidedly sexy, though, even to him, and he purposely tried not to notice those things.

"No," he agreed. "It's Caleb McColl's place. He's our chief

of police. He and his wife are out of town on vacation, so I'm watching his house and animals." At least that was the story. In truth, the McColls had gone to deal with the younger of their two daughters, who'd been in trouble of some sort ever since junior high school, police chief's daughter or not. Lately she'd been ill. Drugs were Dylan's guess, but Caleb insisted her problems came from digestive issues.

Hailey stiffened at his explanation, and Dylan didn't need his old police training to tell him her uneasiness had to do with Caleb's profession. She was hiding something. If she wasn't simply passing through Forgotten, he might have to keep an eye on her—especially with Caleb out of town. Caleb's second-in-command was in charge in the meantime, of course, but Levi was new to the job, and Dylan felt a responsibility since he'd found the woman, even if he no longer wore the badge.

He still hadn't decided if he was going to tell Caleb about finding her in his barn. Taking refuge wasn't something Caleb's family would begrudge her—or anyone—as long as nothing went missing.

Hailey sat without speaking in the chair he'd indicated before, so she'd been paying attention after all, and pulled her yellow dress up to her knee in an oddly intimate gesture. Her dirty, bare feet and calves were pale and too slender, and he knew he should look away, or maybe find something else to do, but he couldn't.

She bent her knee forward and to the side, trying to see the cut better.

"May I?" he asked.

She studied him for several seconds before nodding silently.

Grabbing one of the wet rags he'd laid next to the first aid kit, he slid from his chair onto one knee and began gently rubbing the dirt and dried blood away from her calf. He knew as soon as he uncovered a little more that the cut was deep and the first aid kit wouldn't be enough.

"You need stitches." He watched as more blood leaked from the wound. She had to be in a lot of pain, but she hid it well.

"Stitches?" Her gaze wandered to the first aid kit. "Isn't there some glue in there? That's all the rage now, right?"

"Not for cuts this long and deep. Or at this location. There's a lot of movement so close to the knee, even back here." He was about to explain more when Sable awkwardly arose from her spot by his chair and came over, wanting to get into the action. She pushed into Hailey's good leg.

"Down, girl!" Dylan commanded.

"It's okay." Hailey ran her hand over the eager animal's coat. "She's just making friends."

"She was never much of a watchdog, that's for sure. Caleb says his daughters ruined that with all the friends they always had over. The dog loves pretty much everyone."

"I think she's perfect." The longing in her voice was compelling and strangely hopeless, touching Dylan on a level he didn't understand. "Even if she's fatter than any dog I've ever seen."

"That's because she's pregnant. If you look at her face, you can see she's hardly gained any weight there."

"Pregnant? Huh. I should have guessed. Now that you mention it, she does look ready to nurse a bunch of puppies." She scratched Sable's head, and the dog pushed into her, closing her eyes as if lost in bliss. "She's so soft."

"They normally have eight to twelve pups," he told her. "But I'm pretty sure she's having at least twelve, and probably more."

Hailey gave a low laugh. "And you know that because?"

"I'm her vet."

Hailey met his gaze and then glanced down at her hurt leg. "Oh, so that's why you think this needs stitches."

"I can take you to the doctor."

She shook her head. "No. I'll just bandage it. I-I don't have insurance."

He studied her a moment. Once again, he had the sensation that she was hiding something. While he didn't miss the four years he'd spent as a New York police officer, his honed instincts were one thing he always depended on. "It'll leave a pretty big scar without stitches."

One slender shoulder lifted in a shrug. "I don't mind scars. I can't pay for a doctor."

He made the decision fast. "Tell you what, I can suture it. I'm not licensed to treat people, of course, so technically it'd be like any layperson offering you stitches."

"Except you've done it before."

He nodded. Forgotten had only one overworked doctor and one lay midwife with no professional training except experience and what she gleaned from the doctor, which meant Dylan had been in emergency's way more times than he wanted to admit. He always gave the spiel about not being licensed, of course, though no one ever cared. It was unlikely anyone would try to take his license since he was the only vet serving Forgotten and several other nearby towns.

"I'll get my bag from my car." He left her petting Sable and hurried out to his five-year-old Chevy Tahoe. He'd bought the SUV shortly before coming back to town on a full-time basis after finishing veterinarian school. He had inherited his father's old truck along with his practice, of course, but he used it now only for hauling and for the dirtier jobs. The Tahoe had enough interior room to carry his equipment out of the elements and could double in a pinch to transport smaller animals to the clinic, though so far he'd only transported a few dogs. The Tahoe was his one nod to comfort—or had been until he decided to build his new house.

When he returned to the kitchen, Hailey hadn't moved from the chair. She'd cleaned off more blood from her calf, though, and was once again petting the dog. "Is she close to delivery?"

"Yeah. In fact, I'm going to take her into town instead of leaving her here. Her owners won't be home for another week, and with so many puppies and her sudden lack of an appetite, I think she might deliver before they return. It's her second litter, but they lost a couple pups with the first one because they didn't know she'd had them in the barn, which turned out to be too cold. Someone needs to keep an eye on her."

"Oh, you sweet thing," Hailey crooned, bending over to hug the willing dog. Dylan noticed the effort seemed difficult for her.

"Are you experiencing any other pain?" he asked, voicing a concern that even to him felt exaggerated.

"Maybe I hit a few other things in the river when I fell in." Her comment wasn't exactly an answer.

He pulled on plastic gloves and began irrigating the wound, using rags from the table to catch the falling liquid. "So that's how you did this?" he asked. "Falling into the river?" She'd seemed confused in the barn, and the wound did indicate a trauma that could have caused confusion. She seemed a lot more in control now.

"I was trying to cross the river," she said softly, staring at the dog, who had suddenly discovered a new interest in her water bowl across the room.

He gently patted the wound area with gauze to sop up more blood leakage before swabbing it with disinfectant. "And why were you doing that?" The river, which fed into the large town lake, was pretty wide and for the most part docile, but a few sections were swift and dangerous.

"Trying to get into town." She hesitated a moment and added with a self-deprecating smile, "I didn't realize Forgotten was so far from the bus stop."

He drew back and looked up at her. "The bus? But it only comes on Wednesdays. That was two days ago."

She stared at him for several seconds. "Maybe I did hit my head in the river." Her hand went to her hair, but stopped short, falling to her lap. "Two days. No wonder I'm so hungry."

The words hadn't been directed at him, but he felt guilty for not offering to make her something. Hailey might have been in the barn uninvited, but that was the neighborly thing to do. If Caleb hadn't been out of town, his wife, Natalie, would probably be stuffing Hailey with eggs and pancakes by now. "Do you remember anything else?"

"Of course," she said, too quickly, looking away from him. "I remember everything. I was half asleep before is all."

"You know someone in town?"

She hesitated, as if considering the possibility. "No. I'm just traveling around. I heard the town's name somewhere, and it was unusual enough that it stuck in my head. I wanted to see it for myself."

"It is a great place," he agreed, maybe with a little too much enthusiasm. "Did you hear about the couple who founded the town?"

Smiling, she let her gaze touch his again. "No. But the way you said that, I bet it's an interesting story."

His hand stilled on her leg. "I think so." Even through the plastic gloves, he could feel her warmth. How long had it been since he'd touched a woman so intimately? He swallowed hard and began his story—a story that was important to him not only because he lived in Forgotten, but because it involved his fourth-great grandparents.

"James Morgan, the son of a wealthy Missouri farmer, and Chelsea Fortson, the daughter of an important abolitionist cattle rancher in Missouri, fell in love and wanted to marry, but their fathers were sworn enemies, divided on the issue of slavery, so they separated their children."

"Sounds like Romeo and Juliet," Hailey said with a laugh. She had her elbow on the table now as she watched him, supporting her cheek with her hand. She didn't comment on James's last name, so maybe she hadn't noticed he shared it.

"You aren't the first to make that connection. James was made to travel to Virginia, where his father, who had been elected to office, went in an attempt to influence the politicians in favor of slavery. Chelsea was sent to a territory that would eventually become Kansas to live with relatives, who were on the side of Kansas entering the Union as a free state. James and Chelsea lived apart for three years, with nothing more than secret letters passed between them, aided by loyal friends and servants."

"Three years is a long time," Hailey said.

Was that her stomach growling? Belatedly remembering the granola bar he always kept in his denim jacket, he motioned to the pocket. "I have a granola bar in there if you're hungry." He hoped it wasn't expired.

She rewarded him with a huge smile that did funny things to his stomach. She dug the granola bar out, ripping open the wrapper with her fingers and biting into it. He glimpsed the reddened skin around her right wrist and wondered if it was something else that had happened in the river.

"So did they ever get together?" she asked, covering her mouth delicately with her hand as she spoke, her words only slightly garbled by her mouthful of granola bar.

Dylan pulled his mind back to the story. "James eventually put together enough funds to get himself to Kansas and ask Chelsea to run away with him. She packed a bag and left that same night. When their marriage was discovered, they were both disowned by their families. That might have been the end of it, but they married around the same time Kansas was formed and became a free state, so it wasn't enough for James's father to simply take away his inheritance. He was furious at his son's betrayal, which he considered an affront to his entire way of life, and he sent a posse after him."

Hailey had taken another bite of the granola bar, but she stopped chewing and stared at him. "That's terrible. Did they get him?"

"Yes. They found James and shot him, but Chelsea, eight months pregnant with her first child, threw herself in front of him, and they took pity on her and didn't finish the job. They left him to bleed out in her arms."

"He didn't die, did he?" Her eyes beckoned to him eagerly, begging for verification.

"No, Chelsea stopped the bleeding and called for a doctor. James's leg had to be amputated, and he nearly died of infection, but Chelsea slowly nursed him back to health, all the while keeping his survival a secret."

"What about the family she'd been staying with? Wouldn't they help?"

"They'd been told to disown her, and they did, but Chelsea wrote to her father, begging for his help and forgiveness and telling him about his grandchild. Only years later did she learn that he'd died after being shot himself by his pro-slavery enemies. Her brother inherited everything and tore up her letter so he wouldn't have to share. So Chelsea earned a living making ravioli at a restaurant during the day and sewing dresses late into the night until James was finally well enough to come out of hiding. By then, they wanted nothing to do with their families, and they took off to the northern part of Kansas near the border of what would become Nebraska. They began to farm."

"Here, you mean."

He nodded. "When people who passed through the area asked where they were from, they said they'd been gone so long, they'd forgotten, because they didn't want word to ever get back to their families. They ended up having thirteen children, and most of them married people from nearby towns and stayed close to farm the land. Other people passing through also began staying, and the town became known as Forgotten, a place of new life for all those who had been or wanted to be forgotten."

Hailey's grin was wistful. "So it was a happy ending. But that's too bad about their families."

Dylan wetted another section of gauze with disinfectant for a final cleaning of her leg. "They made their own family, I guess, but I sometimes wonder what might have happened if their parents wouldn't have been so angry. Maybe they could have come to a resolution."

When Dylan had chosen the police academy after college instead of veterinarian school as he'd always planned, his father had been supportive. If he hadn't, maybe Dylan wouldn't have changed his mind and returned to Forgotten at all. He only wished he would have come back for good before the cancer that had shadowed their last years and eventually taken his father's life.

Hailey looked thoughtful. "Maybe. Or maybe the differences were simply too great."

He wondered if she was talking about her own situation, but when his silence didn't evoke more information, he said, "I need to get a better view while I'm doing the stitches, unless you want to look like Frankenstein. The table's too small, I think, but if you'll come and lie down on the couch in the other room, I'll be able to do a better job."

Her smile grew wide and teasing. "Come lie down on the couch or you'll look like Frankenstein—that's something you don't usually hear the first time you meet a guy."

Long-forgotten emotions rushed through him at the words. This wasn't a date, and there hadn't been any subtext in his invitation to lie down on the couch, but he couldn't deny that he was attracted to this woman he knew practically nothing about.

"I don't suppose it is," he recovered enough to say. "But it probably won't be the last time I say something that weird."

She laughed. "I bet in your line of work, a lot of strange things happen."

"I guess so." If he was honest, neither of his jobs had ever involved a woman as beautiful as Hailey.

She didn't let out a peep as he deadened her leg and began stitching with the finest sutures he had. On animals, fur would always hide most scars, but this scar would be with her all her life. He made each stitch carefully, close together and even, taking more time and care than he would for even the most delicate of creatures.

When he finished, he covered the area with an oversized, non-stick bandage he didn't normally have to use with his furry patients. "Keep this on for the next day or two, and don't get it wet," he told her. "After that, you can take it off and rub in a little antibiotic cream periodically over the next week or so. Make sure you keep it moist, even if you're only putting on petroleum jelly. You'll need the stitches removed in about ten days." He paused and then added, "If you're still in town, I'd be glad to do it. You could do it yourself with a fingernail clipper if you had a better view."

She laughed as she swung her legs to the floor and came to a sitting position. "I'm pretty limber—well, usually. Today, I feel stiff."

"That's normal after a fall." The words felt awkward, and her low laugh made him wonder if he'd said something stupid. Why did he feel so distracted around her?

Her next words put him at ease. "You sounded like a doctor when you said that."

His turn to laugh. "My patients are animals, but I have to deal with their owners too, so I guess I switched into doctor mode."

"I like it. It's reassuring."

The words made him feel happy in a way that was all out of proportion to the simple meaning. Clamping down on the emotion, he reminded himself that he knew next to nothing about her, not even her last name. Finding refuge in the McColl barn might have been logical after her adventure in the river, but coming to Forgotten the way she had wasn't typical. When he'd been at the NYPD, the only people who'd done stuff like that were those who had something to hide.

"Well, since I'm in doctor mode," he said. "I noticed your wrist earlier. Maybe I should bandage it too."

A line of stress appeared between her brow. "It doesn't hurt . . . much." She pulled back the sleeve of his jacket that went halfway to her fingers, revealing a red welt, scratches, and thin, dark bruises that went the entire way around her wrist.

"How did you do this?"

She stared at it. "Must have been in the river."

A lie, but he didn't know if she lied purposefully or if she didn't remember. Because no way had those bruises happened in the river. He guessed most of those marks had come from some kind of strap or restraint.

He rubbed a bit of antibiotic cream on her wrist and taped a piece of gauze around the entire area, more to hide the marks than to help them heal. Only time could do that. The memory of whatever happened, if she had one, might take far longer to mend.

He offered a hand to help her stand. "We should get you into town."

She looked paler than she had when he'd first found her, though she seemed physically stronger. He knew exactly where to take her where he could make sure she'd be both taken care of and watched. After that, she'd be out of his life, whoever she was, and he could go back to trying to forget his time in New York.

CHAPTER 3

Hailey was feeling better now, though all the water was weighing a bit heavily on her bladder. She was almost sure Dylan didn't plan to turn her into the police chief for sneaking into his barn. Almost. He'd stitched her up, after all. Maybe that was small-town hospitality, both the stitches and thinking it was okay to sleep in someone's barn.

She still didn't remember going into the barn, though, and nothing before getting off the bus and the short conversation with the bus driver when she exited. The old man had been worried about her, maybe with good reason. Lack of insurance hadn't been the only reason she hadn't wanted to go to the doctor. A doctor meant questions and maybe an official report. If she was running from something, that was likely the quickest way to be found.

Didn't she want to be found?

Dread fell over her at the thought. A throat-choking dread

that made her want to curl up in a ball and cry. The feeling lasted only a few seconds, and then sanity set in. Or insanity, depending on the point of view. Hailey was where she needed to be, and she didn't need to tell anyone a thing about her missing memories—or the money she'd found in her belt. Forgotten was not only going to be her motto, it was going to be her home for the foreseeable future. She had to trust herself.

"You okay?" Dylan's question came with a little bit of a country drawl, as if the words meant more out here somehow and fewer were needed.

She nodded firmly. "Yeah, I'm okay. Thank you." Sable was on the bench seat between them, her head on Hailey's knee, and Hailey stroked her soft fur, glad for the comforting contact.

Dylan took his eyes briefly from the road, as if making sure she really was okay, and a tremble ran through her. She remembered too vividly his touch on her leg and how it had been hard to think about anything else. Even the shot he'd given her had been so gentle, his touch like that of a lover. Not that she was looking for a lover. For all she knew, she had an attentive boyfriend or a family out there somewhere.

At that thought, the constant low ache in her stomach grew worse. "You don't have any aspirin or anything, do you?" she asked.

"I have a bottle of Ibuprofen in the glove box."

She tilted her head at him. "Not in your med kit?"

His laugh was warm. "I treat animals, not people. Pain killers for animals mostly involve shots. The pills are for me. I get headaches if I don't sleep enough."

"Which I bet happens when you're called out in the middle of the night." She opened the glove box and dug past a wool beanie, a charging cable, and several loose batteries to find a nearly full bottle of pills at the very back. As she shook one onto her hand, he handed her a heavy metal bottle.

"Water," he said.

She swallowed a small mouthful, enjoying the coolness but already feeling sloshy inside from her earlier guzzling. She definitely needed to use the restroom again.

They drove in silence until a green sign came up on the right side of the road. *Forgotten,* it read, *Population 3786.*

"Almost four thousand people," she said, having no concept of how big that number was in terms of towns. "I thought the picture at the farmhouse said fourteen hundred."

His smile sent another curl of excitement through her. "That was a picture of Caleb's father in the town's early days. Before I was born. We're small but not the smallest around. The next town to the west has only fifteen hundred. Our biggest neighbor to the north, Panna Creek, has just over eight thousand, mostly because they have a hospital and a Walmart, both of which employ a lot of people. We've got the best specialty shops, though, so they come here for those. It's worth the twenty- to thirty-minute drive, depending on what side of the city they're coming from."

"What kind of shops?" A few small, widely-spaced houses had appeared now on either side of the road, but no businesses yet.

"Custom dresses, an herb store, homemade ice cream, a ravioli restaurant, a pizzeria, a hair salon, and a café that sells the best gooey butter cake in the state. They also have those things in Panna Creek, but ours are better." No missing the pride in his voice there.

"And a vet, right?"

"Right." He grinned. "I'm the only vet for all the towns

around here. At least I will be until you report me for practicing medicine without a license."

She couldn't help snorting at that. "I'm not going to report you." She hoped saying that would encourage him not to report her either. "I owe you for helping me." Her face flushed as she remembered again the touch of his hand on her leg. That was silly, since he probably hadn't given her any thought whatsoever as a woman.

He didn't reply, and she found herself thankful as she stared out the window. The road was still only one car wide both ways, but commercial buildings now sprang up on either side as if by magic, replacing residential houses. She saw a burger place, a gas station, a novelty shop, and an herb store—all of the buildings well-kept and quaint, with wide sidewalks in front of them, trees, and the occasional bench. Some of the businesses were obviously converted from what must have once been the mansions of some early residents.

"That's the town hall," Dylan said, pointing at a large building set back further than most.

The town hall had been constructed in the same style as some of the older houses but carried the gleam of new construction. A large polished boulder with a metal plaque she was too far away to read, a small pioneer cabin, and beautiful flowerbeds decorated the grounds. She loved it all.

The very last building right after a park was a lovely old house set back from the road with a huge sign that read, *Butter Cake Café*. Her mouth watered in anticipation.

"Is there a hotel in town?" she asked as he passed the café and pulled into the small parking lot behind it. She hadn't seen one so far, and until this minute, she hadn't thought about where she'd stay if Forgotten didn't have a hotel.

"There's a motel on First Street," he said, "which is a block east of here. But depending on how long you're staying, you might want to talk to Maggie. I don't know if you noticed the smaller writing under the café sign, but it's also a bed and breakfast."

She hadn't noticed. "Who's Maggie?"

"Maggie Tremblay. She owns the café, but she also has rooms to rent. Might be a little cheaper than the hotel because you have the option to do your own cleaning." He'd parked the car but avoided her eyes as he spoke, which made her stomach clench. He didn't trust her—the realization came in a rush. Why did that hurt her feelings? She didn't need him, not anymore. Taking her into town was enough.

After a moment of silence, he asked, "So how long you going to be in town?"

"I'm not sure." Until she knew why she was here, how could she plan a future? Her hand tightened on the dog's golden fur, and the softness soothed her.

He turned off his engine and came around, opening her door before she could do it herself. She took her hand from Sable and scooted to the outside edge of the bench, a little concerned about the way his face swam. She stifled the urge to vomit.

"Are you okay?"

"Yeah, of course." Her hand went to her backpack, pulling it onto one shoulder. She stretched out her feet and slid from his SUV. It seemed a long way to the ground, but she managed by grabbing onto the door.

"Stay, Sable," Dylan said when the dog stood up and wagged her tail eagerly. "You know how Maggie feels about dogs in her café. I'm going to have to sweet talk her into letting you stay until I finish my morning rounds." Sable let out a resigned whimper and lay back down on the seat on her side, stretching out to take up the place where Hailey had sat.

To Hailey, Dylan added, "I don't have time to take her to the clinic and set up a camera, and the last thing I need is her birthing in my SUV. That's why I'm hoping Maggie will let her stay in her garage or something. My receptionist isn't in until after lunch, and I can't drop Sable at her house now because she's in Panna Creek this morning."

Hailey managed a stiff smile, sensing that the reason he didn't have time was because of her. She walked a few feet, noting with detachment that the café was swaying. She passed two round tables with umbrellas, heading to the back entrance adorned with a painted wooden welcome sign. To the side of the door, a narrow flight of uncovered steps went up to a second floor.

"Hailey?" Dylan's voice came to her from far away.

She pulled her attention back to him, feeling hot and flushed, which this time had nothing to do with her attraction to him. "They sell food here, right?" she asked. "Not just cake?" He was meeting her eyes now, and that made her feel more confident. He couldn't know what she was hiding. She didn't even know.

"Yep." Again, the slow drawl that seemed to speak to her on another level. "That's part of why we're here."

They walked to the door, and he opened it for her like a gentleman. Hailey barely had time to note the dozen tables and the long bar before the heavenly smell descended on her like an epiphany. She let out a contented sigh.

"I know, right?" Dylan said with a laugh. "I feel that way every time I come in here for lunch."

Hailey's stomach growled, and she hurried past a table full of patrons to grab a seat at the bar, her hands pressed on the countertop to stop the swaying. Dylan, who'd paused for a moment to exchange a greeting with someone, caught up to her as a slender woman with a thick roll of jet-black hair wound up on her head came to stand in front of her on the other side of the bar.

"Hey, Dylan," the woman said, her voice as smooth as silk.

"Hey," he returned.

"You're early today. Who's your friend?"

"This is Hailey. She's new to town." He lowered his voice and leaned over the counter. "She had a little accident in the river. Cut up her leg. Can you bring her the works?"

"You poor thing." The woman put her hand on Hailey's fingers that barely poked out from the sleeve of Dylan's jacket, startling her with the warmth. Her eyes were deep and dark and kind. "I'll get you something right away." She glanced at Dylan. "You having anything?"

"Maybe some coffee," he said. "Thanks, Maggie."

This was the owner of the café, then, though Hailey didn't care who she was if she brought her food. Checking to make sure the money in the pocket of her backpack was still there, she let it slide from her shoulder to the floor. Her bladder was complaining again, but she wouldn't attempt walking to the bathroom until she had something to eat. The granola bar seemed ages ago, little more than an insufficient appetizer. Had she really gone two days without food? She strained to remember, but a piercing discomfort in her head made her shelve the matter for the time being.

Dylan waited until an oversized plate, jam-packed with steaming eggs, bacon, pancakes, hash browns and biscuits, was in front of Hailey before he stepped around the end of the counter and began talking in a low, urgent voice with Maggie. He was probably telling her about the barn and her falling into the river, though it was entirely possible they were only discussing the dog. Their heads were close together, and Dylan's familiarity with the woman made Hailey wonder if they had something going on. Maggie's age was hard to determine, but if she was older than Dylan, it wasn't by much, and she was beautiful in an earthy, abandoned sort of way that Hailey thought was probably appealing to most men.

The food was good, loaded with carbs. Hailey wolfed it down, but before she was half-finished, her stomach began to ache and she slowed down. She purposefully didn't look at Dylan, who was still talking to Maggie, holding a cup of coffee in his hands.

A soft, high-pitched ding sounded, and the front door to the café opened behind her. Glancing around, Hailey watched as an older woman with short, brown hair and an even older man sporting a head of thin but curly white hair came into the café. They called a hello to the people at the table near the back door before making their way to the bar. Hailey adjusted her dress to make sure her dirty feet were well hidden.

"Good morning," said the woman as she sat next to Hailey, turning smiling blue eyes in her direction.

Hailey looked around to see if someone was behind her. No one. "Good morning," Hailey murmured.

Maggie left Dylan and approached the other side of the counter. "Good morning, Ronica, Fletcher," she said in her smooth, cheerful voice. "The usual? It'll be ready in a bit. Just finishing the next batch of bacon."

"Fletcher shouldn't even be having bacon," said Ronica. "The doctor said last week that his cholesterol was high."

Fletcher took a newspaper from under his skinny, bare arm and cleared his throat. "My father and grandfather lived past ninety without anyone telling them not to eat bacon, and so will I. That whole cholesterol stuff is a bunch of malarkey, and you know it."

She rolled her eyes. "Fine. Die and see if I care."

"I'll outlive you yet." Fletcher put on a pair of reading glasses, flicked his paper open, and began reading.

Ronica didn't respond to that, but a haunted expression crossed her face that looked similar to the expression Hailey had noticed on her own face in the farmhouse mirror. *There's more to the story,* she thought, a tense pit forming in her stomach.

"I'll bring your coffees now," Maggie said, a smile tugging at her lips at what was probably an argument she'd heard repeated dozens of times. "And I'll hurry with the food because I know Ronica's due at the salon today."

Ronica touched the roots of her hair. "It's that obvious, huh?"

"No, sweetie, you always get it styled on Fridays after breakfast. Your color is fine." Maggie laughed, and Ronica joined her.

"In that case, bring me a side of bacon as well. I'm getting too predictable." Ronica looked over at Hailey and winked, as if they were friends. No trace of a haunted expression, so maybe Hailey had imagined it. She smiled and took another bite.

Dylan came up beside her. "How's the food? Looks like you're making good headway."

"Wonderful," she said in a whisper, "but could you watch it for me? I need to use the restroom."

His warm chuckle reached to the end of her toes. "Sure, but there's no need. We're all practically family here."

That was his reassuring doctor voice again, and she was grateful. She was even more grateful that her legs didn't collapse as she grabbed her backpack and escaped to the bathroom. No one stared, so maybe they didn't notice or care about her bare feet. After relieving her bladder and putting on a new pad, she pulled out the elastic in her long hair, thinking that might be part of the reason her head still ached so much. She scrubbed her fingertips over her scalp, loosening it. The motion seemed to help a bit, though her hair needed a good wash, not so much for oil but for the dirt that stained and stiffened the strands.

When she returned to the bar and climbed onto her seat, feeling better but still dizzy, Ronica held out her hand to Hailey. "Dylan tells us you're new in town. So let's make this official. I'm Ronica Wilson. Well, Veronica, really, but everyone calls me Ronica. And this is my husband, Fletcher."

Hailey was ready for the required response. "I'm Hailey Waters," she said, shaking Ronica's hand and nodding at Fletcher. Waters seemed appropriate since despite all the water she'd drunk, she still felt thirsty. "I'm not sure how long I'll be here. Probably at least a few weeks."

"Only a few weeks? Well, you know what? I thought the same thing when I came thirty years ago to visit my aunt." She winked at Hailey, glancing down at her left hand as if checking for a wedding ring. "Maybe we can convince you to stay. I'll introduce you to my son later. He's a farmer."

"Everyone's a farmer here or married to one," Fletcher stated without looking up from his newspaper. "Except Doc Sayer and Maggie here. Oh, and Dylan."

"No, dear," Ronica said, with a hint of worn patience. "That was in the old days. There's only a handful of farmers and ranchers now. With the turkey factory and Walmart over in Panna Creek, we're getting to be downright city folks." She turned back to Hailey. "Anyway, our son Jeremy has just built a new home next to ours. It's lovely."

Maggie saved Hailey from responding by bringing their

food. Hailey's thumb went to her ring finger, as if automatically checking for a ring there. She felt relieved there wasn't one, and also no mark on her sun-reddened skin to show that one had ever been there. She took another bite of eggs that were now on the verge of cold, but still so good. She followed that mouthful by an entire slice of bacon and a second biscuit, swallowing as fast as she could chew.

"Better now?" Dylan asked, his voice amused.

She glanced at him to find his brown eyes watching her intently. It was kind of embarrassing. Was he worried she'd take off with something?

She nodded, and he continued, "Maggie says she's glad to let you stay."

Her gut clenched with worry. She had a nice amount of money, but without ID, she had no way to earn more. She'd have to figure something out, or she'd be sleeping in barns once her money ran out.

"How much is a room?" she asked.

"Don't worry. She said she can work something out with you."

Next to her, Ronica let out a little squeal, drawing their attention. She pressed close to her husband, looking at his newspaper. "That senator will be the next governor of Nebraska," she said. "Mark my words. My, but he is one good-looking man, even if he is too liberal in my book, whooey!" She waved her hands to fan her face. "If I were twenty years younger . . ."

"He'd still be married," Fletcher grumbled, trying to turn the page.

"Wait!" Ronica squinted at the words, finally grabbing Fletcher's glasses from his face and peering closer at the print. "It says his wife had a fall and was taken to the hospital. Oh, I hope their baby is okay. I'm betting it will be a girl." Ronica read in silence for a moment while Fletcher cleared his throat and waited impatiently.

Hailey paused before eating the last biscuit, suddenly curious if the senator's wife was okay. It was a lot better than worrying about how she was going to make a living.

"Oh, she's fine," Ronica said after a while with a long sigh. "They'll be keeping her a few days for observation." She winked conspiratorially at Hailey. "I'm from Nebraska," she said, "so I like to keep up on politics."

Fletcher snorted. "You mean gossip."

Ronica laughed. "He's right, I confess. Politics are boring, but Brice Granville will be the governor of Nebraska before he's forty, mark my words. He's too handsome and compelling not to be."

"He'd have to be fifty at least before that happens." Fletcher tried to turn the page, but Ronica pulled the newspaper closer.

"I'm not done yet." She held the paper toward Hailey. "See how attractive he is?"

But Hailey could no longer see the paper or anything beyond the middle of her vision, which meant her plate. Blackness ate at that too, tearing the scene away, bit by bit, as if it were all a dream. She felt herself falling and grabbed for the bar. Her fingers missed. She waited to hit the ground.

Arms closed around her, strong arms that made her feel safe. She was sure it was Dylan, who'd been calmly drinking his coffee beside her. "I've got you," his voice whispered.

Those were the same words Dylan had used in the barn, but now they weren't spoken in his slight drawl. Instead, it was that other voice that made her want to run, the voice that had taken everything.

She had to get away. Now.

For a moment, she struggled, flailing her limbs. But the arms around her were unmovable. Her determination vanished as the voice and the sensation of being held dissolved into nothingness.

CHAPTER 4

Dylan caught Hailey as she fell. Barely, and only because he'd recognized the expression on her face. He'd seen it before in enough of the owners of his non-human patients to know it was coming. Hailey was light in his arms, as if she weighed nothing. With her billowy dress, he hadn't really known what to expect.

Maggie hurried around the counter and checked the right side of Hailey's neck for a pulse.

"I can feel she's breathing," he said a little impatiently, "but does she feel hot to you?"

She'd been shivering earlier when he offered his jacket, but fevers were strange that way, making you hot one moment and cold the next. That didn't change from animals to humans. She'd recently taken a pain reliever, though, so she shouldn't be very hot.

Maggie felt her forehead. "If she has a fever, it's not too bad."

"She took a pain killer a half hour ago."

"Want me to call Doc Sayer?" Ronica had her phone out. She and Fletcher and the other people in the café were all standing around staring. Dylan felt the urge to hide Hailey from them. He tucked his jacket more tightly around her, noting the tiny patch of brown on her neck where Maggie had felt for her pulse—a birthmark, he was sure, though he hadn't noticed it before. It made her more human somehow, more real.

"Let's get her upstairs," Maggie said, as another group of people entered the café. She served some of the best food around, and the closer it got to lunchtime, the more people would wander in. "If she's not looking better after lunch, we can call Doc Sayer." She stood swiftly before adding to Ronica, "Keisha won't be in for another hour, so tell everyone I'll be right back down."

"Sure," Ronica said. "And I can pour coffee as people come in."

Maggie nodded. "Good idea. Thank you. I'll be right back."

The small crowd split for Dylan as he followed Maggie toward the back door, where an inner staircase led to the second floor. Aside from Maggie's own suite, there was another room with a private bathroom and two additional rooms that shared a bathroom. Dylan had stayed here himself a few times when visiting his father from New York. As far as he knew, only one of the cheaper bedrooms was currently being rented by a developer from out of town.

Maggie led the way down the hall to the last room on the left that faced the front of the café, opposite her own suite. This was the room with the private bath where he'd stayed, but it had changed. The queen-sized bed now had a canopy frame and gauzy, off-white curtains that were tied to the canopy poles like something from a Disney princess movie, and there were two new paintings on the walls.

"Put her on the bed," Maggie said.

Hailey was already stirring. Dylan laid her on top of the covers as she blinked her eyes open.

"What happened?" she asked, her voice nearly inaudible. With her hair spread out on the pillow, wearing that yellow dress and his jacket, her feet dirty and her leg bandaged, she looked small and defenseless.

"You passed out, that's what." Maggie took a lap blanket from the chair by the desk in the corner and spread it over her. "And I know it's not because of my food. Do you need a doctor?"

"No. Please." Hailey came up on one elbow. "I'm just tired. It's been a long couple of days. I'm sorry to inconvenience you."

Maggie snorted inelegantly. "It's no inconvenience, just a blip. Dylan told me you got off the bus two days ago. Didn't you see the pay phone at the stop?" Her voice was gently chiding. "We do have a taxi service in town, you know."

Hailey bit her lip and shook her head, then winced and brought a hand to her temple. "I didn't see one."

"Well, that's all water under the bridge now. You rest up. I'll be back to check on you later. Feel free to clean up in the adjoining bathroom if you get to feeling better. There are fresh towels in the cupboard, and I'll bring you a change of clothes. The key to the door is on the desk if you want to leave your things here and go out for any reason." Maggie smiled and headed for the door, where she paused and stared back at Dylan. "You might as well bring in the mutt," she said, ushering him out the door with a sweeping motion. "It can keep her company."

"Sable is not a mutt," Dylan protested but not too strongly

because he was grateful to Maggie for watching Sable until he had time to set things up for her at the clinic. In the meantime, Hailey might enjoy the dog's company.

He glanced back when he reached the door, expecting to find Hailey watching them, but she'd curled up under the blanket and closed her eyes. Her face was nearly covered with her mass of blond hair. He was strangely reluctant to leave her.

"She'll be all right," Maggie said, firmly shutting the door behind them.

Dylan nodded as they walked down the hallway. "It's a puzzle, her stepping off the bus like that, falling into the river, and wandering around for two days. When I first found her, I got the impression she didn't even know her name."

They'd reached the top of the stairs, and Maggie paused. "She wouldn't be the first person who came to Forgotten to hide for one reason or another. It doesn't make her a criminal."

Dylan could sense the underlying meaning in Maggie's tone. She'd come from out of nowhere thirteen years ago while he was still in New York and bought the café, rebranding it and changing the menu. But by the time he'd returned to town, she fit in so well that he sometimes forgot she wasn't a native. Her speech was more cultured than ninety percent of residents in their small town, and she occasionally referenced things he'd never experienced firsthand, but that was part of her charm. If she had a secret past, he doubted he'd ever learn about it from her.

"No," he said, "but coming here doesn't give her a pass either. And when I told her whose barn she'd stumbled into, she definitely looked nervous."

"Well, you can always report finding her to Levi at the station."

"I still might, but you know as well as I do that he doesn't have a whole lot of experience. Neither do any of the others." They had four salaried full-time officers in Forgotten, who doubled as firefighters, and three volunteer part-timers, but all of the officers except the chief were new on the job. Which meant the city still depended on the county sheriff's department for help with law enforcement more than Chief McColl liked, especially when he was out of town. If Hailey was on the up and up, Dylan didn't want her pulled into a senseless investigation.

"Let's give her a little time. I'm sure we'll find out more. Unless you feel she's dangerous."

"She did ward me off with a pitchfork," Dylan said, his mouth twitching upward with the memory, "but I know you carry a gun, and I'd bet against her any day if it comes to that."

Maggie laughed and tossed her head, causing a few black hairs to stray from her tight knot. It suited her better that way. Half the time, he didn't know if she was flirting with him or simply teasing. She was an attractive woman, more compelling than beautiful with her raven hair and eyes almost as equally dark, but she'd never indicated that she wanted more from their relationship. For his part, the five years she had on him weren't a problem, but he liked their friendship exactly the way it was. Romance was too complicated. He didn't want to worry about another woman.

Or losing one.

"Don't worry," Maggie repeated, boxing his arm. "Go save an animal or two and come back fast for the dog."

"If she starts to deliver, give me a call."

"It wouldn't be my first time."

"Good. I'll have my receptionist run over some food when she comes in, but you probably won't be able to get her to eat any more until dinner."

Nodding, Maggie walked with him to the outside staircase and stood in the doorway while he retrieved Sable, who promptly began investigating the parking lot, finding a strip of grass to mark her territory. Dylan used the time to retrieve her leash and take it up to Maggie. When Maggie whistled, Sable lumbered up the stairs, wagging her tail. She knew Maggie, of course. Everyone in town did.

Back in his Tahoe, Dylan had to wait for a few people to park before he could pull out. The morning rush was coming to the Butter Cake Café, and though it wouldn't be all that many people, he felt a little guilty for adding to Maggie's burden. But he felt good about helping Caleb with his animals and stitching up Hailey, who was either too naive or too stubborn to seek help. Which, now that he thought about it, meant she wasn't all that different from his regular patients.

His next stop was supposed to be a herd check on one of the dairy farms, but a new text from Jeremy Wilson begging him to come and check out his cow who was "moaning and acting really weird" was a higher priority. Neither Ronica nor Fletcher had mentioned anything about the cow at the café, so that made Dylan more curious about Jeremy's semi-frantic text. Jeremy had worked his family farm with ranch hands even before his father's health had begun to decline, but now he had to do it without his father's experience.

The Wilson farm was only a few miles away, and when Dylan arrived, he pulled up to the newer of the two houses on the property. Jeremy might have followed in his father's footsteps, but he'd grown tired of living under his parents' roof and had built the house next door last year. His parents thought the move was senseless, since they had plenty of room and Jeremy would inherit the house one day, but Dylan suspected Jeremy's move was a good one if he ever wanted to have a family. No woman he knew wanted to live with a mother-in-law, no matter how friendly.

As Dylan exited the Tahoe in front of Jeremy's new house, Jeremy himself came outside, chewing on a sandwich. His blond hair poked out from under his brown cowboy hat, his muscled chest strained at his soiled T-shirt, and tiny bits of hay poked from his full beard. His pants had fared a little better in the morning's work, but his boots were caked in mud.

"Thanks for coming out so fast," Jeremy said, extending his sandwich-free hand to Dylan. He'd been six years behind Dylan in school, and every time they met, Dylan had a glimpse of the scrawny, scab-covered child he'd once been.

"How's Moona Lisa doing?"

"No change since my text. But I did come in to grab some grub. You want to follow me out to the barn?"

Dylan nodded. "You got rope? I have some if we need it."

"Plenty."

Dylan climbed back in his SUV, remembering how Ronica had talked to Hailey about Jeremy. With his impressive physique and landholdings, Jeremy was a popular bachelor among the single ladies in town. For some reason, that bothered Dylan now. He couldn't see Hailey with this man.

Not that it was any of his business.

They were greeted outside the barn by two barking dogs which Jeremy sent away with a terse order.

"You've checked her for cuts?" Dylan asked.

"Yeah, as much as she'll let me. She kicked me good on the shin. I wouldn't worry so much, but my mom loves this cow. Haven't even dared tell her yet."

"You managed to milk her last night, though, right?"

"Yep. Not today, though. She's too upset."

Not milking the cow would eventually cause mastitis, if she didn't already have it, so they needed to take care of her as soon as possible. Striding to the barn, Dylan found the animal in the back of her stall, lowing in a way that told him she was in pain.

"Whoa," Jeremy said, "She's a lot bigger than when I checked on her an hour ago. She looks like she's blowing up."

Moona Lisa was a lovely black Holstein with white patches on her face, torso, and front right leg. The patch on her face looked almost like a visor. Normally she was good-natured, but today her side facing them was grotesquely extended, and her breathing was excessively labored. No wonder she'd kicked Jeremy.

"It's bloat. Good thing you called me." Dylan knew he had to act immediately or the gas inside her rumen would expand until she suffocated. "Has she been in one of your fields?"

Jeremy shook his head, frowning. "Not that I know, but my dad was out here this morning before they went into the Butter Cake. He might have let her out. It wouldn't be the first time."

Dylan felt for him. Watching his own father crumble under the weight of cancer had been hard, but losing a parent to dementia had to be worse. "You're going to need a lock for the gate."

"But you can help her, right? Man, I feel like such an idiot. If my dad was in his right mind, he would have known."

"Don't beat yourself up over it. You grow corn and alfalfa, not raise cattle. Get the rope. I'll get what I need from the car. We need to do this fast, or we'll lose her." Dylan was already heading for the barn door. There was no time for a stomach tube. He'd have to use the more dangerous trocar method.

After a quick sprint to the Tahoe, Dylan moved cautiously

into the pen. "Easy, Moona Lisa," Dylan said as he laid his hands on the cow's side.

Jeremy moved in beside him, holding a rope. On cattle and milk farms, they normally had a metal stall to contain the animals during treatment. Here, they'd have to use a little ingenuity and brute strength. When Moona Lisa's head was tied to his satisfaction, Dylan looped another rope around her girth near her back legs and sent Jeremy into the next stall to tie it down. Then he felt the cow's ribs near the top of her side, searching for the right place to cut. A couple ounces of sterilizer rubbed into the spot, and he was ready.

His knife went through her hide with barely a flicker of notice, but she lurched violently as he shoved the corkscrew trocar through her muscle and into her rumen. He pushed hard, bracing her as she struggled against the ropes. A hissing sound began through the trocar as he finished screwing it in. Almost immediately the tension in the cow's body eased.

"There, that feels better now, doesn't it?" he said to her.

Moona Lisa looked at him, stretching out her neck and straining to free her head as if to show how unimpressed she was. He knew why. Her swollen udder signaled there was more she needed before she could be comfortable.

"You can loosen her," he called over the stall to Jeremy. "But toss me a bucket. I want to make sure she isn't getting mastitis."

After checking her udder and the color of the milk, Dylan was satisfied that she was all right. "Make sure you get all the milk out," he told Jeremy. "She's overdue for a good milking."

"What about the trocar?"

"Leave it in for three or four weeks, then simply take it out. Let me know if it tries to come out before or if she starts to bloat again. There's nothing else you really need to do except watch for infection while it heals. I'll give her an antibiotic to help with that, but you won't be able to use the milk for the next forty-eight hours. If I'd gotten here a little earlier, we could have used a stomach tube and avoided all that."

"I had no idea it was bloat." Jeremy took off his hat and scratched at his blond hair. "Or that my dad had taken her out."

Dylan finished giving the antibiotics and moved away from the cow, letting Jeremy take his place. He clapped a hand on the other man's shoulder. "I'm sorry. I did see your father just now at the Butter Cake. He looked good."

"More like an elegant college professor than a farmer with dementia," Jeremy agreed. "He's aged well, that's for sure. His body, at least." He smiled sadly before adding more brightly, "Got a text from my mom about a new woman in town. Do you believe her? She wants grandkids so bad that she's taken to setting me up with strangers."

"Mothers," Dylan empathized, squelching a pang in his chest. But he didn't really know. The only childhood memories he had of his mother involved her perfume and one happy day at the lake.

"But it's why I built the house, after all," Jeremy continued. "I ain't gettin' any younger. Maybe I'll ask her out. Should be a little fun, at least."

Dylan bristled internally, remembering how vulnerable Hailey had looked lying in bed, but he only nodded and motioned to the cow. "You take care of Moona Lisa. I'll see myself out."

He craned his neck as he passed Jeremy's house. His decision to build it was part of what had given Dylan the idea to build his own place near the lake. He currently lived in the apartment in the clinic, as his father had before him, even when he'd been married to Dylan's mother. It was a good setup, especially since most of their business consisted of large animals and onsite visits. But everyone knew where to find him when he wasn't out on appointments and didn't hesitate to bang loudly on his door in the middle of the night in what weren't true emergencies. Putting a little distance between him and work, and encouraging customers to use his emergency hotline instead of his regular line would be a good thing.

He also wanted to expand the clinic and hire a small-animal assistant in addition to the part-time receptionist he employed. More small animals were coming in these days, and it was difficult to keep up on all the clinic work as he did his normal rounds.

If he was honest, however, those weren't the real reasons he wanted to build a new house on the lake property. He wanted a place that didn't remind him of loss. He shook his head—he didn't want to think about that now.

Dylan proceeded to his regularly scheduled appointment at the dairy farm, where the corral was full of mud, and he had to pull on his waders from his box in the back of his SUV. Everything looked good except one calf who sounded on the verge of respiratory illness, which meant isolation and antibiotics so it wouldn't spread. He'd have to return soon and check up on the animals again.

His next plan had been to go back to his clinic and prepare for the small animal immunizations he had scheduled after lunch, but he was suddenly curious about the bus stop. Whether Hailey had come north from Nebraska or south from deeper into Kansas, there was only one stop north of Forgotten. He'd driven past it a million times driving to and from Panna Creek, but he couldn't really remember it now.

Six minutes later, he pulled over at the solitary shack marking the crossroad by the bus stop. The place was barely more than a bathroom with a small lean-to attached that featured a rough bench. The glass or plastic that had once made up most of the front was long gone.

He walked around the bus stop, seeing that while the payphone worked, the phone book had been torn away. The bathroom was worse. There was no longer tissue in the single toilet stall, the sink was cracked, and the water leaked from the mineral-encrusted tap. He'd have to bring the condition of the stop up at the next town meeting. If this was the first glimpse of Forgotten visitors saw, it was enough to warn them off forever.

He was curious about the path Hailey might have taken to the McColl farm, and he drove slowly along the edge of the road with the window rolled down, looking for signs of her passing—a shoe, a suitcase, a purse. There was nothing.

About five miles toward town, a new sound reached his ears, but it wasn't until he turned off the engine that he recognized what it was—the river. This was the closest point it ever came to the road, and it was a straight line from here to Chief McColl's place.

Leaving the Tahoe, Dylan struck off across the road, knowing it was futile but not being able to help himself. All his instincts told him Hailey was hiding something, and if he could find a clue, maybe he could help her.

Help her or protect the town? He really didn't know. But at some point, he'd stopped wanting to wash his hands of her. In fact, with every second that passed, his desire to see her again increased.

He came to the river in less than three minutes, shaking his head. The water was deep here, the channel narrow. Not a good place to cross. He followed the river, knowing it widened farther on. If Hailey had entered the water here, she would have had to float until the water slowed down enough for her to climb out on the other side.

He came upon a sandal quite suddenly, one with a two-inch-heel. Under a thick covering of mud, it was flesh-colored, a size seven. He searched a little more and gazed across the river, but its mate was nowhere to be found.

At least this part of her story is real, he thought. She could have cut her leg on a branch or rock in the river, but he didn't see anything that could have injured her wrist. He was even more sure *that* hadn't been an accident. Who had hurt her? Or was she hiding something she'd done?

Before he could begin to know any of that, he'd have to find out who she was and where she'd come from. That meant a trip to the police station, but would Levi do a search for him without strings? There was also the question of her privacy. Nothing was quiet in a small town, even if he wanted it to be.

No, it would be better to call his ex-partner in New York. Hector Sanchez had been a rock during the aftermath of what happened with Bristol, and he was still a good friend that Dylan could trust. And at least that way he'd know if Hailey matched the description of a wanted criminal.

He'd take pictures of the sandal and send that too, because while the brand could be commonly sold everywhere, it might lead to pinpointing her origination. Once he had a better idea of what he was looking at, he would decide then what to do about Hailey Waters.

CHAPTER 5

Hailey awoke shivering. She was lying in a bed under a blanket, but she still felt cold. Her body seemed to hurt everywhere. Even rolling over onto her back sent waves of discomfort everywhere. A moan escaped her mouth.

A jingling sounded as something heavy jumped onto the bed. Fear rippled through her—a bright, copper-tasting fear that made all her muscles clench. But then a wet nose shoved into her neck.

"Ah, Sable." Hailey's arms went around the dog. "You scared me."

The dog pushed against her and lay down, looking awkward with her huge belly. Hailey had to loosen her hold to make room, but she kept petting the animal's silky fur, her emotions stabilizing.

Memories came rushing back—the barn, the farmhouse, the wonderful food. "Oh, I passed out. How embarrassing." She let out a long groan, and Sable took that as a sign to lick her.

Hailey laughed. "Stop that." Pulling herself to a seated position, she looked around the room. It was pretty in a generic sort of way, with beige shutters, curtains, and blankets. Only the gauzy canopy on the bed frame was slightly upscale, and maybe a little out of place.

Hailey felt groggy and dirty, but moving around seemed to help her soreness. She flicked off the blanket and realized it was only a small one, and that she was on top of the bed's main coverings. Dirt streaked her yellow dress, and the mirror above the desk showed that her hair looked terrible.

As if I haven't washed it for a week, she thought, which might be true.

She probed her mind but found she still didn't remember anything before talking to the bus driver when she got off the bus—and much of that was hazy. Only this morning was crystal clear, especially the memory of Dylan's penetrating gaze.

She gave her head a sharp shake, then winced at the pain the motion caused. Moving slowly, she arose and went to the desk where she found a note and a box of clothing Maggie had put there for her, items left behind by people who'd once stayed at the cafe. Everything smelled of detergent and looked freshly washed. Gratitude surged in her heart. The oversized lion T-shirt and red gym shorts hardly seemed like something she should be wearing all over town, especially when she still felt so cold.

She held up a pair of skinny jeans and a soft, baby blue sweatshirt with no ribbing at the bottom. They smelled fresh and clean. Adding a pair of underwear and a black sports bra that had seen better days, she grabbed her backpack and went to the adjoining bathroom.

"No, Sable, stay. I'm just going to clean up. I'll be right back." She shut the door firmly behind her.

She filled the bathtub with water as hot as she could handle, removed the bandage from her wrist, and lowered her aching body inside, careful to keep the stitched leg out, resting it on the side of the tub. She couldn't remember anything feeling so wonderful—although if she were honest, she couldn't remember anything, so that wasn't much of an endorsement. She added more hot water as needed, staying in the tub until her cramps eased, the water turned pink, and her fingers wrinkled like prunes. Still, she floated on a happy, blissful wave.

Finally, she let out the water and turned on the overhead shower, taken by a sudden, overpowering urge to scrub herself clean. Using cleansers in the wall dispensers, she first washed her hair and then her body. She was getting water on her stitches against the vet's orders, but it wouldn't be for long. She winced as the soap touched the scratches on her wrist.

Staring at it brought a stuttering vision to her mind. A man's hazy face—or was it a doctor's?—talking to her, his voice raised. His hand gripped her wrist. A wrist that had a leather cuff on it.

A gasp escaped her. She crouched in the tub, water pounding on her head. A gaping chasm opened inside her, threatening to pull her under and suffocate her. The hole was so huge, the emotion so great that she no longer knew anything except the emptiness and a heartache she couldn't name. Then rapid images began assaulting her like the stripes of a whip. Voices spoke, but she couldn't hear them. She smelled coppery blood and antiseptic.

"No!" The word burst from her. She crossed her arms tightly over her chest and pushed it all away.

The water poured down as she rocked herself and cried.

Hailey came to herself with a start. The clean smell of soap hit her nostrils as she became aware of hot water raining down on her, sliding over her face and into her mouth. What was she doing hunched down in the tub like this? How long had she been here?

She stood, feeling embarrassed and not quite understanding what had happened. She was probably still half asleep and dreaming—or maybe she'd caught something from falling into the river. She did feel a little feverish, though that might be from the hot water. She dried off, careful of her leg. The bandage was soaked, but the flesh didn't look too soggy underneath. She'd have to find new bandages for both her leg and wrist.

Back in her room, Sable came slowly to her feet from a blanket Maggie had left on the floor for her. The dog's face seemed reproachful, as if upset at being left so long.

"Sorry, sweetie." Hailey fell to her knees and started petting the dog. She was so sweet and soft—and huge. Hailey ran her hand lightly over the dog's stomach, wondering if she'd skitter away, but she only leaned into Hailey.

"I feel a lot better," she confided to the dog. "But my head is pounding, so you're going to stay here while I go buy some painkillers."

She'd only take the loose bills from the backpack with her on this trip. With the locked room, she could stash the money belt here until she could figure out a safer place to store it. No ID probably meant no bank account for now . . . and also no way to earn more money.

She put everything from her backpack in a drawer except the three hundred and twelve dollars and the flimsy plastic water bottle—currently empty. The ten thousand dollars, still inside the money belt, she stuffed between the mattress and box spring, though that seemed a little cliché. Then it was back to the box of clothes to fish out a pair of flip flops that were half an inch too long and a black baseball cap that would help keep the sun from doing more damage.

Satisfied, she started for the door, but Sable was having none of being left behind again, and she whined loudly as Hailey tried to shut the door. She was considering going downstairs to ask Maggie for a length of rope to take the dog with her when the woman herself appeared at the top of the stairs.

"I thought I heard someone up and about," Maggie said, coming toward her.

Hailey gave her a rueful grin. "I thought I'd do a little shopping. I need something for this headache. But Sable's upset about being left inside, and I can't seem to make myself shut the door on her."

"Probably needs to do her thing, what with all those babies sitting on her bladder." Maggie looked thoughtful. "Though I'm not sure if it works for dogs the same way as humans. Anyway, I did come to let her out. We've been a little busier than usual today, so this is the first chance I've had. There's only an hour until we start serving dinner. We stay open until nine on the weekend, so I might not get another chance before then."

"Clear till nine, huh?" Hailey didn't bother hiding her smile.

Maggie returned it with a grin of her own. "Usually it's seven, and we're closed on Sundays. That's part of what I love about living in a small town. Everyone needs time off. And there's always the bar for people who want to stay out later."

"I can take Sable outside with me."

Maggie's smile widened. "That'll be great. But are you hungry? You slept all the way through lunch."

"I could eat." Hailey wasn't as hungry as she'd been earlier, but she wasn't going to turn down food.

"I left the leash somewhere on the desk earlier when I brought Sable in," Maggie said. "If you go on out the back stairs, I'll meet you there with a sandwich to tide you over until dinner. You can eat at the tables on the side of the café or you might want to walk to the park next door if you're feeling up to it. It's a beautiful day out there."

"Thank you. Um, maybe you can put it on my tab?"

Maggie's laugh was deep and throaty. "This one's on me because you're doing me a big favor taking Sable out. I'm not really a dog person. But Dylan's a friend, and so are Sable's owners."

Hailey bent to rub Sable's back. "I think Sable definitely doesn't think of herself as a dog. She's a person."

Again, the throaty laugh. "That is pretty clear. Well, enjoy yourself. We'll talk about the rest later. I'd better get back downstairs." She was gone before Hailey could thank her again.

By the time Hailey found the leash behind the box of clothes, filled up the plastic water bottle in the bathroom, locked her room, and made her way down the outside staircase, Maggie was already placing a white paper lunch sack on the closest of the round tables, along with a tall glass of water and a bottle of Ibuprofen. Sable beelined toward a bowl of dogfood and a water dish set on the cobblestones next to the table. Apparently sleeping the entire afternoon away with Hailey had done good things for her appetite.

Hailey gratefully swallowed two pills and drank the water. "Thank you so much."

"Just let me know if you need anything more." Removing the empty cup and the bottle of painkillers, Maggie disappeared inside the café, using not the back entrance, but a door behind the tables that led into the kitchen.

For a moment, Hailey let the scene seep into her. The area on this side of the house was a slice of heaven, with its border of grass, the cobblestone walkway leading from the rear door of the café to the parking lot, and the huge flowerpots set at advantageous intervals. The sky overhead was clear and the day still warm enough that her sweatshirt was plenty.

She pulled the sandwich from the bag—thick pieces of homemade bread, cheese, meat, and vegetables—and bit through it with a little sigh. Except for a slight heaviness to the bread, it was pure heaven.

After eating half of the sandwich, she put the rest back in the sack and dropped it into her backpack next to the water bottle, ignoring Sable's pleading gaze. "You've had enough, girl. I've heard about dogs and people food, and I'm not going to be responsible for getting you or your babies sick. Come on." Rising, she tugged at the leash. Sable followed willingly, stopping only to mark the grass border to the parking lot.

The park next door was tempting, with its mature trees and bushes, large gazebo, and iron benches set along cobbled walkways. She longed to sit on a bench and watch the teens playing Frisbee on the grass or the family that picnicked with two adorable toddlers. *Later,* she told herself. First, she wanted to walk a little and see her surroundings.

Forgotten's Main Street was at once unfamiliar and familiar to Hailey. All the usual stores seemed to be there—that was the familiar part—but the traffic was slow, and the wide cobbled walkways on either side of the street were picturesque, as if she'd stepped into some quaint European village.

She walked past an ice cream parlor, a flower shop, a toy

and hobby store, a movie theater, and a pizzeria. Next to a small police station, the town hall sat rather majestically. She rested on a bench there, studying the small pioneer log cabin she'd noticed on the drive in. Likely it was a significant landmark and she decided to investigate later. She drank water from her bottle and poured some in her hand for Sable, who wasn't interested. Instead, the dog gave a little whine and stretched out on the grass. Her stomach moved of its own accord, which was both awesome and a little freaky. Hailey hoped the walk hadn't made her that much closer to having the pups.

"We'd better get you back to the café," she said.

First, she needed to find a store where she could get a few supplies. There had been a grocery store across from the park and next to a church, and that should have what she needed. Whistling to Sable, she found a crosswalk.

Everywhere she went, people smiled and nodded, though a few followed her with their gazes curiously. Was it that obvious she was new in town?

She wasn't sure what to do about Sable while she was in Terrell's Grocery store. She was looking around for somewhere to tie the leash when Ronica Wilson, the woman she'd met at the café that morning, came by, this time with another woman instead of her husband. Ronica's shoulder-length hair was styled, and it looked so nice that Hailey wished she had a blow dryer or something to use on her own wilted locks. Maybe there was one under the sink in her room.

"Hello!" Ronica said. "I hope you're feeling better."

"I am. Thank you."

"This is Charlotte Bennett," Ronica continued. "She's the local midwife."

Charlotte smiled, extending a hand. "Well, I'm a lay midwife. I'm mostly self-trained, though I work a lot with Doc Sayer these days." She had beautiful shoulder-length brown hair and bright green eyes that seemed to see everything.

Ronica leaned forward and said in a loud stage whisper, "Doc is great, but when a woman's in labor, Charlotte is what she needs. I only wish she'd been delivering babies when I had Jeremy twenty-nine years ago."

Charlotte laughed. "I was only one at the time."

Hailey smiled. That made the woman close to her age, or maybe a few years older. Wait, or did it? How old was she?

Ronica saw the consternation on her face and glanced at the store, misreading her thoughts. "You need to go inside? I'd be happy to watch Sable for you. In fact, I was going to the park to meet my husband. He's playing chess there with Charlotte's father."

"Sable's been whining," Hailey said. "I'm wondering if that means something."

"It means she's lazy, that's what," Ronica said in a no-nonsense tone. "She'll drop her litter when they're ready, and a little walking will only do her good." She reached for the leash, and Hailey reluctantly gave it over. A day ago, she hadn't even met Sable, and now the dog seemed like her best friend.

"I have a little experience with delivering children and puppies," Charlotte said with a grin. "Don't worry. Sable will be safe with us."

Of course she would. Hailey felt embarrassed. "Thank you," she said. "I came to buy a few things, but I hadn't thought about what to do with her."

"Take your time." Ronica thumbed over her shoulder. "We'll

meet you in the park. You won't be able to miss the stone chess-boards. They're right next to the gazebo." With a chorus of smiles and nods, Ronica and Charlotte headed toward the crosswalk.

Once in the store, Hailey grabbed a bottle of painkillers, gauze and tape to use as bandages, sunscreen, lotion, a mini tube of antibiotic cream, and a small bottle of laundry deter-gent. Those seemed to be the most pressing items on her list. She was almost to the check stand when she remembered the mini fridge in her room and added yogurt, cheese, fruit, and bagels to her basket. In one aisle, she found a large metal bottle that promised to keep water cold for up to twenty-four hours. That would be a lot better than the disposable plastic one she had now. In that same aisle, she saw new flip flops, but a blister was beginning already between her toes, and she needed something different. She'd seen a clothing store across from town hall and a dress shop that might also have shoes, but she'd have to tackle those another day.

Her attention was drawn to a tiny section of makeup. An image of Dylan Morgan flashed to her mind, and impulsively she added eyeshadow and mascara to her cart. At the check stand, she also put in a large chocolate bar, a staple in every woman's diet. She needed one now.

"You must be Maggie's new lodger," said the gum-snapping, blond, ponytailed teen behind the counter. At Hailey's nod, she continued, "I heard what happened at the café this morning. I hope you're feeling better."

A flush ran over Hailey. Did everyone in town already know about her passing out? "I'm fine," she said faintly, hoping that at least no one knew where Dylan had found her. She would prefer to be known as the fainting woman rather than the woman who broke into someone's barn.

"That's good," the teen said, beginning to ring up her groceries. "My friend started fainting once, and it turned out she was anemic." She paused with her hand on the water bottle, a smile spreading across her face. "She got out of a lot of classes, though, so that was cool."

"I bet."

"I'm Dakota." The teen touched her nametag. "What's your name?"

"Hailey."

"So where are you from? I've never been further than Wichita, and that was only once." She sighed with longing.

Hailey had thought about her response to this question at the same time she'd come up with her last name. It had to be somewhere far enough away that no one would ask her something too specific.

"California," she said. "Los Angeles, originally. Right now, I'm traveling around to see a few places."

"That sounds so fun." Dakota finished ringing up and began bagging her groceries. "That'll be fifty-one dollars and eleven cents."

Hailey's stomach gave a sickening lurch at the total. Depending on the cost of her room, she'd be running through her stash a lot faster than she'd anticipated. And then what? Dogwalker, babysitter? Was she even qualified for anything? With an iron resolve, she stamped down the fear inside her.

Dakota went on talking without noticing Hailey's upset. "I'm going to travel around someday. My boyfriend wants to get married right after high school, you know, but I want to see what's out there." She accepted the bills Hailey gave her but hesitated before putting them in the register. "I heard Dylan Morgan found you. How do you know him anyway? Did you

know he used to be a cop in New York? Before he was a vet,
I mean."

Surprise ran up Hailey's spine. "Um, he was? I—" She cut off,
not knowing what she should say. Dylan was a police officer—or
had been. Did that mean he'd report her and ask the local police
department to look into her past?

A clearing throat made them both turn toward the end of
the checkout station where a striking, ebony-skinned woman
in dress pants and high heels stood with a handbasket. Her face
was expertly made up, and her long, iron-straight, black hair was
perfectly in place.

"Oh, hi, Mrs. Campbell," Dakota said brightly. "How are
you today?"

The woman tapped a long fingernail on her basket. "I'm in
a little bit of a hurry, if you don't mind." Her tone was clipped
and unfriendly.

Dakota opened her mouth to respond, then closed it again,
pursing her lips for a moment. What finally did come out,
Hailey guessed, wasn't what she'd really wanted to say. "Almost
finished," the teen announced sweetly, turning back to her
register for Hailey's change, which she handed over with a smile.

Hailey was about to thank the teen when a very tall, stooped
man with white hair appeared next to the clerk, a box cutter in
his hand. He nodded kindly at Hailey before saying, "Is everything all right, Dakota? We don't want to keep the mayor's wife
waiting, do we?" He slipped the box cutter into the pocket of
his blue apron.

"Everything's fine." Dakota reached quickly for the other
woman's basket.

"How are you, Mrs. Campbell?" The old man asked over
Dakota's head.

The woman gave him a nod. "Doing well. Thank you. As you know, I usually do my shopping in Panna Creek at their larger grocery store, but I do like these green olives you stock. Thank you so much for getting them in, Terrell."

"We're here to please," he responded, but Hailey didn't think she imagined the tightness in the man's smile now. He was probably wondering why he'd bothered to stock the olives.

Hailey finished packing all her sacks except for the one with fruit into her backpack and headed to the door. "Thank you," she murmured.

"Come again," Dakota sang out.

Hailey nodded. To her surprise, the old man beat her to the door, opening it for her. "Are you sure you're feeling okay?" he asked, his smile wide and genuine. "I'd be glad to bring whatever you need over to the Butter Cake. Just give me a call."

"Thank you," she said. "I'll remember that."

"Welcome to Forgotten, Miss Hailey. We always have room for a pretty girl like you. We hope you stay awhile."

Hailey grinned, feeling an unexpected warmth at the old man's comments. She did feel welcome. "Maybe I will," she said.

Outside, she found herself humming a tune, one she couldn't place. Oh well. What mattered was the here and now. She'd figure out some way to support herself before her funds ran out.

At the park, she wandered down a cobblestone path. She thought of the couple Dylan had told her about who'd founded the town, and now she wondered if the cobblestones had been their idea. The walkways made everything seem magical somehow.

Had she really bought makeup after thinking about him? There was no way he'd be interested in her. Especially having once been a police officer. There was a story behind that, to be sure, but she doubted he'd be the one to tell her.

Hailey rounded the gazebo and spied Sable, who jerked the leash from Ronica's hand and waddled toward her. "Hey, girl." Hailey knelt and gave the dog a thorough petting.

The midwife was gone, and so were the picnicking family, but the teens were still playing Frisbee. Ronica and her husband, Fletcher, sat on a narrow stone bench before a stone table inlaid with a chessboard. He was carefully placing chess pieces into a wooden case.

Hailey picked up her bag of fruit and approached the couple. "Thank you so much."

"Not a problem." Ronica smiled up at her.

Fletcher paused. "Who are you?" he asked with an engaging smile. "Have we met before?"

"This is Hailey," Ronica said with an apologetic glance at her. "She's staying at the Butter Cake. We met her this morning."

"Oh, no. I'd remember such a pretty young thing." Fletcher stood and added to his wife, "We need to go home. Jeremy is waiting for me to teach him to drive the tractor."

"Yes, dear." Ronica rose and followed him, pausing near Hailey. "Jeremy has known how to drive the tractor for twenty years," she whispered, "but there's no telling Fletcher that now. See you soon. I hope you get feeling better."

"Thanks." Hailey watched the couple leave, an odd lump in her throat. She was beginning to understand Ronica's haunted expression at the café.

Hailey needed to get the yogurt and cheese into the fridge soon, but it was cool outside, and a few minutes of rest here wouldn't make a difference. She set the bag of fruit down on the stone table and dug in her backpack for the sunscreen. Though the bench was in the shade, light bent in all sorts of ways, and she didn't want to risk making her sunburn worse. Removing her hat, she spread the cream all over her face and on her hands and even the tops of her feet. The tight, painful feeling of her skin wasn't as bad as it had been earlier, so that was a good sign.

She followed her dose of sunscreen with the second half of her sandwich. If anything, the hour she'd been walking had improved the taste, though she probably should worry about the meat being out of the refrigerator so long. Inside the bag was also a small orange she hadn't noticed before. She peeled and ate it quickly. Had oranges always tasted so sweet?

Sable squeezed between the bench and the table, laying her head on Hailey's feet. Peace filled her. Wherever she'd been before, coming to Forgotten was a good idea.

Her peace shattered an instant later when she saw Dylan Morgan striding toward her across the grass. He was even more attractive than she remembered, with his easy stride and his taut muscles filling out that green T-shirt. Belatedly, she remembered that she still had his jacket back in her room. She hoped he hadn't needed it.

She ran a hand through her hair, fearing it was plastered to her head because of the baseball hat, and what had possessed her to wear this oversized sweatshirt? Though there hadn't been much of a choice. She'd have to use some of her funds to fix her lack of a wardrobe sooner rather than later. But instead of the small stores in Forgotten, the Walmart in the next city might be a more economical choice—if she could find a ride.

Stop, she told herself. No matter how Dylan made her pulse race, she couldn't forget he'd been a cop and still had a strong connection with the local police chief.

Dylan's smile was bright, though Hailey was sure it was for

the dog and not for her. Sable stood and wagged her tail at his approach but didn't try to pull her leash from under Hailey's leg where she'd anchored it.

He knelt to pet the dog. "Hey, girl, how are you feeling?" Sable pushed her head into his hand and wagged her tail.

"Thanks for taking care of her." This time his smile was for Hailey, and it made her stomach flop.

"Mostly we slept."

"That's what Maggie said, but it's good you took her for a walk. Being active will help her during delivery. And Maggie said she ate too, which is also good because she needs food for those babies." He rose and squinted up at the sun through the trees. "You really should wear your hat. At least for another hour. You need to protect that burn." He picked up her borrowed hat and shoved it unceremoniously on her head, covering even her eyes.

"Thanks," she said, not meaning it. She pushed up the brim so she could see. "And just so you know, I have been wearing it. I only took it off to put on sunscreen." This last she added so she didn't appear to be completely incapable. She didn't point out that he wasn't wearing a hat on that gorgeous dark head of his.

He chuckled and sat on the stone bench on the other side of the table. "Sorry." His voice didn't sound sorry. "But that hat suits you."

"I probably look like a little kid."

"About as old as those kids over there," he agreed, thumbing at the teens, who were gathering their things to leave.

She didn't have a reply to that, so she stayed silent, trying to recapture the peace she'd felt before he'd crashed her party. As they watched the teens stride from the park, laughing and jostling one another, Hailey felt compelled to say, "Thank you for helping me this morning."

"You're welcome."

Another silence, this one less awkward. Hailey breathed in deeply and let it out slowly. "It's so peaceful here."

He nodded. "It's one of the reasons I like Forgotten so much." He waited a few seconds before adding, "Oh, I found this." He passed her a plastic grocery bag that she hadn't noticed he was carrying. As he set it down, the bag fell open.

"You found my sandals?"

"Uh, not exactly. I found one sandal. It was by the river, caked in mud."

Sure enough, there was only one in the sack, and it was pretty much ruined, though someone had done a good job of cleaning off the dirt—probably with a hose of some kind.

"Thanks," she said.

"It was by the river, not far from the bus stop."

A tendril of worry ran through her. "What were you doing by the river?"

"Looking for your sandal." He said it as if she should have known.

Her heart started beating faster. So was this small-town friendliness, or was he checking up on her?

"I looked for the other one too, but it probably floated down to the lake. I'm afraid it's gone forever."

"Lake?"

"Yeah. Forgotten Reservoir. The lake was always here, but in the early nineteen hundreds they built a dam across the outlet to get power, and it expanded in size. It's probably the prettiest lake I've seen."

"Oh, yeah?" She couldn't help rising to the challenge. "And how many lakes have you seen?"

His only answer was a laugh. "Why don't I take you right

now and you can see for yourself? In fact, I was going to get some dinner at the café since I missed lunch. We can take a picnic."

Hailey didn't know what to make of his invitation. This morning when they'd arrived at the café, he'd barely been able to look at her. Now he was asking her to drive to a lake? Either this was more small-town friendliness, or maybe he was as attracted to her as she was to him.

Then again, he might be searching for more clues into her past. Could she risk that even for the chance of a free meal?

No. She opened her mouth to refuse and was surprised at what came out instead: "Okay, but I need to take my groceries back to the café."

"All right." He came to his feet. "Be prepared for awesome."

Hailey couldn't help smiling, squashing that worrying voice inside her. She couldn't exactly spill anything about her past when she couldn't remember it herself, right?

CHAPTER 6

"S houldn't you be at work?" Hailey asked him as they walked across the park to the Butter Cake Café. She was limping slightly, and he'd volunteered to carry her backpack, but she'd given him Sable's leash instead.

"It's almost five. I'm finished for the day. I was up since seven doing rounds, and then four hours at my clinic."

"Plus rescuing strangers in between. That *is* a long day." She laughed, exposing her throat, which he'd already noticed was smooth and creamy and white, the only part of her not reddened from the sun. The oval birthmark was the single mar on the white expanse, and seeing it brought an unexpected longing to his gut that stole his breath with an alacrity that made him feel helpless.

"Yeah," he managed to say, looking away from her. "Why are you limping? That isn't the leg I stitched."

"Blisters. These flip flops were in a box of things Maggie gave me. There were a few other choices in the box, but I'm not sure they're my size. I'm going to have to buy real shoes soon." She kicked off the offending flip flops, scooped them up, and put them inside the sack with her sandal. He was glad to notice her limping stopped.

"How's the leg?" he asked.

"Good. I got it a little wet in the shower, but I bought some bandages and antibiotic cream."

"Let me know if you'd like me to look at it."

She nodded and didn't ask, so he let it go, though he was itching to see if there was something more he could do. Why this woman seemed to bring out every protective urge in his body had to be connected with the way he'd found her—not because he was interested in her.

Then why are you taking her to the lake? a voice inside his head asked. He had no answer.

When they arrived at the café, she said, "I can hurry and put these away and then watch Sable while you get the food."

"No need. I'll tie her to this table and come out here when I'm finished." Sable was already lapping water Maggie had left out for her.

"Okay." Hailey hurried up the outside stairs.

Inside the café, Maggie was in the dining area near the far corner setting down two plates. "Coffee is coming, boys," she was saying to the old Ramos brothers, whose cattle he treated. "But it's going to be a little wait. I don't want to burn the next batch of steaks."

Dylan lifted his eyebrows as she came toward him. "Busier than usual?" he asked.

"My weekend helpers both called in sick, and Keisha started sniffling after lunch. I had to send her home. I can't have her back here infecting my customers."

"Oh, then I guess now isn't a good time to tell you I need dinner for two to go."

She grinned. "It's a great time. Steaks are on, but just so you know, it'll be a while."

Dylan sat on the only free stool at the bar. Others were also waiting, and though no one seemed upset, he suspected impatience wouldn't be long in coming. Maggie would lose business over this. Not the regulars, but people who only came once in a while.

He was still waiting when Hailey came downstairs, this time using the inside staircase. He stared. That special something he'd noticed in her face before had been accentuated somehow. Though he couldn't exactly pinpoint what she'd done, her eyes were darker and more pronounced. She wore a black blouse that was drawn in at the waist and the jeans she'd been in earlier, but her long hair spread out becomingly around her shoulder. On her feet were a pair of clogs, which gave her a few inches of height. She'd also put on a new bandage around her wrist.

Her smile went all the way through him. "They're pretty busy tonight," she said when she reached him.

"Maggie's employees are sick. It's just her. We'll have to wait a bit more."

As if to punctuate his point, Easton Ramos yelled from the corner table, "Hey, Maggie, what about that coffee?"

Hailey glanced over at the man. "I can pour coffee," she said in an undertone. Sweeping past Dylan, she went to the end of the bar and through the opening. There, she washed her hands at the sink embedded in the back counter. Grabbing the full pot and a couple of mugs, she carried them over to the old ranchers, pouring their coffee with flare. "Looks like you have sugar here.

Any milk or cream? I think I saw fresh over there." When they shook their heads, she asked, "Is there anything else?"

Easton Ramos nodded. "Yes, miss. We're almost finished, so we'll want some of Maggie's gooey butter cake. Nobody makes it like she does."

"Okay, I'll be back then." On her return to the counter, she stopped to refill other coffee mugs.

Maggie came from the back with a loaded tray. She took one look at Hailey and said, "There's an apron on a hook inside the kitchen, and a hairband in the container on the shelf above it. Then you can take this tray to the first table left of the front door." She set the steaming tray on the back counter. "They'll need coffee too. There's an order pad next to the register. Let me know if you have a question." She looked at the people waiting at the counter. "Now who's next?"

A man called out his order and pointed to the table next to the old ranchers. "We're sitting over there." Maggie nodded without writing anything down and disappeared into the back.

Hailey came out almost immediately, tying her yellow apron, her long hair in a ponytail. She grabbed the tray Maggie had left. When she passed Dylan this time, she threw something at him with a wink. He looked down to find an apron in his lap. He stared at it and then at her retreating figure for several seconds before he understood.

Well, sure. He could grill steaks, at least, and free Maggie up from some of her work. When he appeared in the kitchen, apron on, Maggie lifted an eyebrow.

"What?" he said. "I can turn steaks and carry out plates."

"Fine. Wash up. Don't let them burn." She set down her spatula and turned to a huge pot of mashed potatoes, adding an entire measuring cup full of melted butter and another larger one of heated milk. By the time he was ready to turn the steaks, she was already giving Hailey another tray to take.

"We need five servings of butter cake," Hailey said. "That's the house specialty, right?"

Maggie chuckled. "Yep. I've got it already out in the display rack on the back counter. Put a dollop of fresh whipped cream from the small fridge on the side of each plate—the side, not on the cake unless they specifically tell you they want it on top. If you run out of cake, there's more in the cupboard above the display. Cut each pan in twelve equal squares. Make sure to choose the pan on the right, though. It's best after sitting for twenty-hours, and that one is closer to being ready." Hailey nodded and disappeared with the tray.

Dylan turned steaks, cut pieces off the spiral-sliced hams, mashed potatoes, and dished out rice. For as many things as he did, a flush-faced Maggie did three more. She was everywhere, making sure orders kept moving. Somewhere along the way, Hailey had learned to take orders and was putting them up in the window that opened to the kitchen. She was also ringing up people at the cash register before they left.

Maggie added three smaller plates of salad to the large tray she was working on. "Take it out," she told him. "No charge for this one. Name's on the order form."

Before he could question that, she grabbed a pair of potholders and pulled out another sliced ham from the oven. Shrugging, he exited the kitchen with the tray.

At the counter the mood was jovial. "Hey, Dylan," called Jeremy Wilson, who'd just happened to come into town for dinner tonight, probably interested in laying eyes on Hailey. "You starting a new career? They say the third time's a charm."

"You never know," Dylan answered flippantly. "Taking care of your Moona Lisa this morning about did me in."

Jeremy laughed. "You should see what he did to my poor cow."

Whatever else he said was lost in laughter as Dylan found the name on the order form—Robinson—and immediately understood why Maggie didn't want to charge them.

Noah Robinson had gone through school with him, all the way from grade school to graduation, and though they hadn't been close, they'd spent enough time together that Dylan considered him a friend. The Robinson family also happened to have a goat and a cat that he saw on a semi-regular basis at the clinic. But he hadn't seen either Noah or his wife, Evelyn, since the funeral of their daughter six months ago. Little Sylvie Robinson had been hit and killed by a car last summer in Panna Creek at the county fair. The couple had another child, a ten-year-old boy, and Dylan hoped seeing them all out together like this was a good sign.

"Hey, Landan," he said to the boy. "How's that goat of yours?"

The child grinned. "Eating everything. Right, Dad?"

Noah Robinson nodded tightly and tried to smile, but it didn't reach his eyes. His face was gray, though he was barely thirty-five.

Dylan understood too well the emotions—the blame, the regrets, the what-ifs. After he'd learned about Bristol, he'd felt the same way. Only leaving the force and burying himself in studies had kept him alive. Of course, Bristol hadn't been a child—or innocent.

"Well, if he eats anything too big, you bring him right in," Dylan said, placing the boy's plate in front of him.

"You're still a vet?" Landan asked. "What are you doing here then?"

Dylan leaned closer and said in a fake whisper. "Believe it or not, I'm trying to get my dinner, and the best way seemed to be helping Maggie since her employees are all sick."

"Oh, that's smart. As long as you don't have to do the dishes. I *hate* doing dishes." The boy dug into his mashed potatoes. "I love these. I've been waiting to come here for months!"

"Thanks, Dylan," Evelyn Robinson said as he finished laying out their plates. Unlike her husband, her smile did reach her eyes, so at least one of them seemed to be dealing with the accident. They'd be all right—eventually.

Dylan placed a hand on Noah's arm and looked directly in those sad eyes. "It gets better."

"Thanks." Noah locked onto his gaze like a drowning man. "I hope you're right."

"I am. And Maggie wants you to know that tonight it's on the house. She's glad to see you back here."

"Much obliged," Noah said with a gracious nod that Dylan envied. He hadn't been so gracious to people after Bristol's death.

Dylan took that as his cue to escape before anyone became emotional. One thing he knew only too well was that after a tragedy, acting normal was the first step in returning to normalcy. That didn't mean there wouldn't always be an emptiness inside, but some days you had to simply put one foot in front of the other until it became normal again to do so. Dylan vowed to keep an eye on Noah, even if that meant making a free house call on their goat. If Maggie could do something, so could he.

Several people were calling for coffee refills, and Hailey was busy at the counter, so Dylan grabbed the pot and went to where the old Ramos brothers were still chatting, though their food and dessert was long gone. When he went to fill a cup, Easton Ramos put his hand over it.

"We want Hailey," he said. "She's one heck of a lot better on the eyes than you are."

"Is that why you're still here?" Dylan said, hoping they took the hint to leave.

"Better believe it. We want her to feel welcome."

Asher Ramos leaned forward and said, "You might want to do the same. You ain't getting any younger, you know."

Shaking his head, Dylan hurried back to the counter. "The Ramos brothers want you to pour their coffee. If those old ranchers give you any hassle, let me know."

"Oh, they're cute. Of course I'll do it."

She darted away, leaving him at the register. He looked helplessly at the customer, someone he only knew from sight but not by name. "Sorry, I'm not sure how to do this."

The man laughed and laid two twenties on his order form. "No problem. Have her ring it up when she gets back—and she can keep the change." His order was only for thirty bucks, so it was a generous tip.

"Thanks."

"Remember that the next time I bring my hunting dogs in for their shots."

"Okay, that's fair." Dylan joined his laughter.

Two more customers paid cash in the same way, and by the time a credit card came up, Hailey was back.

"The extra money is for you," he explained, giving her the pile of orders and bills.

She opened one of the pockets to her apron and showed

him a wad of bills. "A lot of people are leaving tips. I need to ask Maggie what she wants me to do with them."

"I'm sure they're yours—that's the way it usually works." Where was she from if she didn't know that much?

"Well, there's three of us."

He held up his hands. "Not me. I have a day job. This was your idea. It's all yours." He turned back into the kitchen.

Two and a half hours went by at a rapid pace, with Hailey talking and charming the customers, Maggie cooking like a crazy woman, and Dylan trying not to get in their way too much. He took two breaks to check on Sable, and when he came back from a third, there were only two groups of customers in the café.

Maggie emerged from the kitchen. "Thanks, you guys," she said, the flush already receding from her face. "I can handle the rest from here. Only a few diners will be coming in until closing now that the show is about to begin down at the theater. It's mostly just keeping stuff warm at this point. I know it's late, but your dinner's on me. And at least two more meals during the week."

"One dinner is fine," Dylan said. "Glad to help—and besides, I owed you for Sable today. Though you might want to think about hiring a backup instead of those high schoolers you have helping you. Something tells me this absence has more to do with the school dance than illness."

"You can say that again. Though it wouldn't have been such a problem if Keisha could have stayed late." Maggie turned to go back into the kitchen, but Hailey stopped her.

"What should I do with this?" She pulled the wad of bills from her pocket.

"Those are your tips," Maggie said with a smile. "Usually the girls will split tables and ring up their own so they can keep the tips from the customers they helped. There are also usually some on the credit cards, though they have most customers trained to get extra cash to pay them immediately instead of waiting for their paychecks."

"But—" Hailey began.

"It makes up for the very low wages I pay," Maggie said. "And your room tonight is also free. After closing we can talk about the rest."

Hailey smiled. "Okay, then. Thank you."

Maggie turned to Dylan. "You still want two dinners to go?"

Dylan glanced out the window. The sun would set soon, and he knew with regret that the lake visit was out. "I think here will be fine." He looked at Hailey, who nodded. "One for each of us. I was going to show Hailey our reservoir, but we'll do that another time."

"Good idea. Two specials and a dessert of gooey butter cake coming up." Maggie vanished into the kitchen.

"Let's eat outside with Sable," Hailey suggested.

"Sure. But it's cooled off since earlier."

"Right. I'll run up and get my sweatshirt. I can give you back your jacket too."

"I'll let Maggie know."

Ten minutes later, they were at one of the outside tables, the area now lit by a soft flood light and the moon rising in the darkening night. Weariness had crept into Hailey's face, and he felt guilty he hadn't urged her to sit down earlier. Once again, she was wearing the oversized, baby blue sweatshirt, and it was sliding off one slender shoulder. She began eating, her movements much slower than they had been in the café.

Dylan had snacked a bit while working, but he greedily inhaled an entire piece of steak before saying, "If I ever say anything negative about restaurant workers in the future, you have my permission to knock some sense into me. It's a strenuous profession."

Her chuckle sent a thrill racing up his chest and over his shoulders. "I feel the same way."

He paused, fork in the air. "You're a natural. You sure you never did this before?"

"No. I mean, I've entertained before. I know how to pour coffee."

"I saw that little pot-raising thing you do," he admitted. "Drawing out the stream of coffee so long did look fancy."

"Yeah, but I mixed up at least ten orders. I'm glad everyone here is so nice."

"They aren't where you come from?" It was a natural question, but he was more interested in the answer than he should be.

"In Los Angeles everyone is in too much of a hurry."

Los Angeles, huh, he thought. "What did you do there?"

She chewed and swallowed without hurry. "I worked at a charity that provides medical care for children in Africa."

This last bit he knew was a lie as plainly as if she'd announced it. The words seemed practiced and held none of the genuine emotion that had so captured the diners at the café tonight. Not only them, but him too. But why lie about something like that? Or was the lie masking something more important?

For now, he let it pass. Because he'd seen her give up a free evening to help Maggie, even though she should probably be in bed resting after passing out this morning.

For a time they were silent, basking in the glow of a good

deed done and a fantastic meal. He noticed that like him, she was concentrating on the meat—both the generous pieces of ham and the slices of steak Maggie had piled on their plates.

"You one of those carb-counters?" he teased.

"No, but this meat is fantastic. I don't know if I've ever had anything so good. I'm just really craving it, I guess." She'd already finished both pieces of steak and one of the slices of ham.

"Probably to make up for not eating for almost two days. Or maybe you lost more blood from your cut than you thought. Could be why you fainted. You might want to get tested for anemia."

"Maybe."

He opened his mouth to urge her further, but she said, "That family, the one with the little boy. Robinsons, I think? Maggie said not to charge them, and they never did come up to the register. What's their story?"

He tried to swallow past the sudden lump in his throat. "Last fall they lost their five-year-old daughter."

"No." The word came from her lips like a prayer. "How did it happen? No wonder the father looked so sad. The mother too, of course, but she hides it well."

Dylan had to give her credit for noticing. "It was at the county fair in Panna Creek. There was a lot of traffic, and they had to park far away. Her dad was supposed to be watching her, but she tripped and fell into the road somehow. A car hit her. She was a beautiful child. The whole community mourned."

"But for the community, it passes." She rested her elbows on the table and propped her chin on her fists. "Never for them, though."

"Right." He wondered if she'd lost someone, but he didn't want to ruin the night by asking.

The talk moved on to his work, and he described how he did his large animal rounds in the morning and the small animal clinic in the afternoon. "I do a lot of driving," he said. "And the emergencies almost always seem to happen in the evening or the middle of the night."

"Of course. Emergencies always happen after hours." She seemed to have lost interest in her half-eaten food and now bent down to pet Sable. "That's probably when your babies will come, huh, sweetie? In the middle of the night."

"Speaking of which, she needs her beauty sleep. She won't get much after those babies are born." He set his knife and fork together on his plate and pushed back his chair.

"If you want, I can watch her tomorrow," she volunteered.

Dylan squatted by her chair and rubbed Sable's ears. "Actually, I'm not working tomorrow, except for emergencies, and I fixed up a whelping box in one of the cages at the clinic for her. It has a live camera feed, so I can check on her remotely, at least when I'm in range of a cell tower. My receptionist has promised to keep closer to town for the next week. She's had a lot of experience."

"That's good."

Sable lifted her head, causing their hands to slide along her fur and touch. Abruptly, he was aware of Hailey—every bit of her. No, to be fair, he had been aware of her since the minute she'd walked down Maggie's stairs. The curve of her face, the shadows cast by her lashes under the light, the moistness of her lips, the pink glow of her shoulder under the sweatshirt. He also remembered the way she'd donned the apron and poured the coffee. He recalled her fury when she'd aimed the pitchfork at him in the barn.

But the way she was looking at him now about did him in

and made him want to forget the promises he'd made to himself in New York.

Still crouching, he leaned closer. Her eyes were wide, watching him carefully but not pulling away. The moment stretched out between them. He became hyperaware of her top teeth closing on her bottom lip. Was he really going to kiss her? He wanted to. He craved it more than he'd ever craved anything. He needed to taste her lips and investigate the birthmark on her neck.

Now, he told himself.

Between them, Sable uttered a little whine, obviously upset at the lack of attention. Then his phone buzzed in his pocket, and he rocked back on his heels. They both laughed nervously.

"Sorry," he said.

"Better check to make sure it's not an emergency," she quipped. "It is after hours after all."

Laughing, he pulled the phone from his pocket and saw a text from Hector Sanchez displayed on the screen: *Call me when you get a moment.* Dylan had been waiting for that text since he'd found the sandal and made the decision to find out more about Hailey Waters, but did it really have to come in right that minute?

"Is it an emergency?" Hailey asked.

"No. A text from an old friend."

"From New York?"

His heart seemed to skip a beat. The thing he loved most about Forgotten was the friendliness and the way everyone looked out for everyone else. The flip side was that everyone also knew everyone else's business. Someone must have told Hailey about New York, but how much they'd told her, he could only guess. The only consolation he had was that no one here except his dad knew the whole truth about what had driven him back to animal medicine and ultimately home to Forgotten. Which meant she wasn't the only one hiding something.

"Is something wrong?" Hailey asked, stifling a yawn with the back of her hand.

He stood swiftly. "Yeah, I have to call him back. And you look dead on your feet."

"I am a bit sleepy."

The admission sent a tug of desire shooting through him, which both thrilled and confused him. "I still want a raincheck on showing you the lake," he said, his voice oddly hoarse.

"Okay." She smiled up at him, and once more he felt the urge to kiss her, but the moment had passed.

That's a good thing, he told himself. Because he already knew his heart couldn't be trusted, and there was too much he didn't know about this woman.

"Come on, Sable." He undid the end of her leash as the dog lumbered clumsily to her feet. She stretched before looking up at him, her tail waving slightly. "Good night," he added to Hailey. "Tell Maggie thanks for dinner."

"I will. G'night."

He felt her watching him go, her presence like a light in the darkness.

Once in the Tahoe, with Sable settled comfortably on the seat, he drove to the clinic on Second Street, but he didn't go inside. Instead, he pushed the call button on Hector's number.

"Hey," he said, "it's me, Dylan. What do you have?"

"A big fat zero." Annoyance filled Hector's voice. "The description you gave me doesn't match any missing person, escaped prisoner, or person of interest. If she's done something or ran away from someplace, no one knows about it or cares. Not yet, anyway."

"What about people named Hailey Waters? Any hits?"

"Again, there's no one named Hailey Waters wanted for anything. There's a ton of them in the driver's license records, though. Without a picture of her, I can't begin to narrow them down."

"She might be from California, and she might work at a charity there that helps kids get medical treatments."

"You have a company name?"

"No." He didn't add that he was pretty sure she was lying about the job. "I thought maybe if there were some companies that did that sort of thing, we could ask them if she works there."

"We can pursue that if the picture you give me doesn't bring up anything," Hector said. "Because I'm guessing there are a lot of charitable companies. And I'd still need a picture to show them."

"Okay, I'll get you one." Dylan should have already sent Hector a picture, but he'd been out of the cops and robbers game for a long while. Or maybe he'd been sure something would have been on the wire about her.

"I do have some good news," Hector said into the silence. "That sandal you sent me the picture of? The brand isn't widely distributed. I've got both a call and an email out to the company. It happens to be in the Midwest—Nebraska, to be exact. They might ship to California, but they also have outlets in Nebraska and possibly in Kansas. I'll let you know when I have more."

"Thanks. I appreciate it."

For a few seconds, Hector was silent, and then, "What's with this girl? She someone you like? Because you know personal searches like this aren't exactly allowed."

"No," Dylan said, a little too quickly. "It's like I told you, I found her in the chief's barn, and with him out of town, I feel I need to follow up."

"Yeah, yeah, and I know you don't want to involve the police there in case there isn't anything to find. But that doesn't explain what I hear in your voice."

Dylan thought of the evening in the café and the dinner that followed. It had been one of the best nights of his life in a very long time. "I don't know what to say. Maybe you're right."

"I hope it works out, buddy. That whole mess with Bristol? You deserved better."

Dylan steeled himself for the flood of pain that always accompanied her name, but this time it didn't come. Maybe it was Sable's jaw on his thigh or that he was simply too tired. It couldn't possibly be because of Hailey.

"Please keep looking," he told Hector. "Something's off. She's hiding something. I need to protect my town."

Your town? Or you? a voice inside him mocked.

But the voice was wrong.

CHAPTER 7

Hailey forked up a bit of gooey butter cake as she watched Dylan leave. Despite the sweet gooey-ness that satisfied all her sugar cravings, a sadness fell over her. She told herself it was because she'd become used to having Sable around, but maybe it was because her feet ached and her face once again felt tight with the sunburn, despite the lotion she'd slathered on it. At least the cramps had stopped, though the second batch of painkillers she'd taken to get through the night were probably responsible.

The door to the kitchen opened, and Maggie stood in the doorway, looking exhausted but happy. She came with her own piece of gooey butter cake and settled into the spot at the table next to Hailey.

"Dylan's already gone? Well, at least he finished his food." Maggie put his cup and silverware on his plate before stabbing her fork into her cake.

She didn't seem upset at Dylan's departure, so maybe Hailey's initial idea that there might be something between them was wrong. She didn't expect to feel relieved at that, but she was.

"He got a text from New York," she said. "I think he wanted to call whoever it was back."

Maggie pulled a chain from under her white blouse and glanced at the gold watch on the end. "Not yet ten, so I guess it's not all that late there."

"I heard he was a police officer in New York." Hailey knew she was probing, but she didn't care.

Maggie nodded. "That was before he decided to go to veterinarian school like he originally planned. He got off track for that when he was at Cornell University in New York and met his wife. He's a widower, you know."

A pain grew in Hailey's chest, though she didn't understand why. Dylan was simply a man who'd helped her, a man she'd barely met, no matter how sexy or attractive or supportive. "That's terrible," she murmured.

"I don't know many of the details," Maggie said. "No one does. And it's none of my business. I'm only telling you because, well, it might explain some of how he acts."

"I'm only passing through town," Hailey insisted past an odd pain in her chest that was quickly hardening to a numb mound of nothingness. How Dylan acted was none of her concern.

Maggie nodded, forking up a mouthful of cake. After she swallowed, she said, "How are you feeling?"

"Okay," Hailey lied. She didn't understand why her emotions were so volatile. One moment she was flying high, the next she was laughing, then angry, and the next after that she was raging with desire. Even for that time of the month, it seemed . . . off. Not right.

After a few more bites of cake, Maggie said, "I was worried

about you working so hard tonight after what happened this morning. But I really couldn't have done it without you and Dylan. Not without losing customers." Her voice was soothing, like a lullaby to Hailey's heart.

Hailey leaned back in her chair with a little sigh. "It was fun. I slept all day, so I was fine, though I'm tired now. I don't know how you do this every day."

"I take breaks whenever we don't have customers, and everything here shuts down on Sundays, so I rest then. But you picked it up a lot quicker than the high school girls I employ on the weekends." Her laugh was as sweet as her voice.

"I'm glad it worked out. There are a lot of nice people in this town." When Hailey had done a quick check of her tips, they'd totaled nearly sixty dollars. Of course, half of that should have been Dylan's or Maggie's, but she wasn't going to argue.

"Look, about your lodging," Maggie began, setting down her fork. "I normally charge sixty bucks a night for the room with the private bath and breakfast for one, or four hundred a week. Use of the Internet and washing machine is included— you supply your own detergent. There's also a small business center off the dining area where you can use the computer free of charge. If you print, it's ten cents a page for black and white, fifty cents for color."

Hailey nodded, trying to mentally calculate how long her ten thousand dollars would last at those prices. She'd have to pay for at least one other meal a day, and she'd need another fifty a week for incidentals, so even if she could keep her spending to five or six hundred dollars a month, she'd have enough to last maybe a year and a half.

Before she could speak, Maggie continued, "But I could use another hand in the café, so I could pay you to work for me if you're interested. The pay isn't good—full time alone won't pay the rent, but with the tips added in, it'll be enough to pay your room and more while you're here."

Hailey leaned forward, hardly able to believe her luck. This was her answer! She could earn her keep and save her stash for the future. For when she decided what to do. Maybe if she liked it here, she'd even set down roots. "Sure," she said. "I'd like to give it a try."

"Good. You can fill out the tax information tomorrow." Maggie picked up her fork and took another bite of her cake.

The hope drained from Hailey. "But I . . . when I fell into the river. I don't seem to have my ID or anything with me."

"As long as you know your social, it'll be fine."

"I don't know it."

Maggie tilted her head, studying Hailey for a long moment without speaking. "Look, it's okay if you don't want to give it to me right now. I know you're running from something. I can tell."

Was that because Maggie herself had run from something, or was she simply reading into Hailey's expression? It really didn't matter because even if Hailey wanted to give her a social security number, she couldn't remember one to give her. As for Hailey's ID and documents, had she thrown them out on purpose? But why would she do that?

"You don't have to be afraid," Maggie said. "If someone's stalking you, there are ways to deal with it."

Hailey drew her feet onto her chair, wrapping her arms around her knees. Her secret was like a suffocating burden, and she wanted more than anything to share it with this woman who had been nothing but kind.

"It's not that." Hailey's voice was almost inaudible, even to herself. "The truth is, I don't remember."

"Don't remember?" Maggie scooted her chair closer. "Remember what?"

"Why I came here. What I'm supposed to do. My name. I don't remember anything before I spoke to the driver as I got off the bus, and even what happened after that is foggy."

"I see." Maggie studied her for a long moment as if trying to decide whether or not to believe her. "So what *do* you remember?"

"Today." Hailey clearly remembered Dylan standing over her in the barn and everything since. "Every now and then, it's almost as if I see pieces of something else, but then it's gone. And at least once today, I lost a little time."

"Dylan said you hit your head. You might have a temporary amnesia."

Hailey rubbed the bandage on her wrist that was threatening to come off after the busy evening. "Maybe. But I don't have a bump on my head. I think it's more than that. And please don't tell me to go to the doctor. Until I know who I am . . . I can't trust anyone."

Maggie regarded her for a few more seconds, then nodded once, sharply. "Okay, for what it's worth, I think I'd feel the same if it were me. Your secret goes no further than this table. And tell you what, until we figure this out, you can work here for your room and three meals a day. Leftovers on Sundays, of course. Tips are yours to keep."

"But that's . . . I should at least pay you the tips," Hailey protested. "The work won't even cover your normal rental fees. And you don't know anything about me. What if I . . . I might be a fugitive."

Maggie laughed. "Forgetting doesn't change who you are. I saw the way you treated my customers tonight—and that pregnant mutt." She raised her hand. "I know, she's not a mutt. But

I'm willing to take a risk on you. It'll save me paperwork anyway. And if someone needs to rent the room, you can bunk in my suite with me so I won't lose the rent. I have an extra bed."

"But—"

Again, Maggie raised her hand. "Someone took a chance on me once, and I know what that means. Don't let me down."

Hailey nodded, though she couldn't quite bring herself to agree out loud. How could you promise something when you had no track record to show that you could follow through? "Thank you," she said softly.

Maggie inclined her raven head like a queen sitting court. "You're welcome. Now you should go to bed. I won't need you for the weekend because I have a suspicion that my teen workers are suddenly going to recover. Rest up, and we'll finish your training on Monday."

Hailey nodded. "Okay." She started to reach for her plate, but Maggie pulled it toward her. "I'll put some plastic on the rest of this, and you can take it to the fridge in your room in case you'd like to finish it later. But feel free to come downstairs tomorrow for a fresh meal." With a wink, she rose and disappeared through the open kitchen door.

While Hailey waited for Maggie to return with her plate, she remembered something else Maggie had mentioned—the business center. A computer meant a way to access the outside world. Maybe there she could find some answers—and do it before that nosy police-man-turned-vet decided to search for his own answers.

In the meantime, she was better off staying away from him.

CHAPTER 8

Hailey pushed back from the computer in the Butter Cake Café business center with a sigh. She'd visited dozens of news websites and scanned hundreds of articles about fugitives, missing persons, domestic abuse, and unsolved crimes. She didn't match the descriptions in any of them.

Maybe nobody is looking for me, she thought.

But if nothing traumatic had happened, why couldn't she remember? She'd also looked up causes for amnesia. The main reasons were fever, trauma, mental disorder, or drug use. None of them seem to apply to her, but it meant there were other options besides her fall in the river. Somehow that was comforting.

She didn't consider the issue long. In fact, she was starting not to really care. She liked being in Forgotten. She was making new friends, she had a new job, and maybe she could eventually have a dog like Sable. Most of all, she liked being Hailey Waters. What else did she really need to know? Smiling to herself, she stood, hooked her backpack over her shoulder, and walked into the dining room.

For the past few hours, the cafe had been busier than she'd expected on a Saturday in a small town. Many people she recognized from the day before had stopped in at the business center door and waved to her or come in to introduce friends, a lot of whom happened to be young men about her age—good looking ones too.

Yes, she liked Forgotten a lot.

Now, the crowds were gone and only two tables were occupied. Nodding at first one group and then the other, she passed the counter and the two teenage girls manning it and ducked into the kitchen. She'd slept in until ten this morning, and then finished the rest of last night's dinner before coming downstairs, so she wasn't exactly hungry, but the fresh smell of baking bread had spread throughout the café, and it was calling to her.

Maggie turned from a large pot on the stove, looking her up and down. "Good," she said. "I see you're making use of the things I left outside your door this morning."

"I did." Hailey turned around, showing off the dark blue jeans, fuchsia top, and thin gray sweater that zipped from both the top and the bottom. She'd completed the ensemble with a pair of thick-wedged but flirty heels. Maggie had left a note about getting the clothes from the church across the street, who apparently washed and saved them for people in need or to sell at their annual yard sale. Today's hand-me-downs fit much better than the other clothes Maggie had given her in the box yesterday, and she was grateful.

"Thank you so much. But I confess I'm a little afraid someone's going to come up to me and say, 'Hey, that was my top,'" Hailey admitted.

Maggie laughed. "Not a chance. The way you're putting it all together, no one but the pastor's wife and I will ever know. Do the white blouses fit? I like the girls to wear white under the yellow aprons."

So she'd said in the note. The yellow was to represent the gooey butter cake, Maggie had written in neat cursive.

"They'll work great," Hailey said. "I do need a few underthings. You won't be going to the Walmart in Panna Creek today, will you?"

"I wasn't planning on it. But I can take you next week." Maggie hesitated before continuing. "But to tell you the truth, I try to buy locally whenever I can, or when I can't, I at least avoid the large chain stores."

"Isn't that more expensive?"

"Sometimes," she agreed. "But there's quality in both the merchandise and the relationships."

Hailey considered that a moment and nodded. Maybe this was the attitude she'd need if she decided to set down roots here.

"You hungry?" Maggie asked. "I always change soups on Saturdays, and today is potato. It's really good if I do say so myself."

"Only if I can have some of that bread with it." Hailey drew in a deep breath. "That's an amazing smell."

"If you can wait a few minutes, a fresh batch will be coming out of the oven."

"I'll wait." Digging in her pocket, Hailey fished out a painkiller and downed it with a glass of water. She'd be glad when her cycle was over and her head feeling better, so she wouldn't have to keep taking them. "Do you use vitamin C in your bread?"

"It comes in the yeast." Maggie leaned against one of the stainless steel counters that took up the space along the kitchen walls not already occupied by the ovens, grills, or refrigerators. "You know how to make bread?"

Hailey nodded, furrowing her brow. "Yeah, I think so."

"Maybe you can figure out why mine is coming out a little heavy."

"I'd be glad to try."

"It's a deal. You can take a stab at it on Monday. I make it twice a day. A double batch in the morning at six, so it's fresh when we open, and another batch again about this time when the lunch rush is dying down."

"What if I utterly screw it up?"

Maggie laughed. "Then we make another batch. I always have enough to get through the afternoons. I even have some frozen dough for emergencies."

"Okay. I'll try. But what time should I start work?"

"From nine to two would be good for starters, and then for the dinner shift, though if we're not busy, I'll send you home and put you on another day. Or you can help with the bread before we open. Our rush periods are generally around eleven to one and five to six on weekdays, and five to eight on Friday and Saturday nights. If you could be adjustable for a while, until I figure out a schedule that works with Keisha, my other full-time employee, I'd appreciate it."

"Anything's good."

An insistent chime sounded, and Maggie pulled on mitts to remove bread from an oven. Hailey's mouth watered as she saw the fat, round loaves. Minutes later, she was in the dining room at one of the newly vacated tables, slathering a piece of steaming bread with a thick layer of butter. She ate that first without taking a single bite of her soup.

One of the teen employees, whose nametag read *Ingrid,*

came from the counter and sat down opposite her. "So have you seen him?" she asked urgently, her freckled face flushing. She had pale blue eyes that seemed to grow two sizes as she talked. "They say he's gorgeous, but I don't really know because he's always gone by the time I get here, and I leave before he comes back." She fingered the red hair in her side ponytail as she rushed on. "Do you think he'll be going to the Spring Planting Dance? Will you ask him? It's not that I care about him, you understand, but I want to know what he's going to bring to town. Maybe it'll be another factory—and that means more boys that won't leave to find jobs." She heaved a dreamy sigh. "Or maybe it'll be a mall."

Hailey let her spoon fall into her bowl. "I'm sorry. What are we talking about?"

The teen's eyes widened even further. "The developer staying here. I thought you might have run into him."

Hailey shook her head. "Nope, sorry. I didn't know anyone besides Maggie was here. But to be honest, I've spent most of the past two days sleeping."

Ingrid gasped. "That's right. You poor thing. I heard how you fell into the river and would have drowned if Dylan Morgan hadn't jumped in and rescued you. And then how he carried you upstairs after you fainted." Her hands clasped at her chest. "It's so romantic! I bet he's half in love with you already. That happens all the time in the movies. You know, if you save a life, you're responsible for it and all."

"Uh, no. I never heard that." Hailey was tempted to correct the girl about Dylan jumping into the water to save her but decided it didn't really matter. He had stitched her up and brought her into town, and that was close enough.

"Maybe he'll ask you to the dance next Saturday."

"Dance?" Hailey asked.

Ingrid's eyes did the weird widening thing again, as if she'd been watching too much Anne of Green Gables. "You don't know about the Spring Planting Dance? It's a town tradition. Every May on the very last Saturday, the men build a dance floor on the fairgrounds, and we have a dance to celebrate the finish of the spring planting and to bless the winter wheat harvest. It's a huge deal. All the town goes." She glanced behind her at the remaining customers, who were making their way to the counter to pay for their meals, and lowered her voice. "There's a town legend that says if you dance the very last dance with the man you love and kiss him at midnight, that you'll marry and stay together forever. I was thinking about kissing Billy Henderson, but if more families are coming to town, I think I'll wait."

"How old are you?" Hailey asked.

"Sixteen."

"I'd say waiting is a good idea."

"You should kiss Dylan Morgan." Again, Ingrid glanced behind her. "Before someone else does. I mean, the single women in the Ladies Auxiliary take turns bringing him food all the time. They think the way to win a man's heart is through his stomach, and maybe it will be."

"Ingrid!" The other teen employee, a dark-haired Asian girl, waved at her from the counter, where she was ringing up a customer. Another group of diners were entering the cafe.

"Well, let me know if you hear anything from the developer," Ingrid said. "And put in a good word for a mall, okay? I love shopping." She jumped to her feet and hurried to the counter.

Hailey smiled to herself and bit into a second slice of bread.

It was not as hot as the first and not quite as good, and she could feel the same heaviness she'd noted in her sandwich yesterday. Maybe cooking the bread on a stone instead of on those cookie sheets would help. Hailey didn't bother to examine where the idea came from; it simply felt right.

A few moments later, a blond man with impressive muscles bulging under his white, short-sleeved T-shirt slid into the seat across from her. "Hi," he said.

Her eyes wandered up the wide shoulders to the smiling blue eyes she thought she recognized from yesterday. "Hi," she said. "Jeremy, right?"

He nodded. "Jeremy Wilson. I was here last night."

"Yeah, and I met your parents earlier. Nice people." Should she say she was sorry about his dad? Better to wait until he brought it up. "You shaved your beard."

He rubbed his jaw. "It was time, getting a little long. Hey, I'm here with a few friends. Can we join you?" He thumbed over his shoulder at three men near the counter, who waved or nodded as she looked their way. At least two of them had also been here yesterday, but she didn't remember their names.

"Sure," she said, scooting over to the chair next to her.

Jeremy waved to the men, and as they came over, he moved to sit next to Hailey. Two of his friends sank into the open chairs opposite them, while the third snagged a chair from an empty table and pulled it over to the end.

"How long are you going to be in town?" one of them asked.

"Well, I just got a job here at the Butter Cake Café," she said. "So for a while, at least."

A general murmur of approval rose at that, but it was cut short by Ingrid's appearance. "Okay, what will you have?" the girl asked.

"What she's having," Jeremy dipped his head. "And I'd like to pay for hers."

Ingrid grinned. "Then you'll have to take her somewhere else. Hers is on the house."

"Oh, right," Jeremy said amidst the hoots and hollers from the others.

Hailey found herself laughing.

$\mathcal{D}$ylan could have sent a friend to snap a photo of Hailey at the Butter Cake Café, or make up a reason to ask Maggie to do so, but he found himself walking in the door, timing it for after lunch when the café would be dead. He planned to casually ask Maggie where Hailey was, and if she was out, he could always *accidentally* run into her.

To his surprise, there were still customers in the café, and Hailey herself was seated at one of the tables by the large windows, surrounded by none other than Jeremy Wilson and three other men. *Word is spreading about the new woman in town,* Dylan thought with irritation. Jeremy, of course, sat next to Hailey.

Hailey looked happy, and all the men seemed captivated by her words. Dylan had known she was attractive, but it hit him again, and for a moment his step to the counter faltered. *Get a grip,* he told himself.

He sat on a stool and waited for Lisa Whang to take his order. "The regular?" she asked with a bright smile. "It's potato soup, your favorite. And we have new bread just out of the oven."

"Sounds great." He shot a glance at the table where Hailey sat. "But I'm going to sit over at a table today."

She grinned, her dark eyes sparkling knowingly. "You and

everyone else." Her head dipped toward the men around Hailey. "We've had a lot of people coming in to see the fainting woman."

"Right." Why did that irritate him so much?

"She really is pretty." A hint of envy tinged the girl's voice, though he suspected the pretty teen had more than her share of dates. Her parents had immigrated from Korea before she was born, so she was American through and through, but she definitely stood out in a good way here in Forgotten.

"Yeah." He tried not to look around at where Hailey was seated, but he couldn't help himself.

"Go ahead and sit wherever you want. I'll bring it out to you."

"Thanks."

As he made his way past Hailey's table, she glanced at him and he nodded. If she'd been alone, he would have asked to sit down, but there was no room at the table.

"Hey, look who's here," Jeremy said, raising his voice. "It's our vet waiter." His companions chortled.

"How's your cow?" Dylan asked.

Jeremy sobered. "Good. My mom had a fit when she saw the trocar, but she's keeping a closer eye on my dad. She did find him trying to let Moona Lisa into the alfalfa field again today."

"Good catch." Dylan moved past them to the table behind Hailey and Jeremy, only then realizing it would be hard to take a picture of her with her back toward him.

"Why don't you sit with us?" Hailey asked. "We can make room."

He experienced a rush of warmth all out of proportion to her invitation. "Okay," he agreed, with only a hint of reluctance. He wasn't a hermit, but normally he'd prefer to eat alone than with Jeremy's friends, who were six or seven years younger, like Jeremy. Only one was married, and their concerns sometimes seemed juvenile to him, but he'd endure them all for Hailey.

Hailey hopped to her feet, pushed the table out from against the wall, and scooted her chair around it so the back of her head was framed by the window. Jeremy moved his chair over near her and his sandwich plate to where she'd been, leaving his spot open.

"Hailey was telling us about her work in California," Jeremy said as Dylan pulled over another chair. "Her company helped a little girl in Guatemala who had a clubfoot."

"Oh," Hailey said with a little wave of her hand. "She's walking fine now and adopted by a family. Children with disabilities like that often spend their whole lives in an orphanage. No one wants to adopt them. If they get help, it's a completely different story."

Lisa Whang arrived with his soup and bread, but Dylan barely nodded at her as she set it in front of him. Today Hailey sounded sincere about her former job. Had his impression of her lying been wrong last night?

"I might have heard about that," he said. "What's the name of your charity?"

Hailey laughed. "Sorry, but it's all done through anonymous donors. I really can't say any more."

How convenient, he thought, though the others nodded in agreement.

"Ingrid told me about the Spring Planting Dance," Hailey said, changing the subject. "Will you all be going?"

"I'll definitely be there," Jeremy said to Hailey. "Will you save me a dance?"

"Sure."

"I want one too," chimed the other single men.

Dylan was beginning to wish he'd stayed at the clinic. He quickly downed a spoonful of soup.

"What about you, Dylan?" Hailey gave him a heart-stopping smile. "Do you want me to save you a dance? Will you be going?"

"He has to go," Jeremy said. "He's always one of the police volunteers, making sure the drinking stays in check."

"Spoilsport," one of the friends muttered.

"Might not even have time for a dance," Jeremy finished, ignoring his friend.

"I'll dance with you," Dylan ground out. He didn't mean it to sound so unwilling, but Hailey frowned.

"Guess we'll see," she said, which he took to mean, "No way, sucker."

This was why he didn't like to hang out with Jeremy and his annoying friends. Last night everything had gone so well; now she probably wished she hadn't invited him to sit down. He ate a couple more bites of soup and buttered his bread, glancing at the bar longingly.

As if taking the cue, Hailey stood and gathered her dishes. "Well, I've got a little shopping to do before the stores close." She hesitated. "They are open today, right?"

"Until about six." Jeremy stuffed a huge bite of bread in his mouth, likely hoping to finish and go with her. Not a chance as his bowl was still filled with soup—like Dylan's.

"Great. See you around." She swayed to the counter on her heels with a practiced ease Dylan hadn't noticed yesterday. She disappeared into the kitchen.

The guys stared after her, one of them whistling under his

breath. "Way out of your league," the whistler said to Jeremy. Dylan agreed, though the Hailey he'd worked with in the café yesterday had seemed down-to-earth enough.

When Hailey didn't come back from the kitchen, Dylan suspected she'd left by the back door. "Excuse me," he said. "I just remembered something I have to do." He set a bill under his soup bowl, rose quickly, nearly toppling his chair, and headed for the front door.

Outside, he saw Hailey's retreating back on the sidewalk in front of the park and hurried after her. He told himself he was only going because of the picture. His long strides caught him up to her before she'd passed the park.

She glanced over as he fell into step with her. "I wondered if you'd come after me."

"Uh, why?"

"Because that's who you are—a hero. I bet it's why you became a cop and now save animals. But don't worry. You didn't hurt my feelings about the dance. I know Jeremy and his friends are a little much."

He relaxed at that. He didn't think of himself as a hero, but he didn't mind her feeling that way about him. "So how are you feeling?"

"Pretty good. I'm still taking pills for my headache, but it should be gone soon."

They walked in silence for a few seconds before he said, "What kind of shopping are you doing?"

"Clothing." A smile danced around her lips. "Maggie has been very helpful, since my luggage seems to be missing, but my wardrobe needs some accessorizing."

"Joni's Dress shop is the best place in town," he offered. "There's another clothing store too on this street, but Joni's not only makes custom dresses, they also have all the basics. It's not far. I'll show you."

The store was about five minutes down Main and on the other side of the street. Despite her assurances that she was feeling all right, Hailey was walking more slowly by the time they arrived. She paused before going into the store, looking at the dresses on the mannequins in the window. A hand-lettered sign read: *Get your Spring Planting Dance dresses here.*

"It's beautiful," Hailey said.

He followed her gaze to a gauzy pink dress with capped sleeves and a skirt that looked made for the kind of dancing they did in Forgotten—which, he'd learned the hard way, was completely opposite from the way people danced in New York City clubs. For an instant, looking at the dress, he experienced a déjà vu moment of another shopping trip the week before Bristol had been killed. She'd been looking at dresses too, and the one they'd ended up buying was the same one she'd worn on the morning of the day she'd been shot.

Hailey's hand squeezed his arm, her touch pulling him back to the present. "Are you okay? You look like you saw a ghost."

He shook his head. "It's nothing." But it wasn't nothing. His knees were weak, and he felt like throwing up.

She regarded him for a long moment, and as the images faded, his heart kept pounding for yet another reason. "You should come in and sit down," she said.

"I don't even know if they have chairs." He was a hypocrite, he realized. He always shopped local, except for the veterinarian supplies he had to order, but he hadn't set foot in this store since his return to town. Maybe it was because of the dresses in the window or because Panna Creek had more options. "But I do need some new socks."

"Socks." Again, the slight twitch of smile that fascinated him. She was already peeling a bit on her nose, but her lips looked incredibly soft. "Okay then."

Inside the store, Evelyn Robinson looked up from the counter by the wall and smiled. "Hi, Dylan. What can I do for you two?"

"I'm looking for socks," he said.

She pointed at the wall behind him where a display of shoes and socks took up a small corner of the store.

He went over and pretended to study the socks while in reality he was watching the women. Evelyn took Hailey to the back of the store, to the dress racks, where they stopped to pull out a few items. When they headed for the corner with the intimates, he decided he was being too nosy.

Evelyn returned to grab a few items from around the store, including the dress in the window, taking them back to Hailey in the dressing room. Then she helped him choose dress loafers to replace his worn ones and a six-pack of socks. He was considering telling Evelyn to let Hailey know he'd left when she emerged from the dressing room in the pink dress. She was breathtaking.

"What do you think?" she asked. As she spun around in front of him, he tried to unglue his mouth to respond.

"Nice," he said.

Her mouth turned into a little pout. "Only nice? I guess I shouldn't get it for the Spring Planting Dance then."

"Definitely not for that," he said. "Jeremy and his crowd will be drooling all over you."

She laughed, obviously pleased with his answer. "I'll take it," she said.

Evelyn smiled. "Bring it up with the rest when you're ready."

Dylan watched Hailey turn, and for the first time, a beautiful, sexy woman in a dress didn't make him feel sad about Bristol.

"Wait," he called after her. "Let me take a picture."

She turned, put a hand on her hip, and he clicked away.

Immediately, he felt guilty. He'd used the moment of trust between them to snap a picture he was going to send to Hector in New York. *It's for her too,* he thought. Because he still believed she was hiding something, and maybe he could help.

He should have made excuses and left then, but he waited for her in front of the store, pushing off the brick wall as she emerged.

"So you didn't abandon me," she teased.

"No, but there's still time to go to the lake, if you're not doing anything. We can stop by my clinic and get Sable."

Her smile widened. "I need to put these away, and change my shoes, but sure. I'd love to."

Back at the Butter Cake Café, he had Maggie put two sandwiches in a takeout bag for them. When Hailey still wasn't down from her room, he brought up the picture of her on his phone and sent it to Hector. She'd implied that he had a hero complex, but at the moment he felt more like a peeping Tom.

After twenty minutes had passed, he began to worry. She was either taking a really long time getting ready, or she'd changed her mind, or . . .

Or she might have passed out again.

"Maggie," he said, feeling a strange urgency. "Can you check on Hailey? She was just going to change her shoes."

A vertical line appeared on Maggie's lower brow between her eyes. "Sure." With a word to Ingrid, she hurried up her stairs.

CHAPTER 9

A brisk rap on the door made Hailey start. What was she doing sitting on the bed staring off into the distance when there was an incredibly hot guy downstairs in the café waiting for her? After she'd changed to capris and donned the new tan sandals she'd purchased at Joni's Dress Shop, she'd taken another pain killer, filled up her water bottle, and used the bathroom as well. All in record time, or so she'd thought, but the wall clock said more than twenty minutes had passed.

"Coming," she called, hurrying to the door.

"Hey," Maggie said when she opened it. "Are you okay?"

"Yeah. Fine."

"Dylan was worried." She peered closer at Hailey's face. "I like that eye shadow. Very nice."

There was a mirror by the table, and Hailey glanced at it. For a moment, she didn't recognize herself. "Maybe a little too much eye shadow."

"Not when you're going on a date."

"It's not a date. He's trying to prove the lake is the prettiest I've ever seen."

Maggie rolled her eyes. "It's a date. Though frankly, he's probably telling himself the same thing you're telling yourself. But there are at least six women I know of who are after him, and to my knowledge, he hasn't taken a single one to the lake—or anywhere else."

Hailey flushed, or maybe the room was hot. Maybe it was still that stupid sunburn. At least that should be healed soon—her nose was already peeling.

"Thanks for checking on me. I'm ready." She grabbed her backpack that contained only her water, sunscreen, the new lipstick she'd bought at the dress shop counter, and a spare hygiene pad.

She and Maggie had almost reached the stairs when a handsome man in dress slacks and a navy polo shirt appeared at the top of the landing. He was good looking in a corporate sort of way, with trim black hair, deep brown eyes, gorgeous chestnut skin, and ultra-trim facial scruff he probably had to cut daily.

"Oh, you're back," Maggie said with a smile. "Good timing. I'd like you to meet my new boarder, Hailey Waters. Hailey, this is Connor Davis. He's also staying with us."

The developer, Hailey thought, remembering the mostly one-sided conversation with Ingrid. She smiled and nodded.

His smile was beautiful, his skin exotic in this small town where so far she'd only seen two other people with different ethnicities—Lisa, the Asian teen working in the café, and the mayor's wife from the grocery store. He was gorgeous; no wonder Ingrid was all aflutter about him.

"So what's it going to be?" Hailey asked. "A factory or a mall?"

Maggie laughed. "The more important question is if it's going to be here or in Panna Creek."

Connor smiled. "Exactly. And not only those two places, but in any one of these small towns. But I'll tell you what, none of them has gooey butter cake like Maggie."

"As long as it's enough to sway you in our direction," Maggie said.

"Well, with the turkey factory already in town, and things generally on the upswing, Forgotten is a good choice." His gaze swung back to Hailey. "I'm thinking a few more businesses, and maybe then you can get a mall. A very small one." He paused and added. "Have we met before? You look familiar."

Hailey thought a moment. Had she passed him in town today? "No. I don't think so."

"You don't happen to be from Lincoln, do you? Nebraska's my home base."

"No—California."

"I've done work there too. So maybe it was at some function."

Hailey shrugged. "Maybe. But we've met for sure now." She held out her hand to shake his.

"We have indeed." He inclined his head. "A pleasure."

"Remember, there's a lifetime of free gooey butter cake if you choose Forgotten," Maggie said, her voice sounding ready to break into song. "Unless you end up moving here, and then it's only a year of free cake."

Hailey laughed and continued down the stairs with Maggie. "Free gooey butter cake, huh?" she said. "I wouldn't have thought you'd want development here."

"Development is good, as long as it's not too fast," Maggie said. "As it is, too many of our young people leave to find better jobs. I'd like to see more of them staying, even if it does grow our town. We could double or triple in size, and we'd still be a small town. But if they do decide to build something here, you'd best buy land now, before it goes up in price."

"I'll remember that." Would Hailey's ten thousand dollars buy anything in town? It might.

"There you are," Dylan said, coming to meet her, a Butter Cake Café takeout bag in his hand. "I thought you ditched me."

"Not a chance. I'm excited to see this lake." They started out the back entrance together.

"Have fun, you two!" Maggie called after them.

In his SUV, Dylan checked his phone before handing it to her. She saw a large, floor-to-ceiling cage, with a slightly smaller wooden box taking up the entire back corner of the cage. Sable was lying inside this on what looked like a soft blanket.

"No babies yet," he said, "but it looks like she loves the box already."

"That's where she's going to have them?"

"Yep. It's a whelping box. Usually, dogs will birth in the kitchen by the stove or in the barn or wherever the mother likes to hang out, but with so many babies that Sable will be running after, I thought this would be a help to her and the McColls. It'll be something we can move there so Sable won't be so nervous at the change when they get back."

"It's cool that you can check on her whenever you want."

"I took her temperature before I came to the café this afternoon, and it was lower than normal, which means I'd be surprised if those babies stay in more than another twenty-four hours." His grin once again did funny things to her stomach, and he had seriously nice lips. She dragged her eyes back to the dog with effort before he noticed her stare. Not for the first time today, she wondered about his wife and how she'd died.

"You sure she should go to the lake?"

He nodded. "It'll be good for her."

They drove two streets over to the vet clinic. Parking was in the front, with only a half dozen stalls. The lobby was eerily quiet from what she imagined it might be during the week, and no receptionist was at the desk. In the back, past a few examination rooms that could have been for humans, there was a large room with floor-to-ceiling cages. Several of them had canine occupants, all of whom barked as they entered.

"My current patients," he said. "These have to stay until the morning for observation." He stopped to check on only one—a tiny dog with a bandage on its leg and a cone around its neck.

Sable wagged her tail but didn't get up as they entered. "Want to come for a walk?" Dylan coaxed, petting her. Her tail wagged harder.

There was another door at the end of the room, and Hailey looked toward it questioningly. "There's more?"

"My apartment. I live here. Well, for now. I'm building a house."

"It'll be nice to not sleep at work, I'm guessing," she said, bending over to scratch Sable's neck.

"Yeah, everyone knows exactly where to pound on my door in an emergency, never mind that I check my texts regularly. I'm also planning to expand the business." He snapped a leash on Sable's neck and helped her to her feet. "Come on, girl. You still have time. You'll be glad once we get there."

His gentleness made Hailey feel a bit weak inside, as if she had peeked into his soul. Whatever else Dylan might be, he was a kind man.

The drive to the lake was only ten minutes. "There." Dylan pointed through a gap in some trees. "You can see it there. This road leads to the public park at the lake. That smaller road to the right leads to the residential areas."

"Are there a lot of homes around the lake?"

"Not many. Only half is zoned for it, and most of the land is owned by the families of longtime residents. More people used to live out here when the town was founded, but most moved to town when it became more convenient. Lately, people are moving back. Some of the old houses are in ruins, though."

"What about the rest of the lake?" she asked. "Is it all wild?"

"Yes, except for the park. It's used for camping and fishing and such." As he finished speaking, he pulled into the park itself where a sign read *Forgotten Reservoir* and *Chelsea Park*.

"Chelsea," she said. "That's the name of the lady you told me about, the one who founded Forgotten with her husband."

"Yeah, Chelsea Morgan. I'm surprised you remember."

"Morgan? Is that any relation to you?" She'd missed that before.

"She was my fourth-great grandmother. But don't get too excited; there are hundreds of people living here who can say the same, though not any with the name Morgan. Chelsea had mostly daughters."

"I think it's amazing you're related like that." She would have said more, but her mind was quickly entranced by the park. Everywhere she looked it was lush and green and fertile. She saw trees and bushes of all sizes, wildflowers with thick stems, and bright green grass where families were picnicking or playing games. Beyond the grass was a short, rocky beach and then the lake itself, a vibrant turquoise that beckoned to her even from the SUV. Surrounding the park and the lake, like a literal border, was a verdant forest.

"It's like a painting." She pushed open the car door and sucked in a deep breath filled with the scent of growing things. "Only better."

"The trees are mostly bald cypress and sycamores, but there are huge patches of pawpaws. Legend has it that Chelsea brought them with her when she came. The wildlife really loves the fruit."

"You could get lost in that forest," she said, looking down at her sandals. "I definitely need tennis shoes."

"Not for a path I know. Come on."

They emerged from the vehicle, Sable shivering all over with excitement. They cut across the grass, where Dylan paused to catch a stray Frisbee as it was thrown their way. Sable barked at a dog, but the leash Dylan had snapped on prevented her from darting away. Close to the entrance of the park was a pier with a small shack that advertised boat and canoe rental. Further on, teens were pushing each other off another pier into the water, though she guessed the water was still cold this early in the year. They passed barbecue pits and picnic tables. On the far end of the grass was a hard-packed dirt trail that might once have been layered with gravel to stop the encroaching forest.

"So where are we going?" she asked as Dylan turned onto this path.

He smiled, his eyes dark pools with no bottom. "To prove it's the prettiest lake."

"Does this path lead all the way around?"

"No. Well, you can get around the lake, but this trail is over-grown in a lot of areas, so it's easy to lose. Over by the houses, the trail is better." He looked to the front again, and she was relieved to no longer have his eyes on her. Or was she? The sexual tension between them seemed to grow with each stare.

"So, you grew up here," she said. The trail was as easy as he'd promised, and she had no trouble keeping up with his longer gait.

"I did."

"How'd you become a vet?"

"My dad was one. I was giving shots and going on rounds before I could drive. I always knew it was something I wanted to do."

Something was off about that statement. "But you became a policeman."

"That was a detour I took after getting my bachelor's degree. Sometimes you start down a path before you really know where you are headed and what you want. That's what police work was for me."

Sometimes you start down a path before you really know what you want. The words struck a chord in her, but she didn't know why. One thing was certain. Whatever path she'd been on before coming to Forgotten, she was where she wanted to be now.

"So what brought you back here?"

He shrugged. "Being a cop wasn't what I thought it would be, at least it wasn't in New York. Plus, the ambiance was . . ." He trailed off and started again. "I like being out in the open. I like knowing all my neighbors. I love working with animals, and I love medicine—especially figuring out a problem and solving it." He stopped and turned toward her. "I guess I didn't like being a policeman enough to stay."

She wanted to ask what happened to his wife, but he hadn't

mentioned her, so she stayed quiet. "I'm glad you came back," she said with an odd tightening in her chest. "Just in time to sew me up."

He laughed. "I've been back five years." Another long hesitation, and then he added, "You look really pretty today."

Her pulse went from normal to overload in a single heartbeat. How could he do that to her? He was staring at her like he had last night, right before they almost kissed. And why shouldn't they kiss?

"Thank you," she said.

He stepped forward, past her, and her breath caught in her throat. What was he doing? She turned to look and saw that he was pushing past bushes and undergrowth. Sable, in front of him on the leash, had already disappeared.

"What are you doing?"

He glanced back at her, a contented smile on his face that was every bit as compelling as the other expression he'd displayed when he looked ready to kiss her. "We're here—where I wanted to take you. Come on. I'll hold the branches. I'd trim them, but I don't want anyone to remember about this place."

He extended a hand, and she took it. His warmth spread through her like a rush of flame, though she hadn't realized she was cold before he touched her. When she was close, he turned and held back the bushes with the hand that had once held the leash, gesturing her through.

Ducking, she walked through the makeshift tunnel and came out on the bank in front of a small, circular rock pier that jutted out a few feet into the lake. Parts of the pier were crumbling near the edges, but that only added to the magic cast by the trees angled overhead and the moss growing everywhere. On either side of the pier, tree branches swung low over the river, and on those branches, turtles clung—dozens of them, some all in a row. Those closest to where they stood dropped into the water as she stepped onto the pier. The others ignored her.

Dylan laughed at her exclamation. "They're common sliders. We have hundreds here, mostly because they're protected and because there aren't many folks around to bug them."

Sable, who'd gone ahead, finished lapping at the water. With a little whine, she lay down now, panting as if too exhausted by the short walk to even bark at the turtles.

"She's okay," Dylan said, following Hailey's gaze. "But we'll keep an eye on her."

Nodding, Hailey wandered to the far side of the pier, slowly so as not to disturb the turtles, but they slid into the water anyway as she approached.

"They'll come back in a little while," Dylan called. He was near the edge of the pier, taking off his shoes—loafers, she noticed, instead of the work boots he'd worn yesterday. "Come on," he urged, sitting down and sticking his feet into the water. "Just be careful of your stitches."

Smiling, she kicked off her sandals near his shoes and the takeout bag. Settling next to him, she dipped the tips of her toes in—only to pull them right back out. "Oh, that's cold!"

"You'll get used to it. In the summer, people often come to the lake to swim. It's the fastest way to cool off. You'll see if you're still here." His voice sounded like he hoped she would be.

Hailey didn't know if it was the water, his chuckle, or the way he was staring at her that made goose bumps march up her torso and across her shoulders.

He patted the stone next to him. "Scoot closer, into the sun."

It sounded like a great idea, especially because she was hoping he'd kiss her. She scooted almost close enough to feel the heat radiating from him, close enough to nearly touch.

They sat in silence for a while, feet in the water, enjoying the quiet that was broken only by the occasional call of a bird or the plop of a turtle sliding into the lake. Hailey hadn't realized how very far they'd come on the path. The way the lake was shaped, she couldn't even see the park. One lone boat was out on the water. Nothing more. The beautiful turquoise of the water called to her deceptively.

Before I leave here, I'll have to swim just once, she promised herself. That is, if she ever left.

"Okay," she said into the silence. "You win. This is the most beautiful lake I've ever seen."

His eyes met hers. "You sure? That was an easy surrender. There's still a lot more to see."

"I bet." Was it just her, or did his voice hold promise—a promise she wanted to latch onto and hold forever? The emotion seemed like something she hadn't felt before . . . and yet something ominous loomed there as well, like something ready to pounce. Was it fear?

Maybe. She didn't really know him, after all.

"I used to come here with my dad," Dylan said. "We'd fish or explore. We always ate our food here, though. On this side of the lake, anyway."

"So this isn't where you came to make out with the girls?" she teased.

He shrugged and gave another laugh. "Maybe in high school."

"Where is your dad now?" she asked and immediately wished she hadn't as his face turned sorrowful.

"About the time I quit the force and went to veterinary school, he got cancer. I think he had it before I left the force, but he didn't tell me until I made the decision to change careers and come home." Dylan looked at her, smiling faintly. "He wanted my future to be my choice, but if I'd known . . . I don't know. Anyway, I chose to come back, and I spent every minute I had away from school helping him. It was good—having that time, I mean. I know it might sound strange, but it almost made losing him okay, you know?"

"I'm sorry." She laid a hand on his arm.

He shook his head. "Don't be. We made our peace with it. At least we got to say everything we wanted to."

She wondered if that was a subtle reference to his wife, but when he didn't say anymore, she asked, "What about your mom?"

"Oh, my parents separated when I was young. My mother left town. They met in college, but she didn't like it here."

"She left you?" Hailey didn't mean to say it so abruptly, but she knew by the way he stared down into the water that his mother's leaving was something that still bothered him—and probably always would.

"She left us both," he said finally, lifting his gaze. "As an adult I understand why. She and my dad were very different, and aside from a memory or two, she never really seemed happy here. I'm grateful she didn't uproot me from everything I loved when she left. I do regret never having a sibling. I think kids need siblings."

"Do you ever see her?"

"Every now and then. Mostly we talk on the phone. Or send cards." He tried to sound as if it wasn't important, and her heart ached for him. "What about your parents?" he asked.

She shrugged. "There's nothing really to say. Just an average, normal family." She paused only a moment before changing the subject. "You said people in the town own property on the lake. What about your family? I mean, if your family is from here, and you're practically the only Morgan left, it seems only right that you should own a piece of it."

A smile spread across his face. "We own the original homestead of Chelsea and James Morgan. Well, to be exact, we gave their cabin to the town to display, as long as they want it, so now it sits in front of our town hall. But it was originally here at the lake, and we still own the land." He leaned in close and pointed across the lake. "Right over there."

"Nice," she said, seeing nothing but what looked like a tiny dock and layers of trees. This close, his smell was intoxicating, a mix of spicy aftershave and mint. "I saw the cabin. All logs, except for the stone fireplace, right?"

"That's it. There was a lot of disassembling we had to do to get it over there, and we restored a log or two and missing stones—all authentic and right from Forgotten, of course. It pretty much looks exactly like when Chelsea and James raised their thirteen children there."

"Unlucky thirteen," she murmured.

"Not in Forgotten. Thirteen is a lucky number here."

She laughed and lifted her chin to indicate his land across the lake. "Do you camp there?"

"I did. Now it's where I'm building my house—with the help of a contractor from Panna Creek."

"It's a perfect location." She experienced a surge of envy that he had something of Forgotten forever and ever. She wondered why he hadn't taken her to see his own land—did that mean something? Maybe he wasn't ready to trust her. "Does anyone ever sell their land?"

"All the time, here and elsewhere in Forgotten. Well, not as much right now since that developer has been in town." He laughed. "People aren't above hoping he'll buy up their land for more than it's worth. But that will change back once he's finished."

That meant there might be a little house she could buy, if things worked out. "Maggie offered me a job last night," she told him. "I'll be working at the café now."

"That's great. Kind of different from charity work, though, isn't it? You might miss it after a while."

"It's time for a change."

He picked up a small rock from the stone pier and threw it into the lake. The water rippled out in ever-growing waves. She stared at them, mesmerized. She felt like one of those ripples, growing and expanding her horizons.

He offered her a rock. "Do your co-workers know you're bumming around the US?"

She shrugged. "I didn't really tell anyone."

"Not even your parents? Your siblings?"

"Guess I should call. My phone is lost, so I'll have to get a new one."

"It wasn't in your bag? Or were you robbed on the bus?"

The words confused her, and she hated that feeling. "It probably fell into the river." She gazed past him at the takeout bags. "Did you bring something to eat? I think that soup and bread I ate at the Butter Cake is long gone." She wasn't really all that hungry, but she wanted him to stop with the questions. Who cared about the past? She wanted only to focus on the future—and she was beginning to hope that he might be a part of it.

He turned from her with a chuckle, stretching across their shoes to get the bag. "I didn't even get to eat my soup."

That made her laugh. "Why not?"

"Because I went after you." He set the bag in her lap. "Don't get me wrong. I like Jeremy and all, but he and I are in a different place. I only sat there to see how you were doing."

To see how she was doing—as if she were one of his animal patients. "He recently built a new house," she said, injecting a note of admiration into her voice. "But you probably know that."

"It's nice looking. A woman could do a lot worse than Jeremy, if you're looking to stay in Forgotten."

"You think I'm after his house?" The words sputtered out of her, more amused than offended. "Well, he's not bad-looking, I'll give him that. If you like beach-boy farmer types." She almost wished Jeremy was her type because he seemed a lot less complicated than Dylan, and she had the inkling Jeremy was more than a little interested. Unfortunately, Jeremy didn't give her this fluttery feeling inside.

"And you don't like beach-boy farmers?" he asked.

"Maybe."

"Maybe?" He was looking at her in that way again, and she suddenly forgot the bag in her hand. He was closer than before, having somehow shifted when he'd reached for the bag. She could feel the heat of his leg against hers through both their layers of clothing.

"I guess it depends on how I feel when I'm with him." She purposefully leaned toward him, holding his gaze. His eyes were amazing this close—dark and endless and full of desire.

A soft groan escaped his mouth as he abruptly closed the rest of the space between them. That little groan, even more than the first touch of his lips, captured her. It had always been coming to this kiss, she realized, from the first moment she'd pointed that pitchfork at him.

His hands cupped her face, pulling her lips more firmly against his. The pressure opened her mouth. He tasted of warmth and hunger, and an echoing hunger sprang up inside her.

Yet even as she reached her hands out to him, she felt him hesitate and pull back slightly. She nibbled on his lips, urging him on. His kiss deepened, and for long moments of bliss, she knew nothing but the touch and smell of him. The small split in her lip didn't even hurt. It only made her more aware of his touch.

She purposely ignored a looming blackness that seemed to sit just outside of her conscious thought. Only this moment mattered. Only this kiss.

With a soft, frustrated exclamation, he pulled almost force-fully away, giving a shake of his head.

"That would be pretty hard for a beach-boy farmer to beat," she said huskily. She moved her face closer to his, aware of his breath quickening. She waited, their eyes locked and emotions careening back and forth between them.

He put his hands on her arms, gently but firmly holding her back. His eyes stared at her with regret etched across his face.

"What?" she asked with effort. The looming black seemed to be edging closer now that he'd stopped kissing her, a black edged with panic.

"I don't know a thing about you," he said, his voice jagged. "Besides vague references to a job and California, you change the subject when anything personal comes up. You only talk about things that happened in the past two days. Which means I have no idea where you are from or what your family is like. Or if Hailey Waters is even your real name. Every instinct I have is telling me you're hiding something important. What is it? You can tell me."

She climbed slowly to her feet, rage building inside her. How dare he kiss her as if she meant something when all he was really doing was probing for information? "You think because you found me that I owe you my life story? That if I don't spill everything, I'm ungrateful? Well, thank you for finding me in that barn—and for not turning me into the police and for giving me a ride into town. I *really* appreciate it. But I don't owe you anything more than my thanks." She paused before rushing on, "And while we're talking about secrets, you have plenty of your own. I don't see you telling me about your wife—or how she died."

Surprise registered on his face. "She's not a secret."

"No? Then why haven't you mentioned her?" Her hands clenched at her sides. "I'll tell you why. Because you don't trust me yet. And maybe I don't trust you either." It was a lie because she did—strangely—trust him, but she couldn't tell him what was still not clear in her own mind. She needed a few more days to get it straight.

"Everyone has secrets," she continued. "Maggie, for instance. Do you know where she came from and what brought *her* here?"

"No, and I don't need to." His voice was as unyielding as steel. "I'm not planning on kissing Maggie."

She tried to laugh that off. "It was only a kiss, Dylan." A wonderful, soul-searching kiss that she'd never wanted to end, but he didn't have to know that.

"No," he grated. "It wasn't, and you know it. Look, if it's something serious, I can help. I was a police officer for four years. I have contacts."

"I haven't done anything, and I don't need anything. Except to go back to the café."

She walked stiffly past Sable, who looked up at her with forlorn eyes. Ignoring her, Hailey pushed through the bushes to the path, leaving both the man and the dog staring after her.

CHAPTER 10

Dylan cursed under his breath. What was wrong with him? He suspected Hailey was in trouble and confronting her this way wasn't going to make it easier for her to trust him.

"Wait," he called, gathering the bag of food, his socks, and both pair of shoes before hurrying after her. Sable came with him, her leash dragging on the ground behind her.

Dylan's thoughts swam in all directions, the foremost of which was that he shouldn't have kissed Hailey. He should have known better. It was clear she'd gone through some kind of trauma, and that meant she was vulnerable. But she'd been teasing him about that idiot Jeremy, and her lips had been so close, and it had been so very long.

She was almost jogging on the path in front of him, her long hair streaming behind her.

Give her space, he told himself. She wasn't a nervous heifer or skittish goat, but the concept was the same with animals as it was with people. Making them feel trapped only worsened whatever reaction they might be having. Space was supposed to help.

Except when it didn't. It hadn't with Bristol. Maybe if he'd have been more insistent on her letting him into his life, she wouldn't have been in harm's way that last day. She would have been at home in his bed and in his arms.

Maybe. Because he couldn't say for sure. He would never know.

He caught up to Hailey when she reached the park. She was no longer hurrying but walking slowly over the grass, as if her feet hurt from the bits of gravel she'd run across on the dirt path. His did. He kept a good arm's length between them and didn't speak. If she started down the road instead of going to his Tahoe, what would he do? He couldn't exactly throw her over his shoulder like a recalcitrant calf.

She was right that he hadn't told her about Bristol. But he hadn't told Bristol's parents or even his own police chief at the time about the true events surrounding her death. Aside from a handful of police officers belonging to another precinct, only his father knew the whole truth, and Hector, of course. Dylan had planned never to tell anyone—and he worked hard to avoid conversations that might lead to certain questions. But Hailey hadn't pushed or asked about Bristol. It had been him, not her, who'd forced the issue.

Two days. He'd only known her two days.

He began to feel sheepish. Maybe it had been *only* a kiss for her, and next week she'd be kissing Jeremy or some other farmer or cowboy. He needed to chill and go back to his original plan of washing his hands of her. Yes, he still needed to follow up with Hector for the good of the town, but that was all. He couldn't allow himself to be driven by his hormones like a teenager.

Decision made, he bent down and grabbed the end of Sable's leash, nearly dropping both pairs of shoes. When they'd almost reach the parking lot, which was paved but peppered with tiny stones, he held her sandals out in front of her.

She took them without acknowledgment, bending over to slip them on. He did the same with his loafers, hurrying so she wouldn't get too far ahead of him. In the parking lot, he beeped the lock on the remote and sprinted forward to open her door.

Hailey hesitated, but when Sable clambered heavily inside the Tahoe and settled in the middle of the bench seat, she climbed up too, almost as heavily. Dylan hurried around to the driver's door and jumped inside, the key in the ignition before he'd even shut the door.

"Look, I'm sorry," he said.

"It's okay." Her arms, folded protectively over her chest, didn't agree. Sable laid her muzzle on Hailey's leg, and her hand fell to the golden fur.

He'd never wanted to pull anyone into his arms more than he wanted to grab Hailey at that moment. If only he hadn't been such a persistent *hero*—this last he punctuated with a silent snort—he could have been holding and kissing her right now on that pier.

No! He shook his head. He wasn't looking to complicate his life. It was better this way, and he was not going to apologize one more time when she was definitely lying about something.

Dylan left the parking lot a little more quickly than normal, but in all, he was good at restraint. He'd learned that not only on the force but from his marriage to a woman who always wanted more—from him, from life, and even from death. Maybe that was why he'd kept her secret.

His phone started buzzing before he'd made his way back to Main Street. He took it out impatiently as he waited at the stop sign, planning only to glance at it to make sure it wasn't an emergency.

"No," he moaned, reading the text quickly. He glanced over at Hailey, who was watching him warily. "It's an emergency," he explained. "Old Fletcher Wilson removed a trocar that I put in his cow yesterday morning, and she's swelling again. I need to go now."

"I can walk the rest of the way," Hailey said.

"The Wilson farm is north of here. The café is on the way." His eyes fell to Sable.

"She can come with me," Hailey said. "You don't have time to take her back."

"I haven't asked Maggie."

"I'll ask her. Besides, the blanket Maggie put down for her in my room is still there."

Dylan wanted to refuse, maybe more because of his pride than anything. He didn't want to need help, but then Sable was really the McColls problem, not his. Regardless, he either took the dog with him or let her stay with Hailey, and he had no doubt which the dog would prefer.

Which he'd prefer, if he were to admit the truth.

He pulled the SUV onto Main Street, half a block away from the café. "Thank you," he said, knowing it sounded stilted.

She nodded and looked away, but not before he noticed her smirk.

A minute later, he slowed to let Hailey and the dog out in front of the Butter Cake. Her eyes were lowered as she shut the door, her lashes leaving a small shadow under her eyes, exactly as they had on the pier before their kiss. When she looked up, her blue eyes burning into his, he wanted to throw his cell phone out in the middle of the street and kiss her again.

Instead, he sped away, glancing in the rearview mirror to see with some satisfaction that she was still standing in the grass with Sable, staring after the Tahoe.

More cars were out on Main tonight—shop owners heading home or people arriving in town for dinner or a Saturday night movie. He clenched the steering wheel. He should be going to a movie tonight, preferably with an uncomplicated woman, and maybe he would after this emergency. It wasn't as if he didn't have women friends in town. In fact, he still had a half a dozen dishes at the clinic from women in the area that he needed to return.

Of course, with Sable's temperature so low, he really shouldn't go out, especially to any place he'd have to turn off his phone.

He'd passed the Forget Me Not Bar and the houses that lined the north end of Main. He was next to the ball fields on the edge of town when the lights of a police car went on behind him, accompanied by a siren. He pulled over, slamming his fist against the steering wheel in frustration. When the officer climbed out of his car, he saw it was Levi Hughes, second-in-command at the station. He walked with a bit of a swagger, and the cowboy boots he wore were definitely not standard since Police Chief McColl had nixed them after one of his officers had slipped during a foot chase in the rain.

Dylan rolled down his window. "Seriously, Levi? I have an emergency. Ronica's cow Moona Lisa is going to die if I don't get there fast, and I swear I'll tell Ronica that it was your fault."

Levi swiped his dark hair out of his eyes with an impatient hand. "Dang it all, Dylan, I need to give someone a ticket. If I don't, Chief McColl is going to think I haven't been doing anything while he's been away, except call the county sheriff to help find whoever broke into the turkey plant and stole those turkeys. And you know how he feels about that. You're the only one that's been speeding."

"That's because everyone knows you park at the ball fields." Dylan tried not to roll his eyes. Levi was a good man, if young and inexperienced. "Look, you turn on your siren and accompany me to the Wilson farm, and I won't tell Caleb about you wearing those cowboy boots."

"Why, it ain't raining," Levi objected, looking up at the sky.

"No, but you'll be looking at weekends for the rest of the year for not following protocol."

Levi scowled. "That could be considered bribery."

"No, I'm looking out for the town," Dylan said.

Levi wilted and Dylan knew he'd won. "Okay, hold your horses," Levi said. "I'll give you an escort. But you'll tell Ronica and Chief McColl that I saved that darn cow."

Following the wailing police car didn't really save time, but it gave Dylan an impressive entrance to the Wilson farm. Seeing Jeremy out in front of the barn, pacing, reminded him of Hailey's comments about him.

Beach-boy farmer? he thought. *What did that even mean?* Jeremy didn't look like any surfer Dylan knew, except maybe the blond hair that didn't fall into his eyes only because his hat held it back. He was also strong as a bull. Jeremy could throw bales of hay better than anyone and always won those kinds of competitions at the fairs. Maybe that was what she was talking about.

Jeremy lifted a brow at Levi's company. "Little overkill, isn't it?" he said to Dylan.

"Not if she's as bad as this morning."

"I don't think so. I called as soon as I realized what he'd done. Come on." He motioned to both of them and hurried into the barn.

Ronica was in the stall with the cow, who was indeed blowing up again. "Thank the Lord, you're here," she said, one hand on the cow's neck. She looked a little out of place in her nice clothes and hair styled as if she were heading into town. "I told Jeremy to screw it back in, but he's squeamish. Tell me, how can a farmer be squeamish? You need milk and butter for your family. Cows are like the chickens and the pigs. They're necessary, and you've got to take care of them."

"We eat the pigs and chickens, Mom," Jeremy said. "This cow is your baby, not food. I don't want to be responsible for hurting her."

"Well . . ." Ronica scratched Moona Lisa's neck. "I suppose that's true. I'm going to have to put a bell on both her and your dad, if we're going to keep him from letting her into the wrong field." She gave the cow a final pat and sighed. "It's not really his fault. That used to be the right field ten years ago. He remembers that time best these days."

"Where's the trocar?" Dylan asked, coming into the stall. Jeremy started to hand it to him, but Dylan shook his head. "Your mom's right. I'll show you how far to put it in, and then you screw it, just like she said. You do it, or I'm charging you a hundred bucks for a second emergency call. If you can put it in yourself, today's free and I'll only charge you sixty for yesterday."

"A hundred bucks?" groaned Jeremy. "That's a lot of money for five minutes."

Dylan smirked at him. "If you want, you can call someone else." His fees were actually more reasonable than most vets, but he'd rather keep animals safe than get rich off people who often had to sacrifice to afford his services.

"Okay, let's get this over with," Jeremy said.

Dylan handed him gauze and disinfectant from his bag. "Clean the wound with a little sterilizer first—and the trocar as well."

When that was accomplished, Jeremy approached Moona Lisa. He made two half-hearted attempts before Ronica, with an aggrieved sigh, grabbed his hand and shoved the trocar in hard.

"Now screw that," she said, slapping her son on the back.

Even with Jeremy's reluctance, the whole process took less than five minutes.

"Lot easier than I thought," Jeremy admitted.

Levi wrinkled his nose. "Better you than me. Glad I didn't stay on my dad's ranch." He moved toward the stall door, avoiding a huge cow patty on the floor that the straw didn't quite cover.

"Thanks for giving Dylan the police escort," Ronica called after him. "I'll make a dirt cake and bring it to the station on Monday for everyone."

That promise stopped Levi in his tracks by the barn door. Dylan knew why. Aside from Maggie's gooey butter cake, Ronica's Kansas dirt cake was the most prized dessert at all the community events. "Much obliged," he said, touching a hand to an imaginary hat.

After Levi disappeared, Dylan took a few more minutes to make sure the cow was otherwise healthy. "She'll be okay," he told Ronica. "But keep Fletcher out of the barn."

Ronica nodded. "I have a lock I'll put on the stall. Thanks a lot for coming."

They all walked out together to the cars, where Levi was already pulling away in his police cruiser. Dylan grabbed hand wipes from the back of his Tahoe and began scrubbing his hands clean. His stomach was protesting rather loudly now, and he planned to eat not only his sandwich but the one that should have been Hailey's too.

"That new woman, Hailey, is something else, don't you think?" Jeremy said conversationally, as Dylan shut his liftgate. "Both beautiful and smart."

Ronica grinned ear to ear. "Better ask her out before someone else does."

"I took her to the lake this afternoon," Dylan found himself saying. "In fact, I had to leave Chief McColl's dog with her. I'd better go pick her up."

"Is that why you left the café so fast this afternoon?" Jeremy said with a frown. "Chasing after Hailey? I knew something was up. Just so you know, I enjoyed your soup and bread."

Dylan's stomach growled at that, and he thought longingly of the sandwiches on his seat. "Glad you did. Well, I'd better get Sable before she drops those pups in Maggie's café."

"Oo," Ronica said, widening her eyes. "She wouldn't like that."

"No, she wouldn't." Jeremy agreed. "But I think I might go into town myself, Mom, if you've got Dad okay."

"Oh, he's fine," Ronica said. "Watching TV now. He won't budge till bedtime."

Dylan had no doubt that Jeremy would be making a trip to the Butter Cake Café tonight, while Dylan would be home with Sable.

The phone chose that moment to begin buzzing in his pocket, and he climbed inside the Tahoe—probably another emergency. With a nod to the Wilsons, he pulled the phone out as he shut his door. It was Maggie calling, and a rush of worry made Dylan clumsy as he put his finger on the reader to open his phone.

"Hey, Maggie, what's up?"

"It's Sable. She's acting strange and starting to pant. I've got her and Hailey here in my garage with a bunch of old towels, but you better get this dog out of my cafe."

"Is she straining?" he asked.

"I think so." Her voice rose in pitch. "And we both know what that means."

He groaned. "Sorry, but if she's straining, it's better not to move her."

"Well, get over here, at least. I've got a café full of hungry people, and Hailey's never done this before." She paused before adding matter-of-factly, "Natalie McColl is going to be so upset that she missed this. You sure we shouldn't call her?"

"I've already told them it's close, but they can't come back now. They know I'll take good care of Sable." He wasn't about to share the information that the McColl's vacation involved their troubled daughter, though Maggie might already suspect.

"I'm going home for supplies and her whelping box," he told Maggie. "With so many puppies, we're going to need the box. I'll be there in fifteen or twenty. If a pup comes before that, Sable should know what to do." Gathering his prepared supplies wouldn't take long, but moving the box was a different story.

Dylan rolled down his window, waving Jeremy over. "Chief McColl's dog has gone into labor. She's in Maggie's garage with Hailey, and I need a little help getting a whelping box over there, if you're game."

Jeremy nodded. "Sure, I'd like an excuse to see Hailey again."

"I thought you might." Dylan regretted asking him already, but getting the box over there himself would take a lot more time. He should have left Sable at the clinic this evening instead of taking her to the park, but he'd really thought she had at least until nightfall.

"I'll meet you at the clinic," Jeremy said.

Dylan devoured both sandwiches on the way, the gnawing in his stomach finally ceasing. Levi had apparently decided not to set another speed trap because no one pulled him over on the way back into town. A knot of excitement had formed in Dylan's stomach. He enjoyed most aspects of his job, but helping new life come into the world was always amazing, regardless of the animal species.

His phone buzzed as he opened the door to the clinic, and he answered without checking the caller ID, fully expecting Maggie again. But it wasn't Maggie.

"I've run all the checks," Hector said without preamble. "That picture you sent doesn't match any Hailey Waters I can find, not in California or anywhere in the US. Either this Hailey has never had a driver's license or passport, or her name isn't Hailey Waters. If we had a social security number, we could track her more easily. My gut feeling is she's lying about everything. The good news is that a cursory search with the picture doesn't match any open police cases. I even touched base with my contacts at the FBI, and they checked their most wanted cases and came up with no matches either."

"Thanks," he told Hector, motioning for Jeremy to follow him inside the clinic.

"And before you ask, I've spent my whole day off on this. And because I knew you'd bring it up again, I've got the picture out to California charities, but so far no one recognizes her. The next step is to send me her fingerprints, or I could convince my FBI contacts to do a complete facial recognition search, which as you know can take time. But is that really what you want? I'm going to need a convincing reason to use their database."

"Yeah, I know." Dylan stopped outside the cage with Sable's

whelping box, aware of Jeremy's eyes on him. "Can I get back to you on that?" he said. "I've got a dog about ready to give birth to more puppies than you could stuff in your cruiser. It's going to be a long night."

Hector laughed at that. "And this is what you left law enforcement for?"

"Yeah. Thanks for pointing that out. I really appreciate it."

"Anytime. I got a hot date tonight anyway."

"Glad someone does. Don't have too much fun." Dylan hung up as Hector started laughing.

Twenty minutes after Maggie's call, Dylan pulled up outside the Butter Cake Café. He and Jeremy man-handled the whelping box out of his dad's old truck. The automatic garage door was shut, but when he set the box on the ground and tapped, the door began to rise. Hailey stood in front of the space, her slender body revealed a slice at a time, every inch making his mouth water. When it reached her face, he saw relief there. She'd pulled her hair back since the lake and was wearing a large black T-shirt imprinted with a lion that hung halfway down to her knees over her capris.

"Finally!" she said, hands on her hips. "I've been so worried. She's acting crazy. Moving the towels around and panting."

"That's normal." He picked up his end of the whelping box. "It's called nesting. She might settle down a little after she sees this. It's familiar."

Hailey breathed in a deep breath. "Good." As they passed her, she added, "Hi, Jeremy."

"Hey," Jeremy said.

The hesitant way Jeremy spoke reminded Dylan of the first

time Hailey had told him her name, as if she'd been uncertain. He tried not to dwell on what Hector had said about her lying.

With Jeremy's help, it didn't take much effort to set the box near Sable's current nest. The garage had been added much later to the Butter Cake and was only large enough for Maggie's single car, but she'd apparently moved it out to give them more room. Dylan looked briefly at Sable before jogging back to his Tahoe for the rectangular clothes basket full of towels and other supplies.

He'd barely laid out a few blue-backed medical pads over the black rubber lining of the whelping box when Sable came rushing inside it, dragging a towel with her. Dylan threw in a few more. She arranged them a bit, but almost immediately lay down and began panting.

"Won't be long now." Dylan squatted outside the box near Sable's head. "Good girl," he murmured. "You like this box, don't you? Don't worry. You're going to be just fine." She whined and stuck her head out toward him, which he took as an invitation to scratch her. Some dogs wanted to be left completely alone while they gave birth, but others wanted to be near their owners—or in this case their vet. Even so, he'd refrain from touching her too much.

"Thanks," Dylan said to Jeremy. "Appreciate the hand."

Jeremy nodded. "You too. Thanks for helping with Moona Lisa. Again." His gaze drifted to Hailey. "You interested in going to see a movie tonight?"

She stared at him for long seconds without speaking. Then she looked down at her clothes. "That's a nice offer, but I think I'm too worried. I'm going to stick around here with Sable." Her gaze flew to Dylan's. "If that's okay. You don't mind, do you? Or will Sable mind?"

Her question surprised him. He'd expected her to go with

Jeremy, especially after their fight, but suddenly, more than anything, he wanted her to stay.

"Sable won't mind. And I might actually need the help, with as many puppies as I'm anticipating. I think I already told you it might be twelve or more."

"Okay, then I'll stay." She sank down on the cement next to Dylan, reaching out a tentative hand to pat Sable briefly. "You sweet thing." Her gaze wandered back to Jeremy, as if only then remembering he was still there. "Raincheck?" she asked.

"Sure." Jeremy edged toward the garage door, his face tinged with green. "Sure thing. Good luck, you guys."

When he was gone, Hailey jumped up and shut the garage. "She seems to like it closed," she said. "The light isn't all that great, though."

"Not very warm, either, and it'll get colder after the sun goes down." He frowned at the garage, looking around for an electric heater. "Would you ask Maggie if she's got a heater? We won't need to keep it on all the time, but this is going to take all night, and I don't want these babies getting cold."

"Yeah," Hailey stared at Sable, an odd expression on her face. "So many babies. Isn't there a way to know exactly how many?"

He shook his head. "Ultrasound is unreliable, and I don't like to X-ray babies—if it's not good for pregnant humans, it's not that great for dogs either."

"Right." She nodded. "I'll go ask Maggie." She started for the door that led into the café, pausing with her hand on the knob. "Did you . . . get something to eat?"

"I ate both our dinners." He raised his brow, expecting a jab at that, but she only laughed.

"Good. Uh, look, I'm sorry. I'm a little emotional, what with all the changes. I think I overreacted earlier."

"Me too."

She left then, and he stared after her for a moment, until Sable's straining called his attention. The tiniest bit of a puppy was now emerging. He was torn between calling Hailey and keeping quiet, but his dilemma ended when Hailey returned to the garage. He lifted a finger to his lips, and she nodded.

"Maggie will bring the heater out in a bit," she whispered.

After a few more pushes, the puppy was out, and Sable started licking it. Dylan let her do it for a while, but when she started biting the cord, he clamped and cut it himself. "Sometimes the dog can pull on it too much," he explained, "and it'll cause an injury. But licking the pup gets the sack off and helps it start breathing." He left Sable to her mothering, and when the placenta came out a few minutes later, he let her eat it.

"I know it's gross," he said when Hailey wrinkled her nose. "Some vets swear it helps replace the vitamins and store up nutrients. With her being a domesticated dog, I don't think she really needs that, but I'll let her do it as long as she wants. If she gets distracted, we'll remove them, though. If she eats too many, she might throw up."

From his kit, he brought out a clipboard with a birth form and a handful of soft wool strips. "In cases where there are this many babies, I like to mark each one so we can weigh them later and keep an eye on any that might need a little extra care. Some animals instinctively take care of the runts, but not all of them do, and Sable's owners will need to monitor the pups." He passed her the clipboard. "If you don't mind, maybe you can record the color of the strip we put on them and the birth order. And check the box if the placenta was also delivered. It's important to make sure all of them come out."

He donned surgical gloves and picked up the golden

newborn, rubbing its little body with one of the softer towels he'd brought. "Number one is a boy," he said, tying a strip of blue wool around the baby's neck. He placed the baby at one of Sable's nipples, nodding in satisfaction as he began rooting around. Sable gave the pup a few more licks before resting her muzzle on a towel.

"Puppy one. Blue band. Boy," Hailey said as she wrote on the paper. "What if the band falls off?"

"Or Sable rips it off, you mean." He chuckled. "I'll replace them at every weigh-in, if necessary. Some owners paint the puppies' toenails, though none of it will be necessary once they're a bit older, and we know they're all gaining weight and nursing well. It's just a way to keep track, so we don't overlook any of them."

"How long before the next one comes?" The eager way she asked made him laugh. Was it only his perception, or was he doing more laughing since he'd met her?

"Subsequent babies usually come thirty to sixty minutes after each other, but as long as it isn't more than four hours between each birth, we'll be on track."

Her eyes widened. "You weren't kidding about it taking all night then, were you?"

He laughed. "I wasn't. But you can go up to bed any time you need to. I'm used to snoozing in between."

"I bet Maggie has a cot or something we could set up here for you."

"That reminds me," he said, dumping the towels from the clothes basket into a corner of the whelping box, leaving only one to pad the bottom. "When another baby starts to come, we'll need to put this little guy in here, so Sable can get to the new baby. It's not so important with the first few, but with so many coming, it'll get crowded, and they can get trampled as she tries to take care of each new one. She'll want them close and in sight, though, so the basket works well for that." Dylan pulled off his gloves and stuffed them into one of the heavy-duty garbage bags from his pile of supplies.

"Looks like he's latched on." Hailey started to reach out to the baby, but Dylan intercepted her hand.

"Let's give her a moment with him. There will be plenty of time to hold them as more are born, but Sable might feel threatened right now, seeing as it's her only one. I've been taking care of Sable since she was a puppy herself, and I'm even hesitant to interfere too much right now. I don't think she'll bite, but we want her as calm as possible. And to see for herself that we won't take them away."

"Oh, right." Hailey made a face.

"It's okay." He became aware that he was still holding her hand.

A smile crossed her lips. "Penny for your thoughts," she asked. She didn't pull her hand away. The seconds seemed to stretch into minutes.

He couldn't tell her his thoughts. He was thinking she might not be Hailey Waters and that everything she'd told him could be a lie, including why her leg was bleeding in the McColls' barn. Emotions warred inside him as he remembered their kiss, how her mouth had opened to his, as eager for him as he was for her.

She was so beautiful—why was he fighting the attraction? Was it because of her secrets or his?

CHAPTER 11

The sound of the kitchen door opening brought their hands apart. Fighting disappointment, Hailey looked up to see Maggie slip into the garage, bringing with her a heavy-looking object that looked like an old-fashioned wall heater. Dylan jumped up to help her situate it near the whelping box and plug it in.

"Just leave it on this setting," Maggie said, pointing to a dial. "Otherwise, it'll draw too much energy and trip the breaker. It's old but reliable enough." She peered into the box at the first puppy. "So tiny. What's the blue for?"

"Boy, first pup." Hailey showed her the paper, where there were twenty lines with boxes to fill out.

Nodding, Maggie went to the wall, removed a ladder from a hook, and propped it under a shelf. "Looks like you're going to need this." Climbing up the ladder, she pulled out a huge blue beanbag that Dylan rushed to catch. "I also have a camping cot around here somewhere. Ah, here it is." She passed it to Dylan and climbed down. "And is anyone hungry?"

Hailey nodded. "I can make something."

"You've got your hands full. I'll bring you both a snack."

"None for me," Dylan said, sounding regretful. "I just ate."

Maggie smiled. "Some cake then."

"Sure. Look, I'm so sorry about all this." Dylan jerked his head in Sable's direction. "And we won't be able to move them for at least a day or two."

She waved the words away. "Never mind about that. They can stay as long as they need to. But you owe me a favor. This is way bigger than her staying here yesterday."

"Fine. Whatever you need."

"It won't be this week or this month or maybe even this year," Maggie continued, hands on her hips. "But you and the McColls both owe me. Big."

Dylan chuckled. "Okay. I'll be sure to let them know."

A giggling whisper made them all look toward the kitchen door. Ingrid and Lisa were there, straining their necks to get a look at the new puppy.

"Sh, girls," Maggie said. "Plenty of time to see the babies when their momma is no longer in labor. Go on. I'm sure there are tables to clean before we get another rush of customers. Remember, you still owe me for your no-shows last night." The teens vanished obediently.

Dylan set up the cot while Hailey settled on the beanbag. The blue material was a little dusty, but it cupped her body in comfort, and she suddenly felt drowsy. Her cramps had come back with a vengeance after the lake, causing a momentary alarm, but the painkillers had solved that issue.

"She's starting again," Dylan said. "I'm not surprised it's

sooner rather than later. That's a lot of baby weight in there. She's not going to be comfortable for a long time."

They followed the same steps as before, with Dylan clamping the cord before Sable could rip it, then letting her lick the baby and checking to make sure the pup was breathing. This time Hailey tied on the soft strip of wool before writing: *Puppy two. Green band. Boy.*

The next seven puppies each came twenty to forty minutes apart. Hailey had her hands full with keeping the pups safe during the births and helping them start nursing. So far, the females outnumbered the males five to four. Dylan was discarding the placentas now, and Sable was beginning to visibly tire. She lay with her body stretched out so the babies could nurse, her head on a towel and her eyes closed.

When an hour went by and no more babies materialized, Hailey said, "Maybe that's it."

Dylan gave her a cocky smile. "Give me your hand."

She did as he requested, and he laid it gently on Sable's stomach. Hailey sucked in a deep breath as she felt more babies moving. "Oh," she said with a surprised sigh.

He laughed. "They have a little more room now, so they're easier to feel." He grabbed a bowl that they'd been offering Sable water or treats in, but this time she wasn't interested.

Hailey petted Sable's head, and the dog gave a loud sigh. "She's exhausted. Poor thing." All at once, sadness seemed to loom over Hailey, somehow connected with those unseen, writhing bodies that had yet to be born. She hoped her feeling didn't mean something awful awaited poor Sable or the pups.

No sounds came from the café, as Maggie had long ago closed up shop and stopped peeking inside to see how things were moving along. The last time she'd come in, she'd brought water bottles, more snacks, and blankets, one of which Hailey pulled over herself as she snuggled deeper into the beanbag. It was growing colder with each passing hour, and she was glad to be next to the heater, which was on the side of the whelping box. The heat radiated both ways, but even a few feet away, the air became a lot colder.

"Now what?" she asked.

"Now we wait." He wrapped a blanket around his shoulders and sat on the cot in front of the whelping box.

Silence stretched out between them, but it wasn't an uncomfortable one. Hailey let drowsiness spread through her—until Dylan's words brought her sharply back to the present.

"I met her at the start of my fourth year in college," he said. "Her name was Bristol. I was a biology major; she was studying interior design. She was unlike anyone from here—glamorous, sophisticated, and she knew exactly what she wanted from life. And I was a part of that. At least that's what I thought. I fell for her quick and hard. Her dad was a police chief, and his stories and how much she wanted to stay in New York with her family took over for a while." He shook his head with a self-deprecating laugh. "I was young, and New York was so big. Suddenly everything I'd wanted all my life wasn't enough. So I went to the police academy after college instead of veterinary school. Her dad pulled a few strings to get me a job on the force, and we got married."

"Were you happy?" Hailey pulled her knees up to her chest, hugging them. The pain in his face was apparent even in the dim garage.

"For a time. At least I thought so." His tone was matter-of-fact, his face devoid of his normal expressions. That told Hailey more than he probably wanted her to know.

⬤ KISS AT MIDNIGHT
157

"What happened?"

"I think Bristol got bored. She liked to shop and entertain and go out. I worked long hours on the grunt shifts. I thought maybe having a child would help; she thought it was too soon." He paused, his jaw clenching and unclenching. "I didn't know she was cheating on me until one night when I was working late, a gang broke into the apartment of an officer from another precinct, a guy she'd dated before me, and shot them both in his bed."

Hailey couldn't stop the gasp that escaped her throat. "No!"

He nodded. "It was an undercover case he was working, and she got caught in the crossfire. Pure chance. I might never have known. Or maybe she would have left me. At least I finally understood why she wasn't terribly interested in having a child with me."

"I'm so sorry."

He shrugged. "It was eight years ago, and what happened is really her secret, not mine. The officer's undercover work was important enough that his chief made sure the details never made the papers. The media reported that she'd been killed in a drive-by shooting. My dad knew the truth and my partner at the time knew, but I didn't think anyone else needed to live with that picture of her—especially not her parents. Well, her father might have gotten wind of it from his connections, but if he learned the truth, we never talked about it. Maybe he thought they never told me." He offered her a smile. "No one here knows. There's enough gossip already in this town. I don't like to feed the flames."

Which she knew instinctively was his way of telling her that she was the only person in Forgotten who knew about his past. That was a huge trust he'd given her.

"I know about the gossip here," she said. "Only today Ingrid was telling me how she'd heard about me falling into the river and you pulling me out. Thanks for not telling anyone about the barn."

"I did tell Maggie. But she doesn't gossip much."

Hailey let a few seconds go by before saying, "So is the shooting what made you stop being a police officer?"

He contemplated that for a long moment, then shook his head. "Not so much her dying, but more because I'd already realized that I missed my life here." He blew out a breath. "Anyway, she would have hated it here, exactly like my mother did."

Understanding dawned. This was a man who had been abandoned not once but twice in his lifetime by women who should have loved him more. No wonder he'd reacted to her secrets the way he had. But she had another thought that was every bit as enlightening: if his wife had lived and hadn't cheated on him, he'd likely still be in New York working a job he'd grown to hate.

Sometimes you start down a path before you really know where you are headed and what you want, he'd said. She wondered if that was how her life had been as well, if she'd walked away because she'd found her life intolerable. She'd have to learn the truth eventually.

But not today.

Hailey scooted over on the beanbag, patting the place next to her. "It's warmer over here." He stared at her for a long moment before coming swiftly to his feet and joining her on the bag. She tucked the blanket around him, sharing her warmth.

"You're a good man, Dylan Morgan," she said softly. "And probably the sexiest man I've ever met." It was what he needed to hear—she could see it by the response in his eyes. And she meant every word.

"I'm no beach-boy farmer," he said in a completely serious tone, though his dark eyes were dancing again.

"Nope. Definitely not."

The silence fell again, and this time it was filled with sexual tension. She was aware of his hip next to hers, his smell, the five o'clock shadow on his chin. But he didn't try to kiss her, and after what he'd been through, she didn't really blame him.

So now that he'd told her the truth about his time in New York, should she tell him her secret? Her reluctance to do so might be the reason she'd ended up alone in a barn. Is that the way she wanted to live? Without trusting anyone except Maggie? If she knew anything about Dylan, it was that he, deep in his heart, was a hero. That meant she could trust him.

Maybe.

As long as she wasn't an escaped criminal. She couldn't forget the ten thousand dollars she'd found in the money belt. She'd almost made her decision when Sable started straining again.

Dylan jumped up at the same time Hailey did, and both scrambled for puppies, placing them in the basket. Most were sleeping and didn't appear to notice the change in location, but one little male with a yellow wool band whimpered. Hailey put the pup in her lap instead, patting it gently until it settled.

"We won't be able to put them all in the basket soon," she said.

Dylan laughed. "See what I meant about being able to hold them?"

She did.

This new puppy, number ten, didn't start breathing, not even with Sable's ministrations, and Dylan had to suction its mouth.

"Come on, little guy," he murmured, glancing at Hailey's worried face. "Can you pass me a towel?" After a few seconds of vigorous rubbing, the pup sucked in a breath. "There you go. And oops, she's a female, not a little guy after all."

Hailey tied a purple strip around its neck, blowing out a sigh of relief. "Do you lose a lot of them?"

"Not usually when I'm around, but sometimes one will be stillborn, and some die in the first few days when they fail to thrive, which is why I like to use the bands."

"I'm glad she's okay." Hailey wrote the number and color on the clipboard.

The night went on, with resting and talking between births. But now, as if by unspoken agreement—or maybe exhaustion—they kept things between them light, even when sitting together on the beanbag. They took turns refilling their waters and using the restroom. At one point, Hailey fell asleep and missed a couple of births.

She blinked her eyes open at six in the morning to find Dylan looming over her. "Sorry to wake you," he said, "but I think the last pup is coming. Can you hold these?" Dylan had two puppies in his gloved hands, and he tucked them in next to her. "No more room in the basket," he said as he grabbed two more to give her.

Hailey already had the little purple-banded pup on her chest, but she welcomed the others in the routine they'd developed during the night. This time Dylan shouldn't have bothered moving the pups out from underfoot as Sable barely lifted her head when the baby was born.

Dylan quickly cleaned up the pup. "Male," he said, tying on a black camo strip. "Number seventeen." Hailey's hands were full, so he recorded the birth, then gently touched Sable's belly.

"That's it?" Hailey asked.

"I think so. Her uterus is already contracting. I'd do an

ultrasound if we were at the clinic, but I'm fairly certain that's it. And there have been seventeen placentas, so we shouldn't have to worry about extra bleeding."

He rubbed Sable's head. "Good job," he murmured. She lapped a little water when he offered it but otherwise didn't move.

Dylan cleaned up the blue-backed pads and laid down new ones before reaching for the puppies Hailey was holding. He placed them with the others next to Sable, all except the one with the purple band.

"I hate to give her up," Hailey said, kneeling next to the whelping box. "She won't get squished, will she?"

"Not by Sable. That's only a worry in the heat of birth. She'll get squished a lot by her siblings, but that's part of growing and learning." He pulled off his gloves and put them into the garbage bag that was now nearly full of trash. "We'll keep an eye on her. You could always adopt one, you know. You're entitled after this night."

Hailey laughed. "Maggie would love that." She put the baby next to Sable's paw, where it quickly burrowed into the mound of puppies.

"Good point. But there are other places you could rent. Houses, I mean. If you're going to stay in Forgotten."

Hailey sat back on the beanbag with a huge yawn. "You mean like Chelsea Morgan's house?" she teased. "Why don't you ask the mayor if I can stay there?"

A chuckle erupted from his chest. "I guess I should have thought about renting the cabin before we donated it to the town. I mean, who cares about such things as electricity and running water? But seriously, you can find a good deal, if you decide that's what you want."

Suddenly, desperately, Hailey did want to adopt a puppy. "How long before they can leave Sable?" She held herself tensely as she waited for the answer.

"Not for at least eight weeks. They're usually eating solid food well by six weeks, and some people like to give them away then, but in my experience, dogs are always better behaved if they have a few more weeks in a pack, learning from their mother and siblings."

Hailey relaxed. Eight weeks was a lifetime when you could only remember two days. "Okay then. I'll see how the job goes and look into it." Another yawn took her, and she was dizzy again, but who wouldn't be after a night like this?

"Go upstairs to bed," he urged. "I'll crash right here with Sable."

"But you've been up all night too."

"Yep, and it won't be the last time. It kind of goes with the job. Tell you what, I'll take the first shift, and when you wake up, you can peek in on her while I take care of a few things."

Hailey nodded. "Okay."

"But don't hurry or set an alarm. I'm going to stay with her either way right now. I can sleep anywhere."

He offered a hand to help her up from the beanbag, much as he had when he'd found her in the barn. She let him pull her up, amazed at how warm his touch felt on her hand. He tucked a hair that had escaped her ponytail behind her ear, desire clear in his eyes. But things hadn't really changed between them, had they? He'd trusted her with his innermost secret—no, with his dead wife's secret—but if he knew Hailey's, he'd think her a liar or, worse, crazy.

And he'd be right because right now she was uncertain about what was true in her life and what wasn't. That was even scarier than not remembering. In fact, maybe Dylan and his questions were the only thing between her complete self-deception.

His fingers glided over her cheek, burning a path to her lips. She closed her eyes, head swimming either from lack of sleep or from his nearness. Maybe it was a little of both.

She opened her eyes, making her decision. "I don't remember," she said softly.

He stared at her. "Remember what?"

"Anything before I stepped off the bus. My name, why I came. Even after the bus, it's foggy. I don't remember finding the barn."

He didn't respond, and he didn't need to. She saw all she needed to in his eyes. He didn't believe or trust her. How could he when she didn't trust herself?

She backed away from his touch, holding his gaze for long seconds before finally turning and hurrying to the kitchen door.

"Hailey!" he called.

But she didn't stop. Hailey wasn't even her name.

CHAPTER 12

In her dreams, Hailey heard music. She knew it was from the church across the street, whose service, Maggie had told her, began at ten. Hailey had been planning to go, to experience even more of the small town she was beginning to love. She tried opening her eyes, but the music lulled her back to sleep.

She dreamed of a white room and monitors and something around her wrist. Someone was crying. Not the cries of anger or fear, but a keening of deep despair. Her head pounded. She sought the comforting music once more, but looming blackness fell over and consumed her.

She slept.

When she finally regained consciousness, the blackness and the singing and the white room were all gone, but the pounding headache was still there. Her body ached from the night's long vigil, and she was tempted to fall back to sleep. But remembering the puppies and Dylan watching over them, she groggily checked the clock on the wall, blinking away the cobwebs. What she saw startled the sleep from her system. Already two o'clock, which meant she'd been dead to the world, if not her dreams, for almost eight hours.

Yawning, she pushed herself to her feet, experiencing a rush of liquid in the red shorts she wore under the clean white shirt she'd pulled on before falling into bed. Hurrying inside the bathroom, she silently cursed monthly periods. She should have bought bigger pads or used tampons too. Did she normally even use tampons?

Shaking her head at the ridiculous thoughts, she downed a couple of painkillers before standing under a hot shower for probably far too long. She was feeling like a new person when she emerged from the steaming bath and smothered her face and body in lotion. Her face was peeling in earnest now, but there was nothing she could do about that.

She dressed quickly in her newly purchased underclothes and hand-me-down jean shorts. As she contemplated which shirt to wear, her hand fell to her bare stomach. Definitely a little weight there she needed to lose, though, thankfully, it hadn't seemed to spread to the rest of her, except maybe her breasts, which she didn't mind, though they did feel tender, being that time of the month and all.

Groaning, she pulled on a snug black tank, topping it with a bright red shirt that was designed to fall off one shoulder and would hide her belly weight. Maybe she could take Sable for more walks. Of course, Sable was a little busy right now for walks, and by the time the dog was feeling up to it, she and her sweet puppies would be back on the McColl farm.

Pulling her still-wet hair into a messy ponytail and ignoring her makeup, Hailey headed downstairs. The café was completely deserted—no Maggie, no customers, and no employees. She thought it was odd until she remembered Maggie didn't open the café on Sundays, except for birthday parties and church socials.

She stopped in the kitchen long enough to cut herself a slab of bread, buttering it thickly and drizzling on a bit of honey. If she was going to watch Sable, she'd need to be ready to stay awhile. Did Maggie have any books?

She walked to the garage door but stopped short of opening it, experiencing a bout of dread. She'd walked out on Dylan last night, knowing too well that someone like her didn't fit into his life. He wanted truth, clear-cut lines, and someone who would never leave. He hadn't said so in those words, but she felt the knowledge in the way he talked and in the eight years he'd spent alone.

Or maybe not alone. Not committed and alone were two different things, and Hailey was annoyed at herself for wondering who he might have spent time with here in Forgotten.

"Stop it," she whispered and opened the door.

A grinning youth with midnight skin and short-cropped hair blinked up at her. He was kneeling close to Sable's box, two squirming puppies in his lap. "Hi," he called.

"Hi." She moved into the garage, scanning the area for Dylan as her eyes adjusted to the dimmer light. "Who are you?"

"I'm Charlie." He put the puppies back with Sable and jumped to his feet. He was taller and more gangly than she'd noticed at first, all limbs and elbows. "Charlie Campbell. Well, my mom calls me Charles." He grinned again, which turned his handsome face to brilliant. "I work for Dylan cleaning out the pens and stuff at the clinic. I'll be coming in to help Sable here. Those puppies are a long way from being potty trained. We already took Sable outside, and she's eaten real good today." He pointed at the bowl of food next to the box. "She gets as much puppy food as she wants for the next six weeks. It's what she needs for the babies."

"I'm glad you're here." Hailey hadn't known about any of that. "Would you like some bread with honey?"

"Naw, Maggie already gave me bread. I'm stuffed."

She sank down onto the beanbag. "So how long have you been here?"

"Not long. You just missed Dylan," he thumbed at the automatic garage door enthusiastically, which was lifted about waist high. "Well, he left about a half hour ago. I came to help him weigh all the pups first. That's important, you know."

"So I've heard." Hailey smiled. The boy's excitement was catching. "And are they all okay?"

"The purple, yellow, and turquoise weigh less than the others. We have to make sure they're getting their fair share of milk."

Hailey bit into her bread, scanning for the purple-collared pup. No wonder she'd had trouble breathing at birth. At least she was nursing now.

Charlie brushed his hands on his jeans. "Well, I gotta get going."

Hailey swallowed. "Were you waiting for me? Sorry if you were."

"Oh, no." He shook his head. "Sable's fine being checked in on every hour or two. She's being a good mom." He glanced toward the garage door. "But I already stayed too long because Sable's special, and I hate to leave her. Did Dylan tell you he found her in a bag in the stream a few years ago? Could have died right there, but he saved her life. The McColls old dog had died, so he took her there."

"Sounds like Dylan. He likes saving animals—and people."

Charlie's eyes grew wide. "That's right. He saved you from the river too. What a coincidence!"

"No, it wasn't the river. People are mixing up the stories. He found me on the way from the bus stop into town."

"That's a long walk. Good thing he found you."

"Yeah. So you want to be a vet like Dylan?" Hailey took another bite of bread as she waited for a reply.

The boy shoved his hands into his pockets. "I think so. Not sure yet. It's hard because my mom wants me to be a doctor for people, or maybe go into politics like my dad. But that doesn't really interest me."

"Your dad wouldn't be the mayor, would he?"

"Yeah." He grinned. "Have you met him? Everyone loves my dad."

But not his mom so much, Hailey guessed. "No, but I saw your mom in the grocery store last Friday."

"Oh, right." He shrugged. "That's surprising. She doesn't usually go in there."

Hailey thought it best not to answer. "Well, I'm sure you'll figure out what you want to do. You've still got a lot of time."

"Right." He nodded and reached for a black trash bag. "I'll be back later tonight to clean the box again. Gotta keep these little guys comfortable."

"Wait," she said to his retreating back. "Could you let Dylan know I'm going to be here? He doesn't have to hurry back."

"Sure." The boy was staring at her a bit curiously.

"I lost my phone," she felt compelled to explain.

"Oh, yeah. They have some at the electronics store on Broadway. But seriously, my friends and I order them online. Lots cheaper."

"I'll keep that in mind." Without ID, that wasn't going to happen anytime soon.

"Nice to meet you." He gave a polite dip of his head that was probably a credit to his father's upbringing. "Oh, and when you leave Sable, make sure the garage is closed. Don't want her too far from the babies or outside alone."

"I will. Good to meet you, too."

Hailey finished her bread and spent the next two hours watching Sable, holding the pups, and making sure the babies rotated feedings. She found the clipboard from last night on a shelf and saw for herself the puppies' weights. A tight knot of anxiety rose inside when she saw the female with the purple collar was the very lowest weight of all.

She picked up the pup and cuddled her. Like most of her siblings, the pup was a light golden color with a darker gold on the tips of her ears. Her eyes looked like dark pebbles in the gold fluff. "I'll make sure you get what you need," she promised, and then felt a little silly. Hero Dylan was on the job, after all.

"I think I'll call you Pebbles," she said. "I can't keep calling you purple pup. Too impersonal."

One thing led to another, and soon she'd come up with names for all the dogs that began with the color of the collar they wore, jotting them above the color she'd written. Her favorite names were Loki, Topaz, Ruby, Punk, Boomer, and Ollie.

Maggie peeked through the kitchen door as Hailey was placing Pebbles in a prime position to nurse once more. "Hey, there you are. Glad to see you survived last night. Come join us for an afternoon snack."

"Who's us?" Straightening, Hailey walked to the door.

"Oh, just a few friends from the Ladies Auxiliary. We're holding an emergency meeting today about the Spring Planting

Dance. Ronica Wilson coordinates all the official city events, but she always asks the Ladies Auxiliary to help with the food. I mean, everyone who comes to the dance brings something to share, so there's always plenty to eat, but she makes sure there's a variety instead of only donuts."

"You can't go wrong with donuts," Hailey said with a laugh. "Really, I'd help, but I'm watching Sable and the babies until Dylan comes back."

Maggie rolled her eyes. "No one needs to watch her. Dylan certainly isn't giving up *his* entire day to dog-sit. She'll be fine as long as she's protected from any nosy kids." She jabbed a finger at the automatic door button, and the garage door began to close. "There. Now come on, you can check on her in a bit."

"Okay." With a last glance at Sable, Hailey followed Maggie into the kitchen, where two large serving trays were loaded with meats, cheeses, and breads.

"We take turns hosting the Ladies Auxiliary," Maggie said, "And quite frankly, I think that's mostly so people will get in the habit of attending. Even so, only about ten will come each time. Wash your hands and grab a tray, okay?"

By the time Hailey came out with the second tray, the Ladies Auxiliary was underway. They'd pushed together three tables in the middle of the café, and nine women were gathered. Hailey recognized Ronica Wilson, the midwife Charlotte Bennett, Evelyn Robinson from the dress shop, and Mayor Campbell's wife.

The room fell silent as she set the tray on the table. "Hi," she said, nodding.

"This is my boarder and new employee, Hailey Waters," Maggie announced. Murmured greetings rose to meet her. "Hailey, you know Ronica, and this is Olivia Campbell, our mayor's wife." Maggie continued making introductions all around the table, but the only new names Hailey fixed were Keisha Jefferson, who was Maggie's other full-time employee, and Carina Sayer, the doctor's wife.

Hailey nodded at each woman in turn before reaching to fill her plate. She expected them to go on with their planning, but next to her, Carina Sayer said with a slight Hispanic accent that made her sound glamorous, "So did you really fall into the river?"

Hailey lifted her gaze from the piece of cheese in her tongs. "I was trying to cross the river to get into town. I hadn't realized how far it was. I cut my leg pretty badly."

"Can I see it?" the woman asked.

"Sure, I guess." Awkwardly, Hailey stood and backed up from the table, turning to show everyone her leg. She hadn't put the bandage back on today, as Dylan said it wasn't necessary after two days, but she'd remembered the cream on top.

"Dylan did the stitches?" Carina asked, bending over in her chair to peer closer. "He did a great job."

"You're so lucky he got you out of the river," said a pretty young woman with frizzy blond hair. "You have all the luck. I wish it had been me." She heaved a sigh.

Before Hailey could say that Dylan hadn't pulled her from the river, Maggie said, "Now Laina, you'll have your chance to impress Dylan and any other available man at the dance."

"Only if they buy the cakes I submit for the Singles Mix auction," Laina said with a pout. She had beautiful lips, Hailey noticed. She also wore a liberal dose of makeup, which suited her and made Hailey wish she'd taken more time with her own appearance that morning.

"They'll buy them," Maggie assured her.

"Will you be making one, Hailey?" Olivia, the mayor's wife asked. "The cakes always help our budget."

Hailey must have looked puzzled because Carina jumped in to explain. "The Mix is where single women make cakes and donate them. At the dance, single men go to the booth, look at the cakes, and write down their bids without knowing who made them. If they win, they get two dances with the woman." She gave a little roll of her eyes and added in a whisper, "If you ask me, they should have the men make the cakes."

"I think it's a great idea," Maggie said, somehow picking up the whisper. "Men should enter cakes too." Laughter rolled through the room.

"That's ridiculous," Olivia said. "Most of these men don't know the difference between baking powder and baking soda."

"Unfortunately, I have to agree with Olivia," Ronica said. "And they're a lot more likely than women to overpay for a cake."

Olivia nodded at her. "Thank you, Ronica. It's decided then." A couple of the women sighed, but no one objected.

"What about at least opening it up to something besides cake?" Hailey found herself saying. Olivia's granite stare made her immediately wish she'd kept her mouth shut.

Maggie's eyes gleamed. "That's perfect," she said. "That way health-conscious men will be even more inclined to buy, and I for one am tired of having all the Singles Mix cakes competing with my food booth. Any objections?"

Olivia drew in a breath. "It's a break in tradition."

"Tradition, smadition," Laina retorted. "Who cares what food it is? I just want one kiss at midnight."

Keisha snorted in a way that told Hailey they would probably become friends as well as co-workers. "You've kissed at least five guys at midnight at the Spring Planting Dance. It only works with the first true love."

Laina sighed. "Yeah, too bad he left town."

"Does it ever really come true?" Hailey wanted to know. "The kissing at midnight, I mean." The legend couldn't be real, of course, but it would be interesting to see what the women here thought.

Maggie laughed. "Some people say it does; others disagree. But what we do know is that four daughters of Chelsea and James Morgan—the couple who founded the town—kissed their beaus at the very first dance that was held seventeen years after they moved here. One of them was only ten, and it was a dare, but later they all got married to the man—or boy—they kissed."

"Well, I think it's a great idea," Charlotte said. "Opening it up to other baked goods, I mean, not the kissing. It would give more of the single women and men a chance to participate."

The women voted unanimously on the idea, except Olivia Campbell, who, with her arms crossed and her expression sour, abstained from the vote. As they continued with assignments, Hailey tried to stay out of the rest of the planning, eating her way steadily through her plate of snacks. No one else seemed interested in food, so she might as well do Maggie's spread justice.

"What time would you like to man the city food booth?" someone asked.

Hailey looked up to see all eyes on her. "Um . . ."

"A later shift would be best." Ronica glanced down at a paper in front of her. "After all, she's single too, and the Mix winners are announced after the first hour. She'll need time for her two dances. Plus, I know for a fact she's already promised a few dances to some of our bachelors."

Which was true. Even if Dylan avoided her, Hailey would dance with Ronica's son, Jeremy, and his friends. "Just name a time," she said. "But what are we there for exactly? Waving off the flies?"

Ronica laughed. "Sort of. But there's also a nominal charge for each food item. Mostly so the teenagers don't start food fights with it." A few of the women nodded in agreement.

"The proceeds help pay for next year's band," Maggie added. "There will also be food booths from the local establishments, like my cafe, Gandolf's Ravioli, and the pizzeria."

"You won't need me for the Butter Cake's booth?" Hailey asked.

"No, the teens will take care of it. We'll only bring the gooey butter cake."

The conversation went from there to phone-calling assignments, and for the first time, Hailey was grateful to be new in town. No one expected her to call to remind town residents to bring their donations. Or email them, either, as Olivia Campbell volunteered to have her husband's office do.

As the meeting wound down, Hailey slipped away to check on Sable. The dog was sound asleep with her puppies. When she reentered the kitchen, closing the garage door softly behind her, she heard voices near the open door leading into the counter area and dining room. Two voices to be exact, belonging to a man and a woman. She paused, wondering if she should interrupt or maybe retreat to the garage again.

"Thanks for taking care of him while I figured out the rest of the assignments," said the woman, who Hailey was almost sure was Ronica.

"It's always a pleasure to be of help." The man's voice was deep and gentle. "I don't know how we'd put on these events without you. How are you holding up?"

"Okay, I think. It's hard, though remembering . . ."

"How it was," he finished. "I understand that only too well."

"I know you do, and I'm sorry. Maybe things will get better."

His chuckle was sad. "Unfortunately, I think those days are past. There is a light at the end of the tunnel, though. It won't be long."

"I'm glad," Ronica said. "You deserve to be happy."

"So do you. But your journey will be harder."

"Fletcher and I had a lot of good years."

"He was a good man." A brief pause and then he added, "Remember, I'm here if you ever need to talk."

"I know. But I can handle it. I have Jeremy."

"That's good. I wish . . ."

Hailey broke free of whatever had been holding her in place, knowing whatever that the man wished wasn't any of her business. She opened the door to the garage again and shut it more loudly. She hummed to make sure they heard her coming. This time there was silence as she emerged from the kitchen and saw Ronica Wilson with a tall, muscular man with graying black hair and the darkest skin she'd ever seen.

"Hailey," Ronica said. "Have you met Josiah Campbell, the mayor?"

The man dipped his graying head and held out a big hand. "Nice to meet you, Hailey. Welcome to our little town." His hand enveloped hers completely.

"Thank you. I met your son, Charlie, today. Seems like a good kid."

He smiled, reminding her of the boy. "The best. Should have had a dozen more exactly like him."

Hailey laughed, but her thoughts were distracted by the expression on Ronica's face. She practically glowed. Charlie had said that everyone loved his father, and he might be telling the truth. Hailey herself already liked the man.

"Well, I'd best be taking my wife home." Josiah nodded at them before moving away in an oddly graceful movement for someone so tall.

Hailey and Ronica watched him walk from the counter to the door where Olivia Campbell was standing outside the front entrance, talking to Maggie.

"Time for me to get going as well." Ronica turned resolutely and headed to the end of the bar where her husband, Fletcher, now sat reading his newspaper.

"You ready to go?" she asked.

"I haven't had breakfast yet."

"Yes, you have." Her words were as gentle as the mayor's had been with her. "It'll be dinner time soon. Let's go home. I'll make your favorite."

"Peanut butter and jelly?" His hopeful expression reminded Hailey of a child—an oddly elegant child.

"If that's what you want. Sure."

"Okay." He started to slide off his stool but stopped halfway. "Wait, there is something I wanted to show you in here." He reached for his newspaper but didn't pick it up. "But I can't remember. Maybe it's that guy you like."

Ronica laughed. "You're the only guy I like. Come on, honey." She helped him the rest of the way to the floor.

Hailey felt like a voyeur, but they were already leaving, so she waited for them to exit the café before heading back to her room for a bathroom break. As she passed the counter, she saw that Fletcher had forgotten his newspaper.

She'd picked it up and begun walking to the door with it when a headline jumped out at her: *Senator and Wife Grieve Loss of Baby Born Too Early.* The picture was of the same senator Ronica had raved about last Friday, only this time his arm was wrapped around a blond woman in a long coat as they walked through a parking lot. Her face was buried in his chest and his free hand protectively shielded the side of her face that might have otherwise been exposed to the cameras. Hailey couldn't imagine surviving something like that, and having the world watching made it only that much more tragic.

"No," Hailey whispered. "That poor woman."

Maggie came into the café then, took one look at Hailey's face, and asked, "What's wrong?"

"Fletcher forgot his paper." Hailey handed it to her.

Maggie glanced down, and Hailey saw the same emotions play out on her face that Hailey had felt. Or was it something more? Hailey still wondered what had brought Maggie to Forgotten and the secrets she'd alluded to.

"Has Ronica seen this?" Maggie shook the newspaper.

"I don't think so."

Maggie marched to the garbage behind the bar and threw the paper inside. "And she doesn't need to. Not today."

"What's wrong with her husband?"

"Dementia." Maggie shrugged. "Early on-set Alzheimer's, or something like that. It's been a couple of years now. The medicine helped a lot at first, but not so much anymore, though some days when they come in here, he seems completely normal. It's why they come every day now, instead of once a week like they did before it started. She says familiar places help, and he can't exactly go out and tend his fields anymore."

"That's so sad."

"Yeah. She's a strong woman, but it's a lot to have on your plate."

"Maybe she shouldn't be in charge of the dance, then. Isn't that a lot of pressure?"

Maggie gave a gentle snort. "Right now that dance is the only thing keeping her together. And when it's over, we'll start on the next event."

Hailey understood now. "Good plan. Well, I'm going to head upstairs for a bit, but I'll be back to check on the dogs."

"Okay."

Leaving Maggie to stare out the windows of the café, Hailey hurried away, vowing to get back to Sable before Dylan returned.

.

CHAPTER 13

On Monday morning at five, Dylan groaned as his alarm went off under his pillow. At least he *had* a pillow. He had once again spent the night in Maggie's garage with Sable, but this time he'd come prepared with a sleeping bag and pillow to use with the cot.

He stretched and looked around, fighting disappointment to see that besides Sable and the pups, he was alone. The beanbag where Hailey had been sleeping last night when he'd come in from a Sunday night emergency call—thankfully not from the Wilsons about their cow—was empty. She'd probably awakened and read his note about his plan to stay there all night. If not, his sleeping bag, pillow, reading material, and cooler of snacks would have made it obvious.

He'd wanted to talk to her, to straighten things out from the way they had left them on Sunday morning when they were both so exhausted and not thinking straight, but the emergency call had nixed that plan. He sometimes went weeks without an emergency call, but his luck the past weekend had been lousy.

The sleeping bag and actually going to sleep should have made the night more comfortable, but his dreams had been restless, with Hailey featuring in all of them, even if he couldn't exactly remember the details. Not too surprising that his dreams had been of her—being with Hailey in that beanbag had been the highlight of the previous night, one he'd hoped to repeat last night or maybe this morning. But he had no luck at all.

Shaking his head, he stifled a yawn and pulled himself from his makeshift bed. Sable seemed to be adjusting well to having so many puppies, but they weren't out of danger yet. He planned to move Sable back to the clinic today where he could watch her more easily. In the meantime, he'd brought one of his cameras to live-stream her while he and Hailey were both at their jobs. Charlie would also come twice to take Sable out and clean the whelping box, once before and once after school, if Dylan hadn't moved her by then.

He used the ladder to tie a rope on two high shelves opposite each other and clipped the camera to it, directly above the whelping box, winding the power cord up one of the ropes and down the wall to the outlet. Then he connected the camera to the café's free wi-fi and tested it on his phone to make sure he had a decent angle.

After letting Sable outside to do her thing, he knelt and looked over the babies, rotating them to make sure the smaller ones were eating as much as they could hold. Usually the sightless pups would rotate naturally as they filled up on milk, but he wouldn't know for a day or so if they were all regaining their birth weight.

Checking his watch, he saw that he had barely enough time to shower at the clinic before he was due for his next well check at a farm in Panna Creek. He had three farm visits there this morning as farmers and ranchers would often band together and schedule his services at the same time to share the higher farm call fee that he charged outside Forgotten's city limits.

He hurried out to the Tahoe and almost didn't answer the call that came to his phone until a glance at the caller ID told him it was Hector Sanchez.

"Hey," he said, shutting the door and turning on the engine. "So did the dog survive?"

Dylan laughed. "Yeah, she's fine. Sorry for not getting back to you yet. It's been crazy. We ended up with seventeen puppies."

"Remind me never to get a dog. I hope you grabbed a nap somewhere in all that."

"I did. How was your date?"

"I don't kiss and tell," Hector said, "but it was really good. I saw her again yesterday, and we spent all day together, which is why I didn't track you down until now."

Dylan had to smile. "Good. I'm glad someone's having fun." But he'd had fun too. Being with Hailey was like drinking without the hangover in the morning.

"So, what next?" Hector said. "Are we going with facial recognition? I've heard back from over a dozen charities, and so far no ID on the photo."

Dylan rubbed his eyes and tried to concentrate. Sable and work hadn't been the only reason he hadn't called Hector back. After Hailey's confession, he'd been debating with himself if he should ask her permission to research her past. Surely she'd want to know where she came from, but if she didn't, asking would mean a halt to his investigation or the risk of alienating her even more than he already had. Was it really better to ask forgiveness than permission?

Besides, if she didn't have any memory that had to mean trauma of some kind or drug use, and keeping the secret wouldn't do anyone a favor, especially not her. Who was Hailey really? A part of him felt he knew her. He'd spent more time with her in the past weekend than he had with any other woman in the past eight years. But was the face she presented to the world real? Or when she remembered her old life, would she walk away?

Maybe that was what had really stopped him from calling Hector, the thought of her leaving Forgotten. But if Hailey needed help—and it was clear she did—he had no right to let selfishness enter the equation.

"Do it," he said. "And if the FBI won't run the search without an official request, I can have the chief here put in one. He owes me a big favor for helping with his dog last night."

"That might put the investigation on your county sheriff's radar," Hector said, "and wasn't local interference what you were trying to avoid?"

Dylan thought of Levi and his cowboy-boot rebellion. The county sheriff's office was better, but they still had nowhere near the resources Hector had at his fingertips. "You got that right."

"Leave it to me. I'll come up with another excuse to get my FBI contacts on board. This is the first woman you've shown interest in, in what, eight years? I'm not about to let you get involved with a fugitive."

"I'm not involved." Even to himself, it sounded like a lie.

Hector laughed. "Whatever. But you know the routine with facial recognition. It's going to take a few days. Meanwhile, see if you can manage to get me some fingerprints."

Dylan thought of the clipboard Hailey had used, but he

felt ashamed at the thought. "We'll see," he said. "Thanks. I owe you." Dylan hung up, already knowing it was going to be a long day.

On Monday morning, Hailey went into the kitchen where Maggie was making bread. "You're up early," Maggie greeted her. "Especially on a Monday."

"I feel like all I did yesterday was sleep," Hailey admitted. "I'm apparently not used to being up all night." She glanced toward the garage door. "Is Dylan still here?" She craved to see him.

She'd awakened last night in the garage to find him dead to the world in a sleeping bag on the cot. At the time she'd been relieved, but now the need to talk to him festered inside. When he'd called her name Sunday morning, what had he been going to say? She should have stayed to listen.

"He's gone already. He did say that he's planning to move Sable back to the clinic later on today."

"Oh." Hailey fought her disappointment. "Guess that means they're all doing well."

"Or he wants to keep a closer eye on them. With you working now, it won't be so easy, and he's usually in his clinic during the afternoons. Even if he's called away, his receptionist is still there to admit any animals that need attention."

"Yeah. It makes sense."

"I know we said nine, but since you're here, you can help with the bread, if you want."

"I do want. I'll go check on the puppies and be right back, okay?"

At Maggie's nod, Hailey went into the garage. Sable was

standing outside the box, chomping on dog food. She wagged her tail at Hailey but didn't stop eating. All the babies were moving blindly around, as if searching for their mother. After a few more moments of crunching, Sable stepped delicately into the box, moved a few pups over and lay down, licking each in turn.

"Such a good momma, but that's a lot of licking." Hailey made sure that Pebbles and the other two smaller pups were nursing before she returned to the kitchen.

"It's weird how she knows what to do," she said, washing her hands.

"Not weird at all. It's nature. Even humans know what to do instinctively." Maggie shrugged. "The important things anyway. So what do you want to do? Mix up the dough yourself? Do you know a recipe?"

Hailey reached for a yellow apron, tying it over her white blouse. "I'd like to see yours. I'm not sure I know how to do it."

Maggie turned on a tablet that hung in a holder on the wall. "This is my recipe. I usually make a double batch every morning. I've already made one that's about ready to put in the oven. Why don't you do the next batch while I prep the ingredients for breakfast?"

They worked in a comfortable silence. At first, Hailey followed the recipe to the letter, but by the time she'd finished the dough, she was no longer looking at it.

"You really have done this before," Maggie said with a smile.

The real test came when she was putting the bread into the oven. Maggie had formed her loaves on flat metal sheets, but that didn't feel right. "Do you have any baking stones?" Hailey asked.

Maggie thought for a moment. "I have some that I use to make pizza with, but they never really helped with the bread."

"That might be because you need to get them really hot first. With your professional ovens, I think we can do that."

Maggie crossed the kitchen and pulled out a stack of baking stones from a bottom cupboard. "You can at least try. If it makes them lighter than mine, I'll buy more."

Hailey laughed. "And if they fall flat, then what?"

"We sprinkle sauce and cheese over them and call them pizza bread." Maggie's eyes danced. "You might start a new trend."

The bread was barely in the oven when the first customers began trickling into the Butter Cake Café. Since Hailey still wasn't trained, she mostly shadowed Maggie, jumping to pour coffee or clean up tables when needed. She was ringing up an order for Terrell Whiting, the kindly owner of the grocery across from the park, when Maggie appeared beside her with a slice of steaming bread, a wide grin on her face.

The bread looked perfect. Hailey took a bite right there, not minding how hot it was. The heaviness that she'd detected before in Maggie's otherwise perfect bread was gone. She doubted that the regular Joe off the street could tell the difference unless the breads were side-by-side, but she could tell, and so could Maggie.

"I'll order two more stones," Maggie said. "That way we'll have enough to cook an entire batch."

"I think I'll have a slice of that to go," said Terrell. "With butter." He'd already had a slice of the earlier bread with his eggs and bacon, but Hailey didn't blame him.

Maggie went in the back and wrapped up a slice in tinfoil to keep warm. "This one is on the house," she told him.

As they watched him leave, she whispered to Hailey, "His wife is the sweetest woman, but she burns everything she cooks. You know what? Maybe you should make some of this for the Singles Mix auction at the Spring Planting Dance. It'll be light and tasty even when it's cold, and I have it on good information that a lot of the young men in town love fresh-ly-baked bread." She lowered her voice and added, "Including a certain vet."

"Why not?" Hailey laughed. It certainly couldn't make anything worse between her and Dylan. She hoped.

When Keisha came in at ten thirty, shortly before the lunch rush, they hit it off as Hailey had predicted. Keisha had an oddly striking combination of straight, dark brown hair, unusual hazel eyes, and skin the color of warm honey. She was also quick-witted, hard-working, and flirted shamelessly with all the male customers while at the same time deftly avoiding any serious attempts at asking her out. It was a skill Hailey envied.

"So how long have you been in Forgotten?" Hailey asked her when they'd taken care of the lunch rush.

"All my life—twenty-five years." Keisha put one hand on her slender hip. "And before you find out for yourself and judge me for it, you might as well know that I'm Olivia Campbell's niece. My dad was her half brother."

Hailey's mind caught on the word "was," but she didn't know Keisha well enough to ask. "She's a strong woman," Hailey ventured.

"Strong isn't the word I'd use. Let's try rude, stubborn, and downright ornery. She never forgave my dad for convincing her to move to Forgotten, and me by extension."

"Don't worry. I won't hold your relationship with her against you," Hailey promised.

"Good. Now go fill the cups of those guys over there. They're attorneys who used to work in the same firm as my father. And believe me, they only leave a good tip if you flirt with them."

"Got it." Laughing, Hailey grabbed a fresh pitcher of coffee and went out to the dining room.

Dylan hauled himself into the Butter Cake at a little after one in the afternoon, feeling like he been dragged through the mud, which he had been at a ranch in Panna Creek while wrestling a particularly agitated bull. He'd already been home to shower, but he felt frayed, and the large bruise on his left shoulder would take a few weeks to heal. The animal had been successfully treated, of course, and would, unfortunately, live to take him down another day.

The moment he walked into the café and saw Hailey pouring coffee for a table full of fancy, suit-dressed men, his temper worsened. Why had he had ever thought things would go back to normal while she was still here? Forgotten was a small town, and thanks to his interference, she was smack dab in the middle of his daily routine. He'd eaten lunch at the Butter Cake almost every day for the past five years, and in the summers before that. This was his turf, his safety net, and now she was everywhere.

In the four days since he'd found her in that barn, she'd never been far from his mind. She haunted him at every moment and, if his disjointed dreams last night were any indication, she would continue doing so. Worse, he knew he wouldn't change that moment of meeting her even if he could. He was beginning to think he had a fatal attraction for women who would break his heart.

That was the moment he realized he was falling for her, hard and fast, like some college boy who had no idea that women as beautiful as Hailey tended to up and leave.

"The usual?" Keisha asked as he slid into a vacant seat at the bar. He'd timed his entry for after one because most people in this town got up early and would have finished lunch by now.

"Yeah." That meant a steak sandwich with freshly baked bread, barbecue sauce, a heap of fries, and a salad. It didn't sound like nearly enough for how long it had been since his hurried breakfast at the clinic, but Maggie's generous servings were always larger than he expected.

Hailey appeared on the other side of the counter to pour him coffee long before his food arrived. "Sable's doing great," she said. "I've been checking on her. I mean, I saw the camera you set up, but I figured it wasn't as good as going out there. When do you weigh the pups again?"

Dylan had only seen Hailey once on the camera out of the dozens of times he'd checked on Sable, but he wouldn't tell her that. "After I get them back to the clinic. I'm going to move them after I finish eating. I'm a little worried about Maggie's electric bill if I keep that heater on out there any more nights."

"It'll also make sleeping easier for you, I bet." She leaned against the counter, her smile calming something inside him.

"That's for sure." Which reminded him that he'd need help lifting the whelping box into the truck, and he scanned the café to see if there was anyone he knew who could give him a hand.

"I'm going to miss them."

He was going to miss the extra excuse to see her—even if she was only asleep on that beanbag. "You about off? You could come over and help me weigh them."

Her smile widened. "I've actually been working since seven, and we don't seem to be busy. Let me talk to Maggie."

On her way into the kitchen, she passed Keisha carrying a heaping plate of food. "Thanks," he murmured appreciatively as Keisha set it down in front of him. He'd only taken a few gulping bites when Hailey returned, minus her apron.

He grinned. "I'm guessing she said it was okay."

"Let me think. Her exact words were 'Thank you, God' while she clasped her hands together and stared at the ceiling. It's safe to say she won't miss having Sable in her garage."

They both laughed while Dylan stuffed in another bite. "Did Maggie do something different with the bread?" he asked after swallowing. "It tastes mostly the same, but it's lighter somehow— and bigger than usual."

"We used baking stones in the oven instead of pans." Hailey came around the bar. "I'll change while you finish up."

"Wait," Keisha said, coming from a table in the dining room. "You forgot your tips from the attorneys. We added their bill to their account when they ordered, but I just picked these up from their table."

Hailey stared at the handful of bills. "You weren't joking about flirting." She fixed a hard eye on Dylan as she pocketed the money. "Make sure you give Keisha a good tip so she doesn't have to flirt."

"Oh, Dylan and I have an understanding already," Keisha said. "He tips me less than twenty percent, and the next time I give him twenty percent less meat."

"So that's how it works." He looked inside his sandwich. "Guess I passed the test last time."

Hailey laughed. "I'll go change. Be down in a bit." With a wave, she walked away, moving slowly now, as if having lost her steam, which he thought was entirely possible in light of the constant motion at the café. Maybe it was good he'd convinced her to come with him to move Sable and the pups.

Someone sat beside him, and Dylan looked over to see

Connor Davis, the developer who was also staying at the Butter Cake. He was staring fixedly at Hailey's retreating back. *He's probably another admirer,* Dylan thought with a rush of jealousy.

"Hey," he said to Connor. "Haven't seen you around the past few days."

The developer shifted his gaze to Dylan. "I swear I've seen her somewhere before."

So maybe not a conquest after all, and if he had seen Hailey, it might be important.

"But yeah," Connor continued before Dylan could ask. "I've been scouting out all the towns around here. Sometimes a visit and all the accompanying hyperbole take most of the day."

"Hopefully you're coming to the end of your scouting mission." Dylan wasn't sure how he felt about the possibility of Forgotten growing, because he already had more business than he could handle. On the other hand, more business in Panna Creek might attract a vet there, which would be good for everyone.

"I think so," Connor agreed. "At least I have recommendations to take to my investors."

Dylan waited until Connor ordered before saying, "So, you think you know Hailey from somewhere?"

Connor shrugged. "Probably wishful thinking. Maybe she's got one of those faces. They say we all have a doppelganger somewhere. More likely, it's because she is one very fine woman—even when she's not all dressed up."

"She sure is," Dylan agreed. "Well, if you do remember seeing her somewhere, let me know, okay?"

"Sure."

Refocusing on his meal, Dylan thought about Hector and the facial recognition. Depending on how many photos there were of Hailey out there, he'd know who she was soon. Of course, there would likely be a few false positives to investigate. As Connor had suggested, in all the millions of people in the world, some inevitably looked similar, especially based on a single photo, but he'd deal with those and find the real Hailey.

He hoped it wouldn't be something he would regret.

CHAPTER 14

Hailey changed clothes, used the restroom, and took another painkiller for the headache and cramps that were still plaguing her with a vengeance. She felt rather ridiculously happy that Dylan had asked her to help him with Sable, and she didn't want her discomfort to make her terrible company. She tried telling herself that his asking meant nothing, but she was a woman, and she knew the way he looked at her was something special.

Was it possible they could start over right now? Because the moment he'd walked into the café, all her senses had been alerted, as if her body had been aware of his presence even before her brain was.

She spent a little time on her hair and applied more makeup. By the time she went downstairs, Dylan had finished eating and had recruited three men, including the developer, Connor Davis, to help him move the whelping box.

Inside the garage, he handed Hailey a leash, at the end of

which a nervous Sable was pacing. "Just take her out to the grass while we load the box and the puppies."

"Come on, Sable," Hailey urged. The dog went with her easily enough, though she kept looking back to the automatic garage door that was open all the way.

"Just keep the box even, boys," she heard Dylan call. "We don't want any of these puppies to slip out."

They emerged from the garage, walking carefully. Within seconds the whelping box was settled in the back of a large pickup truck so old and battered, Hailey wasn't quite sure what color it was. He must have used the same truck to bring the box to the café in the first place, but she hadn't noticed it before. She led Sable over to the tailgate, where Dylan helped the dog into the box. Sable started licking all the puppies again, as if she'd been away for hours.

"I'm going to drive really slow," Dylan said. "If you can get in the back and keep hold of her leash, that would be great." He offered Hailey a hand into the truck bed, which she accepted.

His touch sent an electric shock racing through her body. "Um, any particular instructions?" she asked, hoping she didn't sound as distracted as she felt.

"Nope. Bang on the cab if there's a problem."

"I can do that." The box took up almost the entire width of the bed, so she had to step carefully to get up front between the cab and the box. She slapped the top of the cab. "Like this?" When he nodded, she added, "I didn't know you had a truck too."

He winked at her. "It came with the clinic." Which meant it had been his dad's. She felt a rush of nostalgia for him. Sorrow followed that she couldn't remember her own father, which also made him out of reach.

The other three men climbed inside another truck and drove

off first while Dylan followed, keeping his vehicle at a walking pace. Sable stopped her furious licking and stood up in the box to look around.

"It's okay," Hailey said, choking up on the leash in case Sable decided to jump. But the dog only stretched out her neck to peer around the front of the truck.

At the clinic, they followed the same procedure in reverse. After Dylan thanked the men, Hailey crouched on the floor inside the cage next to the box and laughed at how Sable had started licking her pups again.

"She'll settle down," Dylan promised. "That's her way of checking them all. I'd better fill up her water dish, though."

When he returned with a water hose taken from a hook on the wall, he was also carrying the portable scale. "I have an appointment at two-thirty, but that leaves us almost thirty minutes to weigh them."

"Good. I've been worried about Pebbles," she confessed. "Loki and Topaz too, but her mostly."

He blinked at her. "You named the puppies?"

"Well, yeah, but they're only temporary names." She picked up the clipboard and stood, offering it to him. "I couldn't keep calling them colors."

Dylan took the clipboard, glancing at the names and chuckling before handing it back. "Good idea, but now you'll have to adopt one of them; you know that, right?"

She hoped so. Placing the clipboard on the floor, she bent down to pick up her favorite pup. "Let's weigh Pebbles first." She held her breath as he did so. "Well?"

"She lost a little since yesterday, but only a little, so it's great news. She'll regain her birth weight soon, I'm guessing. And then more from there."

"Good."

"Why'd you name her Pebbles?"

"Her eyes look like pebbles." She laughed. "But they all do, I guess."

"So there's not a Bamm-Bamm?"

She scrunched up her face in apology. "Well, yeah. There is. I was running out of creative names." She placed Pebbles back and scooped up another.

"I actually loved the Flintstones movies," he said. "You know, the one with live actors. I grew up watching them."

Hailey nodded but had no other response. She remembered there were movies about the Flintstones, but she didn't remember seeing any of them. She might have hated them for all she knew.

One by one, they weighed the puppies, with Dylan giving nods or adorable grunts of satisfaction with each one. "I think they're all on the right track. Just need to keep making sure those smallest ones get enough milk. Another week and we won't have to worry at all, I'm betting. Well, actually, I won't have to after Friday. The McColls have raised enough puppies to take them all on." He stood and laid the last puppy by Sable, who promptly started licking it.

Hailey stared at the wriggling mound of puppies, tightness growing in her chest. Why did watching them both thrill and sadden her?

"Is something wrong?"

She looked up to see Dylan standing near where she sat balanced on the edge of the whelping box. She knew she should get up and walk the two blocks back to the café, but she was suddenly too tired to move.

She shrugged. "Not really. I was thinking—how do I remember the Flintstones but not seeing any movies? How can

I not remember my parents or where I grew up?" She sighed. "I just . . . I want things to be normal. I don't want to be crazy."

He sank to the floor in front of her, his face sympathetic. That face was so familiar now, from the brown eyes and the scar in his eyebrow, to the strong square jaw and hair that swept over his brow. He hadn't shaved today—and probably not yesterday either—and she wondered how his rugged face would feel under her fingers.

"You're not crazy," he said. "I still think you hit your head. At some point, you're probably going to have to see a doctor."

She forced a grin. "You're a doctor."

"I mean a people doctor." His chuckle made her relax. Whatever had passed between them, he obviously had processed her confession. "You do seem to remember where you worked," he added. "I mean, the first time you mentioned it, I could have sworn you made it up. But when you were telling Jeremy about the little girl—I believed you. Maybe your memory is coming back in pieces."

"No." She bit down on her bottom lip for a moment before adding, "I know I made the job up. I didn't want anyone to think I was crazy because I can't remember what I do for work."

"Why did you choose that?"

She shrugged. "Because it's something I wish I did. I love children, and saving them from a lifetime of misery sounds like a better contribution to society than pouring coffee somewhere."

"Not necessarily." He shifted to lean back on the bars of the cage, stretching out his legs over the currently clean floor. He looked sideways at her. "I mean, after all, a lot of people go into the Butter Cake Café every bit as much for a smile and a kind word as they do for food. I know I do. I could make lunch here for myself, or order out, but people need people."

Hailey wasn't convinced. Should she tell him she'd made up her name from the hay he'd found her in and the water she'd gulped afterward? No. She couldn't bear to. He was smart enough to realize that for himself.

"So," he said into the silence that was broken only by the occasional puppy squeak. "What do you think they're like?"

"Who?"

"Your parents. If they could be anything, what would you have them be?"

She sat beside him and stretched out her own legs. "Okay, I'll play. They're active people. My dad owns a sports shop because he loves the outdoors. And since we're from California, he surfs. He also likes to go on safari in Africa and used to take me with him when I was young. That's how I got interested in charities."

"Nice," he said. "And your mom?"

"She's harder to pinpoint. I think she stayed at home with me when I was younger. Now she's probably going on trips with my dad or her friends, playing tennis, or hanging out with her grandkids."

"Oh, you have siblings, do you?" His words hinted at laughter.

She laughed. "Why not? I'll order up two. I have a brother who became an attorney and is no fun, and a sister who is now a partner with my dad at the shop and who can beat anyone playing HORSE."

He arched his left brow, the one with the missing patch of hair. "Do you play too?"

"Yes, but I always lose."

They both laughed, and Hailey said, "Thanks, I do feel better, even if it's not true. Or probably not, at least. Not even the California part."

His intent stare made her start thinking about their kiss at the lake again. Was he also thinking of that, or was he thinking she was crazy? When he spoke, she was fairly sure it was the latter.

"You could go see Doc Sayer. Unlike most of the people in this town, he's discreet. Or you could always go to someone in Panna Creek."

She thought about that, a hard knot of anxiety forming in her stomach. "What if it's not a physical reason? Wouldn't I need a shrink?" Surely that possibility hadn't escaped his attention.

"That doesn't mean you're crazy, but Doc Sayer can make a recommendation."

Had he forgotten her money situation? It wasn't as if she had health insurance or a fantastically well-paying job. Of course, she did have that ten thousand dollars. Was it even hers? What would he say if he knew?

"I need a little more time to decide," she said. "Meanwhile, I want to do normal things for a change. And talk about normal things. Like how did you get this scar?" She reached up and touched the edge of his eyebrow.

His brow lifted again, most likely to tell her he realized she was purposefully changing the subject, but he let her do it. "It happened at the lake. There's a spot with rocks where people jump off in the summer. One year when I was thirteen, we had a drought, and there wasn't as much water, but I, being the know-it-all kid I was, didn't listen to the adults and dived in anyway. Somehow, I hit my face on a rock. It was only my dad's medical training that probably prevented more scarring."

"It makes you look tough." Not that he needed help for that. He didn't have the crazy bulk Jeremy did, but he filled out his shirt better than most.

"Tell that to the bull that about ran me over this morning." He pulled down the neck of his blue tee, revealing an ugly black and red bruise.

She gasped. "Maybe you should see a doctor." She leaned forward to examine it, but he pulled the shirt back into place.

"I did an X-ray already. I'm okay."

"Right." She shook her head and laughed. "Of course you did." She lifted her pant leg to show him her stitches. "From what Doc Sayer's wife says, you're really good at these."

"She's right." He leaned closer, studying the sutures. "It's healing nicely. You've done a good job keeping it moist."

"Thanks." She folded back the pantleg and looked up at him.

He was watching her, his dark eyes curiously soft. Her silly heart raced in response before she could warn it not to read too much into his expression. The world seemed to fade away. They were no longer in an animal cage with Sable and seventeen puppies. They were alone, with hot, rushing wind around them, standing on the edge of a cliff that would either lead them to the biggest thrill of their lives or crash them on the rocks below.

"Doctor?" An older woman with her hair in a tight knot at the back of her head stuck her head in from the door that led to the hallway with the exam rooms. Hailey recognized her from the Ladies Auxiliary, but she couldn't remember her name. "Your two-thirty is here. He looks really bad."

"Put him in one," Dylan said.

"Will do." She nodded at Hailey. "Hi, there, I'm Maeve, the receptionist here. We met at the Butter Cake Café yesterday, but I'm sure with so many women there, you didn't fix my name. And I didn't get to say, but welcome to Forgotten."

"Thank you. I appreciate that." Hailey gave her a smile.

"Might as well prep one of the cages in quarantine in case

Mrs. Cox will let me keep her dog." Dylan climbed to his feet. "His liver failure isn't contagious, but I don't want him in here with Sable."

"Okey dokey." Maeve disappeared.

Dylan extended a hand to Hailey to help her rise, for which she was grateful, even if the touch of his skin sent her back onto that imaginary cliff.

"Thanks for letting me help." She took a step toward the open cage door.

He met her at the opening, his hands going out to take both of hers. "Hey, let's do something normal tonight. Go to a movie, grab a pizza. What do you say?"

Her heartbeat rushed in her ears. She might have forgotten a lot, but she knew that expression in his eyes. She'd seen it at the lake right before he'd kissed her. "I'd like that. I'd like it a lot."

"Okay, I'll pick you up at six."

"I might still be at the café. I worked earlier than I was supposed to this morning, but I'm supposed to be available for the dinner shift."

"I doubt Maggie will need you that long. Most everything except the gas station, the theater, and the bar closes down by seven on weekdays here. But I can order out if you don't get off that early. I don't mind waiting."

"Okay. See you then."

"Wait, I can drive you back to the café."

"No. I can walk. It's only two blocks." She didn't feel like walking as much as she wanted to take a nap, but that only meant she needed it more. "I need exercise after all of Maggie's good food. Go take care of your patient. See you tonight."

Dylan walked Hailey through the examination room hallway to the door of the reception room. He stopped there, but his eyes followed her as she moved slowly toward the door. He should have insisted on driving her. She looked exhausted. What if that hit on her head had caused more serious damage than memory loss?

With effort, he pushed down the unreasonable burst of panic. She'd be okay. Tonight he'd convince her to see the doctor. Whatever she decided, he needed to take things slow. No memories meant she had little experience to compare with, and he didn't want to take advantage. She needed to decide for herself—about the doctor and her memories. About him. This last would be the hardest. Every second they were together, he could barely stop himself from kissing her.

Turning his attention to the desk, he saw Mrs. Cox standing at the counter talking to Maeve instead of waiting in an exam room. Her huge Saint Bernard was at her side as he had been for the past ten years. The old guy wouldn't last much longer. He was already mostly blind, and now his liver was failing. He'd lost a lot of weight in the past six months, but his stomach was bloated with fluid. If Dylan left it, he'd stop breathing, but draining the fluid would cause other serious issues. He'd have to help Mrs. Cox make hard decisions today because it was clear this dog was in a lot of pain.

"Hi," he greeted Mrs. Cox.

She blinked at him, her wrinkled eyes reddened with tears. "I can't get Muffin to walk any further, I'm afraid. You may have to see him here."

He took her hand, relieving it of the leash she held. "I'll get a cart and take care of him. Why don't you go back with Maeve and take a peek at the new puppies Chief McColl's dog had this weekend? You won't believe how many of them there are."

"Puppies?" Mrs. Cox said slowly. "Seems like yesterday Muffin was a puppy. Weighed a whole pound and a half at birth."

"These aren't quite that big," Dylan said, "But they're really cute."

Mrs. Cox smiled at him, grasping at his hand. "I know what you're trying to do. Distract an old woman. You're a good man, Doctor Morgan. I'll go and look at them." She bent over and patted her dog. "Momma's going to be back in a bit. You stay with the good doctor."

Most days Dylan loved his job, but sometimes, like now, it was hard.

He'd barely managed to get the huge dog into an exam room when a text came through from Hector. *We're in the queue. It'll take a few days, but we'll have an answer soon, if there is one to be had. But what will you do if it comes back with nothing but false hits?*

Dylan didn't respond because he didn't know. He was more concerned that his search *would* lead back to wherever Hailey had come from, because knowing might lead to her leaving.

He already couldn't imagine Forgotten without her.

CHAPTER 15

*A*fter making it back to the café, Hailey told Maggie about her movie invitation, and she was more than happy to let Hailey leave when she needed to.

"Things are dead now," Maggie added, eyeing her closely. "Why don't you go upstairs and take a little nap? You can come down later to help."

Hailey took a hot bath before falling asleep for an hour. She awoke with a start at fifteen to five, feeling groggier than when she'd drifted off. Her long hair had also dried funny, so she had to comb a little water through it before reapplying her makeup and hurrying downstairs to work the remaining hour she owed Maggie for the day.

The café had only three tables of customers, with no one at the bar or waiting to pay, and at the moment, Keisha was cleaning the counters. When Hailey went into the kitchen to ask what she should do and apologize for not coming down sooner, Maggie took one look at her hair and ordered her back upstairs.

"You can't go out looking like that," she said. "Don't you have a curling iron? And you should put on a little more makeup. Go on now over to Terrell's. You'll help with the bread in the morning and work tomorrow night to make up the time. And for goodness sake put on something a little more dressy than jeans!"

Before Hailey knew what happened, she was at Terrell's Grocery buying a twelve-dollar curling iron, blush, and a bottle of makeup base to cover up her peeling skin. Back in her room, she fought her hair into submission and put on the base and blush, only to wipe most of it back off. She didn't want to look as if she were throwing herself at Dylan.

As she stared into the mirror debating what to try next, she experienced an odd stuttering, where one moment she saw herself and the next she stared at another, more beautiful woman that was somehow also her. She wore expensive-looking jewelry and a little black dress, the perfection marred only by a glittering teardrop on an eyelash. The image of the woman scissored back and forth with her own image several times, as if her mind couldn't decide which was real.

Grasping the bathroom counter and struggling for breath, Hailey closed her eyes. She stayed that way until she could breathe normally again. Opening her eyes, she found only herself staring back. Whatever the vision, Hailey didn't want it to return. That beautiful, sad woman couldn't be her. Maybe she did have a sister after all.

Sighing, she put on a little lip balm, topping it with lipstick. She didn't look too bad, and the gentle curls had done a lot toward fixing her hair. Next, she needed to decide what to wear. A skirt seemed too formal, so she pulled on a pair of black pants that were a little tight, but a loose navy blouse made it work. The new tan sandals weren't a good match, but they were all she had. There had been a small black purse in the things from the church that Maggie had given her, so she put her personal items in that instead of the backpack.

Despite her excitement, she was beginning to regret agreeing to this normal night out. She was tired, and being with Dylan meant more questions. At the same time, she hungered to be with him. She rubbed her left thumb on the base of her left ring finger before realizing what she was doing. Again. Was this a nervous habit, or something more?

Shaking the thoughts away, she threw a black sweater over her arm, locked her door, and hurried downstairs to find Dylan already at the bar talking to Maggie and Keisha. His eyes met hers and caught, as if unable to look away. That was how she felt. He'd changed into black dress slacks and a gray button-down shirt that was open at the neck to show part of his chest. His hair still looped over in a wave at the top, but it was apparent he'd showered and combed it into place.

"Is that aftershave I'm smelling?" Keisha said with a hooting laugh.

"Is it too much?" Dylan asked, still not taking his gaze from Hailey. Her heartbeat quickened. He'd shaved and put on aftershave, which meant this "normal" night wasn't exactly normal. Good, because she was excited too.

Keisha rolled her eyes. "I'm saying that if you looked like this more often when you came in here, you'd have women falling at your feet."

Maggie laughed. "Don't tell him that, or he'll never dress up again. Do you know how many casseroles from the single women in the Ladies Auxiliary already end up at his clinic?"

"And I appreciate every single one." Dylan rose from the barstool.

Keisha turned to Hailey. "Uh-huh, girl. Now that's what I'm talking about. You look marvelous."

Hailey couldn't help flushing at the comment. "Thanks."

"Shall we?" Dylan pointed at the back entrance. "I'm parked out back."

Hailey was glad to escape the watchful stares of the other women. "Sorry about that," she said.

He laughed. "They're just having fun." He opened his SUV door for her. "So, are you hungry?"

She wasn't really, but she hadn't eaten since lunch, so she nodded. "I wonder if I like pizza."

He froze, his hand at the ignition, and lifted his gaze to hers. For a moment, neither of them spoke. Then they both burst out laughing. Not casual laughing but deep, gut-wrenching laughs that made tears come to her eyes.

"If you didn't before, you have a second stab at it," Dylan choked out.

"Well, this time, I'll be sure to get it right."

"What if you hate pepperoni but like Canadian bacon? Mushrooms, but no pineapple?"

"Wait, they put pineapple on pizza?" she deadpanned. They both started laughing again.

It really wasn't funny, if she thought about it. But for the entire drive to the restaurant, all it took was for one of them to look at the other, and they would erupt into new spasms of laughter.

Once at the Hot Stone Pizzeria, she was glad she hadn't worn jeans. From what she'd learned so far about Forgotten, there wasn't a really upscale restaurant in town, not even the ravioli restaurant, which boasted a self-serve salad bar, but Hot Stone was a lot nicer than she'd expected. Comfortable bench seats nestled inside tall mahogany booths, and dark lighting gave the place a private, romantic air that she hadn't expected from a pizza parlor. A waitress seated them in a back corner, where they were several booths away from other diners, and handed them menus.

"Shall we get the works?" Dylan asked her, his voice slightly strained.

Hailey looked at him, barely able to keep a straight face. "Do your worst."

The waitress was barely out of sight when they exploded into laughter again.

The pizza turned out to be fabulous, with Hailey liking everything on it, though the pizza itself was so large, they could never finish it in one sitting. "Can you take it back to the clinic?" she asked.

"I have a cooler in the Tahoe," he said. "We'll store it there for now. We might want a snack after the movies. There will be literally nothing open by then except the gas station and the bar, and there's nothing better than cold pizza." He took out his phone and moved to sit next to her. "Smile. Let's take this as proof that we had a perfectly ordinary night out with great pizza. Grab another slice and bite down on three. One, two, three!"

Hailey bit down and laughed, nearly losing her mouthful. He took three more pictures, even managing to catch one of her squirting soda from her mouth.

Leaving his vehicle at the pizzeria, they went next door. The movie theater was playing a sci-fi thriller Hailey hadn't heard of before. Dylan wanted drinks and popcorn, which she was sure she couldn't eat, but he put a hand to his heart as if wounded at the very notion of watching a movie without popcorn. That made her laugh and agree. Minutes later, they were walking down an aisle, with her carrying the huge tub while he balanced the drinks.

The movie was full of action, and Hailey had the notion it might be a film she'd have enjoyed, if she hadn't started dropping off. Several times she found herself startled awake with the action sequences, and the last time, she realized she was resting her head on Dylan's shoulder and his arm was around her. The pounding in her heart when she discovered that had nothing to do with the aliens on the screen being obliterated by the good guys. No, that was a mix of passion and embarrassment.

Had she been snoring? If so, hopefully the sounds from the movie covered it. But what did it say about her that she was on a date with an incredibly hot, intelligent man, and she was sleeping? Not exactly the way to his heart, she was sure.

She sat up and gulped her soda, hoping the caffeine would help her stay awake. It probably wouldn't help the achiness that was once again over coming her. With a rush of panic, she realized she hadn't put her painkillers inside her purse.

Dylan leaned over and whispered, "You okay?"

The concern in his voice smoothed away her panic. "Yes. Stop hogging the popcorn." He chuckled as she grabbed a handful from the tub.

The movie was almost over, and she needed to stop taking painkillers anyway. Either that or go see a doctor and ask if this was normal for a monthly cycle. It didn't feel normal, but she had no way to compare the experience. She was definitely *not* going to bring it up with Dylan, even if he did have a medical background and had been married before.

She was able to finish the last part of the movie without sleeping again. Dylan kept his arm around her, and she felt safe and content. After the movie, they wandered back in the direction of his SUV. Faint stars were beginning to appear in the twilight sky, and she had to stop to stare. "I don't remember seeing so many stars before." She hadn't meant the note of sadness, but it was there. Would he notice?

Dylan stared upward. "That's nothing. I know a place where they seem to be hung right in front of your face."

"Really?"

He nodded. "It's only a little after nine. Why don't we go?"

Hailey had to be at work at seven, but she felt more rested now after all the carbs and her snooze during the movie. Another hour or two wouldn't hurt. "Okay," she said, giving him a smile.

He leaned past her and opened the door to the SUV, sending her pulse racing. He was almost as close as they'd been at the lake. But to her disappointment, he didn't try to kiss her.

They drove in silence for a while, but it wasn't long before she recognized where they were going. "The pier at the lake?" she asked.

"Not exactly."

Near the reservoir, he took the fork leading to the private homes instead of to the park. Her heart was thudding again. Was it roasting in this cab, or was that her imagination? After another five minutes, he pulled to a stop and began slowly up a gravel road wide enough for only one vehicle. "I'll need to have this paved, I think," he said. "But only after the house is built. Some of the trucks are pretty heavy, and I don't want them to damage it before it's finished. We already had to take out a couple trees to get the equipment in."

A house rose up in front of them, fully roofed and partially sided, but missing doors and windows. It was every bit as large as the Butter Cake Café but decidedly more modern. No work had been done on what would become the yard, but the wildness of the forest here was magical.

"It's beautiful," she said.

He nodded. "I think so. Wait until you see where I'm going to put the fireplace."

Inside the house, only framing met her gaze, making it hard to imagine what it would be like. The future kitchen, which seemed rather large for a bachelor, opened onto what would become a family room. Framing for a huge fireplace was in place, but that was all.

"I'm having it custom made by a local woodworker. That and the bookshelves on each side. He's finished as much as he can without moving it here, but we don't want to put it in until the doors and windows are installed later this week. I come to check on the house every night, but I still sometimes find kids here."

They wandered around, Dylan excitedly showing her the four bedrooms and laundry room. It was apparent to her, even if not to him, that he planned at some point to put his past behind him, which included a new marriage and a family.

Did she dare hope she might be around when he was ready to move on? Because she also wanted a family more than anything. Another thought, more troubling, was quick to follow. What if she wasn't free? Was it possible she'd run from a family that was already hers? Maybe a husband or even kids?

A thick mass of heaviness formed in her stomach. She didn't think she was the type to walk out on a commitment, but how did she know? That might mean being here with Dylan could be very, very wrong. But she wore no ring, and there were no press releases or television interviews about her. No one had reported someone like her missing. On her Internet search there had been missing children, missing teens, missing husbands, and even missing wives, but they weren't her. Her face wasn't on any posters, and no one begged television audiences for her safe return. If she did have a family somewhere, they certainly didn't care that she was gone.

They walked to the other side of the family room where a sliding door would be someday, and down a dirt path that soon intersected with a cobbled pathway. "The original house was over there," Dylan said, pointing beyond a new-looking shed in front of them. "I was going to build my house there, but then I'd have had to ruin more of the original cobbled walk and uproot all the roses Chelsea Morgan planted. I couldn't do that, so I'm going to have a garden there. Not sure exactly what kind but, you know, a place to read and . . ."

"And watch the kids play," she said.

Dylan's eyes rested on her face. "I hope so." Tension crackled in the air between them. His desire or hers? She couldn't tell which, but her hands clenched at her sides. Maybe she had no right to feel anything for him.

He turned to unlock the shed with a key from his pocket. Inside, he removed a large sleeping bag. "Since we began construction, I occasionally sleep in the house to keep an eye on things, so I stash this here. It's really warm."

"Hard to see stars inside the house," she teased. "Now that it has a roof, anyway."

"That's why we're not going back inside." Tucking the folded sleeping bag under his arm, he took her hand. "The path's a little hard to see until we get through the trees. But I've been down it a million times."

He pulled her along the trail. The cobbled path needed repairing, but he knew exactly where to move to the side and which branches to duck under. Within minutes they broke from the trees and found themselves at the side of the lake. He didn't let go, though, pulling her out onto a long, sturdy wood dock where a rowboat was moored. The blackness of the lake was broken only by the reflection of the moon.

"I finished rebuilding this last year," he told her, finally stopping to let her look around. "I'm out here more summer nights in July and August than you can imagine, but I use a net tent to keep off the mosquitos. My dad and I used to do the same thing when I was a boy. Come on, let's go to the end." He practically sprinted down the dock, and Hailey had to hurry to keep up. She laughed at his excitement.

"What?" He said as they came to a stop.

"I'm trying to imagine you as a boy, coming here. How many times did you run all the way to the end and jump in?"

"Every summer day, most likely. I'd ride my bike here if my dad couldn't get away."

His dad, not his mom, she thought. "You sound independent."

"Dad was away on emergencies a lot, or it seemed that way to me." As he spoke, he was unzipping the sleeping bag and laying it out on the dock.

"You've been having a lot of those yourself."

"Only this week." He stretched out on the bag. "Come on." He patted the spot next to him. "The light's almost completely gone. You'll miss the show."

She lay down and gazed up into the sky. More and more stars were appearing everywhere above them, large and small, and he was right—it seemed as if she could reach up and take one in her hands. Her chest filled with wonder.

"It's amazing," she said with a sigh.

"Even when I was in New York, coming here and looking at the stars made the journey worth it."

"It would." She had no idea how far she'd come to see it, but she would never forget now that she had. Or would she? Her breath whooshed out of her at the thought.

I have to know. She shivered with the realization.

Without speaking, Dylan reached past her and grabbed the edge of the sleeping bag, pulling it over her. He did the same on his side. She hadn't been cold but being this close to him was intoxicating. They lay there for long moments, staring up at the stars and making up names for them because the only constellation either of them knew was the Big Dipper.

After a while, Dylan retrieved the cooler, and to her surprise, instead of offering her leftover pizza, he pulled out a bottle of wine.

"Really?" She lifted a brow.

"Why not? Can you think of a better place?"

She laughed. "No, I really can't."

Having no cups, he opened the bottle and offered her the first drink. She drank deeply and handed it back. "That's really good. If I'd known we were going to end up here, I wouldn't have almost pitchforked you." Her comment made him laugh, as she'd intended, but he nearly choked on a mouthful of wine.

They sat on the dock, drinking and making up names for the constellations, like Greedy Brother Steals Bread, Lone Star Finds a Friend, and Baby Does a Summersault. Hailey laughed more than she thought possible, and the wine made her body aches fade. After a time, she noticed Dylan was no longer taking turns with the wine and realized it had to be because he was driving. The knowledge made her feel safe.

She wished the night would never end. She wanted to stay right here with this man who not only had saved her but had given her a second chance at telling the truth about her memory. She was already half in love with him. At least it *felt* like love.

"Have another drink." He passed her the bottle again, his fingers touching hers. She reached for it, but he didn't let go. Their fingers touched. Their eyes locked. Neither of them moved.

"It feels like it was meant to be, me walking into the barn," he said, his voice hoarse as if it cost him to say it, as if he were afraid of her response.

She dropped both her gaze and her hand. "What if I'm a convict or wanted for a crime? Did you think of that? Maybe you were right to be worried about me."

He considered her comment for far too long. She was about to stand up and ask him to take her home when he set down the bottle and placed both hands on her shoulders.

"Hailey," he said. "Look at me."

Reluctantly, she lifted her gaze to his. He stared deeply into her eyes. "I've gotten to know you pretty well in the past few days. The Hailey I know is a kind, giving, and loving person. Whatever you've been in your life, you're not a criminal."

He was so close. A few inches more and they'd be kissing.

She opened her mouth. "There's something I haven't told you."

She hadn't realized he was still moving closer until he stopped. "Something you remembered?"

She thought of the woman in the mirror but shook her head. "When you found me, I was wearing a money belt. It has ten thousand dollars in it. What if it's not mine? I haven't dared to spend any of it." There, he'd either take her to the police station now or help her figure out what to do.

"What if it *is* yours?" He took her hand and rubbed it gently. "A lot of people save money and take it when they move or go on a trip."

"I think I have to know."

He nodded. "It would be good to find out. And we can talk about that as much as you'd like. But could it be later? And can I kiss you right now? Because I don't know if I can wait a second longer."

"If you don't kiss me, I'll never forgive you." She couldn't even think about the fact that she might not be free.

His lips landed on hers, hard and searching. Hailey opened her mouth to his, tasting wine and heat and desire. Flashes of delicious heat fluttered through and over and around her. For long moments they kissed, sitting on the pier, turned toward each other. Hailey let the sleeping bag slip from her shoulders. She was too hot now anyway.

And dizzy too. So deliciously dizzy. Had she drunk too much wine? She didn't think so, but who cared if she had? At some point, she'd have to stop him, though at the moment, she couldn't remember why. All she knew was that his touch made her heart pound as if it would fly right out of her chest.

He pulled her over on his lap, and she straddled him. They were still kissing, tongues hot and demanding. He gave a little moan, which urged her on. The hard lines of his body told her just how physically demanding his job was, from his solid chest to the arms that pressed her against him. He felt so good.

He lifted his hands to her face, cupping it tenderly. But almost immediately, he started to pull back. "No," she murmured.

"But you're burning up." He kissed her again, then rested his cheek against hers. "I'm serious. Either you're having an allergic reaction, or you're sick."

"No, I'm just . . ." She couldn't remember what she was. "I do feel a little strange." It wasn't the throwing up kind of strange, but the kind where you wanted to be in bed with a handful of painkillers, a pile of blankets, and no noise, except maybe for the breathing of the man you loved.

His face wavered in front of her. "Dylan?"

"I'm here."

"I think you're right—I am coming down with something."

Still holding her face in his hands, he said, "I'm sorry." He kissed her again.

She tried to pull away. "You'll get it too."

"Little late for that," he drawled with a chuckle that sent a wave of desire shooting through her. "Besides, I'm due for a vacation."

That made her laugh. "Somehow lying on a beach or something sounds more fun than lying around in bed."

"That depends on what you're doing in bed." His tone was casual but his eyes telling.

She laughed again. "I guess that's true."

He jumped to his feet and pulled her up with him, steadying her tightly against his body. "You go home and get some sleep. We'll have plenty of time later to talk about that." Before she could answer, he turned and hunched over a bit. "Climb on my back."

"What about the cooler?"

"I'll come back for everything after I get you to the car."

She wrapped her arms and legs around him and laughed as he jogged up the pier and into the trees. He opened the SUV and set her gently inside, as if he considered her precious cargo. *We've come a long way since our last time here at the lake,* she thought.

She rested as he drove to the café, where he walked her up the back stairs to the door. "I had a good time," she said, reluctant to let him leave.

He grinned. "Normal?"

"Oh, no. Not even close to normal."

"Good." He gave her a lingering kiss that made her feel as if she were the only woman in the world. What had made her so lucky to come to this town and to the barn where he'd found her? Her life before couldn't have been all that bad if he was her reward.

"You get better," he said, his voice low and incredibly sexy. "Next time, we'll spend the whole night watching the stars."

His promise gave her the courage to let him leave, waving as he flashed his lights for her to go inside. She obeyed, feeling oddly out of breath. The pain was back in her stomach, and there was a full feeling too. Could it be the wine?

At her room door, she fumbled for her keys, dropping them. In the next instant, she was somehow falling onto the floor, her head banging against the wall. Sighing, she tried to get up. That was when she saw the blood between her legs. At first only a small patch, but that quickly grew. She'd changed her pad at the restaurant and then later after the movie. This didn't make any sense.

She tried to get up, but then it didn't matter. Her eyes closed. She let the heat and dizziness take her.

CHAPTER 16

Maggie heard the thump in the hallway and opened her bedroom door. She wasn't sure what she was expecting to find in the hallway, but she needed to check, even though she might end up embarrassing herself if Dylan and Hailey were out there together.

What she found was far worse. Hailey was on the floor in the hallway, half sprawled, half sitting against the wall, her head lolling to the side. Maggie knelt beside her.

"Hailey," she whispered urgently. "Are you okay?"

There was no response, though Hailey hadn't exactly fainted. She was still trying to hold up her head.

"Hailey!" she repeated.

"I'm sorry," Hailey whispered. "Maybe it's the blood."

Blood? What did that even mean? Then she saw the blood spreading down Hailey's pants.

"What happened?" Maggie asked. "Did someone hurt you?

We need to call the ambulance. Or better yet, Doc Sayer. He's a lot closer."

"No!" Hailey's hands went out on either side, steadying herself. Her breath was coming fast. "It's my cycle, that's all. I need to change . . ." She didn't finish. "I have a fever, I think. I feel like I'm going to pass out. My-my heart is pounding."

Maggie checked her neck, and sure enough, her heart was beating furiously. Her flesh was hot and clammy. "How long have you been on your cycle?"

Hailey gave the slightest shrug. "Since I got off the bus. Isn't it supposed to stop? I shouldn't be going to the bathroom every hour, should I?"

"Definitely not." Maggie grabbed the keys on the floor and opened her door. "Let's get you to the bed. I'll call the doctor."

"It's just a period. Or the flu. Please don't call him. I need to rest is all."

"No, something else is going on." Maggie considered waking her other boarder to ask for help getting Hailey inside, but when she dragged Hailey to her feet, she could support her weight.

Instead of going to the bed, Hailey went into the bathroom. "Don't shut the door all the way." Maggie thought for a moment and added, "I'll call Charlotte. She's a midwife, and she knows about these things."

"I'm not pregnant."

"Are you sure?"

The utter silence behind the partially closed door told Maggie all she needed to know.

While Hailey changed, Maggie called Charlotte, explaining the situation as quickly as she could. "I've seen something like this before," she added. "It might be a miscarriage."

"Look, keep her calm and give her fluids. I'm going to stop by the doctor's office and grab the portable ultrasound."

"Please hurry." Maggie stifled the fear in her heart. Bleeding to death was a very real possibility in a town without a hospital. Was she making a mistake by not calling Doc Sayer or an ambulance to take Hailey to Panna Creek?

Maggie helped Hailey drink water and tucked blankets around her, which she pushed off. Her forehead was hot, but Maggie didn't dare leave her to find a thermometer.

To her relief, Charlotte arrived more quickly than Maggie expected. Charlotte leaned over Hailey. "Hi, Hailey, it's Charlotte. Does anything hurt?"

Hailey's eyes came open. "Not right now."

"I'm going to check a few things." Charlotte shone a light into Hailey's eyes and checked her pupils. "Dilated," she said, her face grave. "With the fever and confusion, that could mean shock." She put on a blood pressure cuff and frowned but didn't say anything about the reading. "Okay, I'm going to prick your finger to test the level of iron in your blood."

Hailey didn't react to the prick.

Next, Charlotte gently massaged Hailey's torso between her waist and pelvic bone. "Your lower stomach does seem a little extended," Charlotte said. "Does this hurt?"

Hailey winced at the pressure on her belly. "I guess so."

"Maggie said you've been bleeding a lot. How much?"

"I don't know. It's been heavy."

"Have you had cramps? A headache?"

Hailey nodded. "I've been taking painkillers since Friday."

Charlotte's brow creased, but she didn't respond to that. Hailey closed her eyes.

Charlotte moved away from the bed, motioning to Maggie.

"Her blood pressure is dangerously low, and her iron is low as well. With all the symptoms, I think it's safe to say she's hemorrhaging inside—probably in her uterus. I'll see what I can with the ultrasound, but if she's hemorrhaging, we'll need to talk to Doc Sayer for a recommendation. She may need a D&C."

"I should call him now," Maggie said. "Give him a heads up."

Charlotte gave a shake of her head. "I already called his house, and Carina said he's out on a call right now—Fletcher Wilson apparently forgot how to use a knife and nearly cut off a finger, so Doc's out there now. Anyway, depending on what I see with the ultrasound, Doc may want us to go to the hospital in Panna Creek instead of treating her himself. So let's do the ultrasound first. He should be finished with Fletcher by then."

Charlotte set up the equipment. "This gel is going to be a little cold."

"It's okay," Hailey murmured. Maggie didn't know what disturbed her more, Hailey's lolling head or the fact that she didn't react to the cold.

Charlotte moved the wand around Hailey's exposed stomach, nodding. "There's something there," she said in a low voice to Maggie. "But there's no heartbeat, and it doesn't look like an embryo sack. I don't have official training in ultrasound—everything I know about them, I've learned from Doc, so I think we need to ask him what to do. I don't know what this is, but I'm sure it's causing the problem."

Maggie took out her phone and called Doc. She let it ring until it went to voicemail. "He's not answering, so either he's in a dead zone, or he can't get to his cell phone."

"We need to find him." Charlotte's voice was calm but

urgent. "I have a tincture I can give her for hemorrhage, and it might have been enough a couple of days ago, but I think this is going to need something much stronger."

Maggie thought quickly. "I'll call Dylan. He can get out to the Wilson place and find Doc Sayer. It'll still be faster than calling for the ambulance in Panna Creek." She was already dialing as she spoke.

He answered right away, but sleepily. "Maggie? Is everything okay?"

"Hailey's sick. I need you to go find Doc Sayer. He was making a house call at the Wilsons. Fletcher cut himself. Either Doc's put his phone aside, or they have a dead zone out there."

"Service is usually good at their house," Dylan said, already sounding more awake. "But how's Hailey? What should I tell Doc?"

"Tell him we think it's an internal hemorrhage. And she's not doing well. Charlotte's here helping. You should hurry." Over on the bed, Hailey was gagging on something Charlotte had given her.

"On my way," Dylan muttered. "Call you when I find him."

Maggie heard a door slam from his end before the line went dead.

Dylan revved his engine a little too hard and burned rubber outside the clinic as he sped away, cursing under his breath.

He knew that Hailey had been exhausted. He'd seen that much during the movie. Why had he pushed her to go to the lake? But he knew why. He'd wanted to show his house to her, something he'd never wanted to show a woman before tonight. And he'd wanted to share the stars with her from his special place on his dock. Most of all, he'd wanted to taste her lips again. What a selfish fool.

The Tahoe ate the miles to the Wilson farm steadily, but still far too slowly for Dylan. He pushed harder on the gas, hoping to see the lights of a police car chasing him so he could get Levi to give him an escort. No such luck tonight.

Hemorrhage? She could have damaged herself when she fell into the river, but wouldn't it have either healed or gotten worse before now? She had been pale today, and not nearly as energetic as she'd been during their night together with Sable. Maybe she'd been in trouble then, but he'd been too concerned about what she was hiding to notice what was right in front of his face. The alcohol he'd given her on his dock tonight could have also thinned her blood enough to worsen the hemorrhage, especially if she'd had problems with drinking in the past.

He hit the steering wheel and cursed. What if he lost her now when they were finally figuring things out?

At last he pulled up outside Ronica Wilson's house, which looked low slung and rather dingy compared to her son's newer one. He was relieved to see Doc Sayer's silver sedan parked outside.

"God, help me," he muttered. Though with the way he'd been swearing, he wasn't too sure God would be listening at this point.

Wrenching open the door, he jumped out, leaving the door open and the keys inside as he hurried up the walk. The porch light was on, but the front window was dark. He rang the doorbell three times. When that didn't bring immediate results, he banged on the door. Then he almost fell inside as it swung open, revealing Jeremy Wilson.

"What's with all the racket?" Jeremy growled. "It's practically the middle of the night."

"Hardly," snorted Dylan. "I need Doc."

"He's in the kitchen having a cup of hot chocolate with us. You know how my mom is. After he stitched up—"

Dylan pushed past him, not caring to hear the rest. He hurried through the darkened living room to a hallway and finally to the kitchen where Ronica and Doc were at a small round table. Fletcher was nowhere to be seen.

Dylan stopped in the doorway with Jeremy, who was following close behind and slammed into him. "Doc, you have to come with me now," he said. "They tried to call you, but you didn't answer."

Doc stood immediately and started in his direction. "I left my bag in the living room. What's the problem?"

"It's Hailey, the new woman at the café. Charlotte's there, but Maggie says they think it's internal bleeding." He shrugged. "Maybe it was from the fall into the river."

"Oh, no!" gasped Ronica. "Hurry then. The poor thing."

Once again, Dylan shoved past a surprised Jeremy, with Doc following close behind. By the time Dylan hit the door, he was running. On the way back into town, he called Maggie to let her know help was coming.

When he finally got to the Butter Cake, he jumped from the Tahoe and ran up the outside stairs, waiting impatiently for Doc to hurry up the stairs after him. Maggie motioned to them as they entered, but she only let Doc pass into Hailey's room.

"You stay here," she told Dylan, a restraining hand on his chest. He had no choice but to remain in the hallway as Maggie shut the door in his face.

Doc was inside the room for less than three minutes. When he emerged, his face was grave. "I'll need your help to get her over to my office. I've given her a shot to help stabilize her, but I'll need to do a . . ." he hesitated before rushing on, "a procedure."

"Will she be okay?" Dylan asked, panic slicing through him.

"I think so," Doc said. "But we need to hurry."

"What kind of a procedure," Dylan wanted to know. "I can help."

Doc shook his head. "Not necessary. Charlotte and I will do it."

It was obvious no one wanted to tell him exactly what was wrong with Hailey, and Dylan stifled irritation at all of them and their ridiculous privacy rules.

"It's female stuff," Maggie elaborated.

Big help there. Female problems could cover a host of issues, Dylan well knew. He was about to protest when Maggie extended her hand and added, "Stop standing there looking angry and give me your keys. I'll put blankets in the back of your car and ride with her to Doc's."

Dylan handed his keys over and followed Doc into the room where Charlotte was tucking a blanket around Hailey. He scooped her up, holding her tightly to his chest. "I got you," he murmured.

She cracked an eye. "What are you doing here? I'm fine. I'm just . . ." Whatever she was going to say was lost as her eyes rolled up in her head and she passed out.

Dylan wanted to scream as he had on the day they'd told him about Bristol, but he kept it inside. *Focus,* he told himself. *Get her to the doctor's office.*

In the end, it was Doc and Charlotte who rode in the back of the Tahoe with Hailey while Maggie followed in Doc's sedan.

Once at the office, Dylan carried Hailey inside and laid her on an examining table. Then he was banished again to pace in the front waiting room.

Guilt ate at him. Had keeping Hailey out late made things worse and maybe precipitated her attack?

Whatever had happened, it was serious. And though most of his worry was for Hailey, he couldn't stop a very selfish thought from floating to the surface of his mind: why did all the important women in his life end up leaving him?

Hailey drifted in a sea of comfort. Her breathing was slowing, and the panic she'd felt outside her door at Maggie's had eased. Maybe she'd had a panic attack about kissing Dylan or what their relationship might be leading to. She wanted to laugh at that but couldn't find the strength. Maybe after a good night's sleep.

Hailey was aware of Maggie's voice around her, constant and soothing like music. Hailey really had to ask her about that. Maybe she had missed her calling in life.

Someone—Maggie?—lifted her head, and cool liquid touched her lips. She pulled away. She wanted to sleep, to drift off and forget.

Hands ran over Hailey's body. Strong, competent hands that pushed at her sore stomach. She wanted to shove them aside, but she felt too weak.

Voices floated over her. Their words were very interesting, but her exhaustion was more compelling. That and the beating of her heart, which seemed to radiate in her ears and throughout the room.

More talking, and then someone leaned over and said in her

ear, "Hailey, it's time to wake up." It was a man's voice, and the seriousness of his tone frightened her.

She opened her eyes and was surprised to see a man she didn't know standing over her. He wore a white jacket that screamed medical doctor. Had Maggie gone ahead and called him without her permission? She stared wildly around the unfamiliar room, her breathing coming rapidly again. Where had Dylan gone? Feeling his arms around her and his whispered, "I got you" had made her feel safe. But he wasn't here now.

A monitor somewhere beeped, causing a feeling of dread and loss to fill her entire being. "No," she whimpered.

Maggie's face came into view, her face close to Hailey's. "It's going to be okay. Just listen to the doctor. I promise you, it's going to be okay."

"Okay," Hailey repeated, wanting to trust her.

The doctor's face replaced Maggie's. "You should be feeling a lot better now with the shot I gave you for your fever, if a bit groggy, but you are going to need immediate surgery." The doctor tilted his head as his intense gaze penetrated her lethargy. "You have some tissue inside your uterus, and that is causing the excessive bleeding. I need to do what's commonly called a D&C to take it out. It's in a good position for this, and we can do it right here. I don't believe there will be any lasting problem after we finish. You shouldn't have any trouble getting pregnant in the future, though sometimes complications do happen. But if we don't remove the tissue, you will likely bleed to death or lose your uterus because of the infection. I've tried a few other things, and so far nothing has affected the bleeding in any significant way. Do you understand?"

"Yes," Hailey said. "Do it."

"You will only be partially sedated during the procedure,

but you shouldn't feel any pain," the doctor added. "You let me know if you do."

"Okay, but how . . . how did it happen?" Hailey managed to ask. "I've been feeling fine, except for the headache and cramps." It didn't make sense.

His expression didn't change, but there was a slight catch in his voice as he said, "It's called late postpartum hemorrhage, or PPH. It's rare, but it can happen up to twelve weeks after giving birth. I'm thinking for you it's been less than four weeks."

She gasped. "Birth?"

"Yes. You had a baby. I don't know how far along in the pregnancy you were, but judging from the signs, it was probably in the last trimester. Do you remember having a child?"

Hailey stared at him, the word reverberating in her head: *a child, a child, a child, a child.* He was saying that she had a baby. That she'd been pregnant and had given birth. What kind of person didn't remember such a thing? And if it was true, where was her baby?

A scream bubbled up in her throat.

"Stop. You're scaring her." Maggie brought her face close to Hailey's until their cheeks touched, and her lips were close to Hailey's ears. Her hands gripped Hailey's. "Listen to me. You're going to be okay. Everything is going to be okay. You focus on that. Nothing else. Everything is going to be okay. Don't worry about a thing. Just hold onto my hands and remember that you're going to be okay." She dragged out the last words, punctuating each one and filling it with meaning.

Hailey latched onto the earnest tone, to the melodic voice that slowly pushed away those two other, more troublesome words. Maggie was a good person, and Hailey would trust her. She clung tightly to Maggie's hands as the doctor injected something into an IV hanging next to her. Then she shut her eyes and let the tears run down her face.

Minutes ticked into hours as Dylan paced in the waiting room. His phone buzzed with messages from his clients and even two from Hector in New York, but he didn't look at or respond to any of them. Why was it taking so long? His mind dredged up a dozen reasons that a procedure for "female issues" would be necessary and a hundred ways that fixing them could go wrong. Most of those included permanent sterility, which made him feel sick. Hailey had said she loved children. He himself still hoped to have at least a couple of them someday. Though he and Hailey weren't a couple—yet—the thoughts were enough to drive him insane.

Finally, Doc and Charlotte emerged from the room, their faces still grave. "Is she . . ." Dylan asked, not able to finish.

Doc heaved a sigh. "She'll be fine." He looked at Charlotte, whose brown hair was doing its best to escape the long braid she wore. "Thanks for the assist. If you'll stay here with her for an hour, I'd really like to get home and peek in on my kids and kiss my wife, if she's still awake. I'm sure Hailey's stable, but I'd like to give it another hour and check her one more time before I send her home."

"Sure." Charlotte nodded. "Be glad to."

With a nod at Dylan, the doctor headed toward the front door to the office. Dylan didn't move after him. "Can I see her?" he asked Charlotte.

"I don't see why not." She put a hand on his arm. "Don't look so worried. She'll be okay. You did good, finding Doc so fast. I admit that I was out of my depth." She gave a wistful smile. "Maybe it's time I get some additional training."

"I was out with her," Dylan said, barely hearing Charlotte's words. "I should have known it was serious."

Her green eyes pinned him into place. "Don't beat yourself up about it. She's lucky you two went out. Because if she'd done this while she was sleeping, she might never have woken up."

Dylan stared at her. "It's that serious? What does she have? Why won't anyone say? I'm a doctor for crying out loud, even if my patients are mostly four-legged."

Charlotte shook her head. "Not my place to explain. You'll have to ask her." She hesitated before adding, "But if I were you, I'd save it until later. She doesn't need a lot of questions right now, especially when she doesn't know any of the answers."

Dylan nearly growled at that. He deserved to know what was going on, and Hailey needed to tell him. He wouldn't be yanked around like this!

Behind Charlotte, Maggie opened the door to the room, where he could see Hailey stretched out on a table, covered by the blanket from the café. Hailey was propped up on pillows, looking small and forlorn . . . and so incredibly beautiful.

A protective urge grew inside him, obliterating all his outrage. She was here. She was okay, and that was all that mattered. Not his pride or his questions or his fears. Only she mattered. Only making her smile again mattered.

He went into the room, a tentative smile on his face. "Hey," he said.

"I told you he was still out there," Maggie told Hailey. "I'll leave you two alone for a bit while Charlotte and I make a pot of tea in the break room." She moved toward Dylan, leaning toward him. "No stress!" she whispered. "Got it?" She swept on past before he could respond.

Dylan moved around the exam table. Hailey wasn't looking at him, but he knew her well enough to recognize the embarrassment on her face. He eased himself up on the edge of the table and put an arm around her without saying another word.

She leaned into him, and he took that as his cue to pull her onto his lap as he moved further onto the table, careful not to pull on the IV still in her arm. With a little sigh, her head nestled against his shoulder, her face pressed into his neck. Moments later, he felt her tears as she began to sob—a heartbreaking sob that he understood instinctively but couldn't name.

"It's okay," he murmured, his lips in her hair. "I've got you. Just hold on tight." He tightened his own hold on her body. He never wanted to let go.

CHAPTER 17

D ylan woke early the next morning, stiff from spending the past few hours in a chair in Hailey's room. When the doctor had finally released her to go home, Dylan had insisted on carrying her up the stairs at the café, and then he hadn't been able to bring himself to leave.

He'd checked on her breathing every few minutes and her blood pressure every half hour until she finally slapped him away with a smile. A couple of times, he'd woken up not in his chair but holding her on the bed. That part was the best, though not exactly the way he'd thought they'd spend their first night in a bed together.

At least he'd made her smile. Underneath the smile, though, there was a sadness in her expression that hadn't been there before. But he didn't ask because he didn't want to bring back the tears. She would talk to him when she was ready. He had to trust her, trust the relationship they were building.

She was sleeping soundly now, and he was certain himself that she was physically fine. He could leave her in Maggie's care and get to work.

Yet he lingered. For long moments, he stood over Hailey, watching her sleep. He'd never imagined when he found her in the barn that she'd come to mean this much to him. But she did, and he knew there was no going back. Kissing her cheek, he slipped out of her room and down the back stairs. If people saw him sneaking out this early, there would be talk, but he didn't care.

Back at his clinic, he checked on Sable and the pups, the only current overnight occupants besides an ornery cat who he'd had to stitch up yesterday after a run-in with a car. He grabbed a couple of leftover slices of pizza and his work boots, opting to skip his shower in favor of his first appointment at a ranch thirty miles west of town. He'd have to shower anyway before he went back to check on Hailey. In the meantime, the rancher and his cattle wouldn't care if he smelled fresh.

In the Tahoe, he rolled down the windows and turned up the CD volume to keep himself awake, then set off for the ranch. The music and the wind were probably why he missed another text from Hector, adding to the others he'd ignored, but he got it when he pulled up at the ranch where he planned to vaccinate a thousand head of cattle.

Hector answered his return call immediately. "You'd think you were a doctor or something, the way you don't answer texts," Hector said.

"Sorry it took me so long, but there was an emergency," Dylan said. "I also had a date last night."

"A real date where you paid for a meal the girl didn't make and where you actually had fun?"

"Something like that."

"It's her, isn't it? This Hailey Waters."

Dylan closed his eyes, grimacing. "Yeah. So what do you have?" He hoped Hector wasn't going to burst the contented bubble he'd constructed during the drive—one that had him imagining falling asleep next to Hailey every night. Though he hadn't been with Hailey last night for romantic reasons, he'd liked it more than he wanted to admit.

"Unfortunately, the news isn't extraordinary," Hector told him. "I texted last night—twice—because we came back with two hits. In the meantime, during your very rude silence, I researched them, and that's why I texted this morning. I don't believe either of the hits is the woman you're looking for, so I'm calling to make sure you didn't get all excited. Though you should probably verify my findings, since you know what she looks like in person and all I have is a single photo. The database search isn't complete yet, so we could still come up with more hits, but if we don't, it probably means she's not there."

"She still could be. Isn't there a small percentage of times the person won't be found even if they're in the database?"

"True, but it's only like fifteen percent. It might have helped if we'd put in another picture or two. Anyway, they'll let me know if they find more hits. In the meantime, should I text you the information on the two women? One lives in California, no criminal record or anything, and she's not missing. I still jumped on social media, and if it's her, she's different from the woman in the picture you sent. I mean, I can see a faint resemblance in the face, but nothing else matches. The second hit is closer to your neck of the woods in Nebraska, and the resemblance is better. By the way, I was kind of excited about the Nebraska connection at first because of the sandal you found, but it turns out the sandal company ships all over the US, which means it's no proof of anything. And the Nebraska woman isn't missing, either, so a double dead end. She's a senator's wife or something."

Senator? Dylan's interest triggered at that, but he didn't know what it meant. It was as if something he knew hovered out of memory. "I would like to see the information," he told Hector.

"Okay, but remember, this is off the books. If this turns up trouble, we go through your chief and proper channels. Whatever happens, I never gave you this information."

"Of course."

Hector laughed. "I'm just yanking your chain. I've always wanted to say something like that. We've nothing to worry about with these two. They're definitely not your Hailey Waters. Oops, speaking of chiefs, mine is coming this way. Later." The phone went dead.

"Thanks," Dylan said, more to himself than to Hector.

He knew he should get out of the Tahoe and get to work, but he didn't. He waited until the texts came through with not only the names but links to social media for both women and news articles for the second. Like Hector, he quickly dismissed the woman in California. To be her, Hailey would have had to dye her hair and lose sixty pounds since the last publicly shared post a week earlier. The woman also didn't have that certain something Hailey possessed in abundance—the cast of her eyes or the jutting of her cheek bones that had appealed to him from the first day.

The second woman was a different story. Seeing her profile picture and the public posts and new articles made a great yawning pit form in his stomach. She was Hannah Waterford Granville, age twenty-eight, wife of Senator Brice Granville, one of Nebraska's forty-nine unicameral senators, not to be confused with Nebraska's two US senators serving in Washington DC. Brice was one of the youngest senators, a powerful, upcoming politician who had eyes on the governorship and maybe someday something more. There weren't nearly as many pictures of Hannah as there were of Brice, but in every one of them, Dylan couldn't miss Hailey's distinct features. Hannah Granville was definitely his Hailey.

His Hailey. When had he started thinking of her that way?

Hannah was beautiful, and the cameras loved her. But she was often caught from the side while turning away. Camera shy, a few of the articles said—and the reporters loved her even more for not seeking attention. He saw her reading to children, talking to other women at several charity dinners, and walking with a stocky attorney said to be her father.

Her dad's an attorney, Dylan thought. That was a far cry from the surf shop owner she had made up, but she *had* given the attorney role to her boring, make-believe brother.

That was when he landed on a page with a rare photograph of her holding onto the arm of her husband, a man who wasn't nearly her equal in looks, but who radiated power and confidence. In the picture, her face was as expressionless as Dylan had ever seen it, and the swell of her stomach was obvious. Hannah Granville, the reporter wrote, was expecting her first daughter.

The last news article showed the couple again together, Hannah wearing a long coat, her face hidden as her husband, arm protectively around her, shielded her from reporters as she left the hospital after tragically losing her daughter during an unexpected birth nearly three months before the child was due.

Everything matched up. Hailey's appearance, her strange hemorrhage last night, and the reason she didn't want to remember. The name, especially her maiden name, was uncannily close to her made-up name. This might also explain why Hailey had fainted that first day when Ronica Wilson had been talking about a senator from Nebraska—Dylan hadn't paid much attention, but it had to be the same man. And Connor, the developer from Lincoln, had said Hailey looked familiar, as she probably was to many of the residents of that city. Even the small birthmark on her neck was clearly visible in at least two photographs.

Only one thing didn't add up: the date on the last article had been Saturday when Hailey had definitely not been in Lincoln Nebraska because she'd been kissing him at the lake. That date stopped his whirling emotions and gave him hope.

During their joking around about her family yesterday, Hailey had come up with a sister. Maybe she was a twin. It was possible. Wasn't it? He desperately hoped so.

He scanned the articles again for mentions of her family, but they were mostly about Brice Granville. Even his public page on Facebook showed videos of him in the Nebraska legislature, usually speaking passionately. His wife was only shown in the occasional still photo. One link led to a recent article that told how Senator Granville's approval rating had skyrocketed since the news broke about the couple losing the baby. By contrast, Hannah Granville's personal Facebook profile was private, and only a few public pictures, most of them years old, were available to him. A quick search of Hannah Granville's father, Frank Waterford, brought up a law firm and a brief bio that didn't mention his family.

She has to be a twin, he thought. It was the only explanation. Either that or Hailey could be married and have another life that would take her away from Forgotten.

Dylan climbed from the Tahoe like a man in a dream. He could show this to Hailey, but would it do more damage than good? And there was still the possibility that the woman wasn't related at all. Stranger things had happened.

But his heart already knew.

By the time he'd vaccinated half the cattle, he'd made a decision. Removing his gloves, he reached for his phone to call his receptionist, Maeve Smithson.

"I need you to reschedule all my afternoon appointments. If there's any you can't reschedule, move them up to my lunch hour. And call Chris Berrett in Junction City to see if he'll be on call for possible emergencies here."

"Are you sure? Dr. Berrett? Your clients hate him."

"They hate his personality, but they trust his veterinarian skills." *And with any luck there won't be an emergency,* he thought.

"Okay, but you'll regret it the next time you have to drive an hour and a half to cover him."

Dylan already knew that. "Remind me to make an offer to one of those new vets I've been looking at. I need a partner."

"Now that's something I can agree on. But why am I doing all this? What's going on?"

He hadn't anticipated her question and didn't really know what to say. "I have to drive to Lincoln this afternoon on a personal matter." He hoped his tone made it clear it was none of her business. The last thing he needed was the entire town gossiping about what he'd found. He didn't even know if he was going to tell Hailey.

"Okay," Maeve said. "You let me know if you need anything more." A little sniff told him he'd have to spring for chocolates or something for evoking the personal card.

That was the price for privacy in Forgotten, where no one actually ever forgot. Except Hailey.

Hailey slept late and when she awoke, she felt better physically than she could ever remember feeling. She didn't have a headache, her body aches were gone, and she wasn't pouring out blood—only a little cramping and spotting today. No need for pain killers, which surprised her.

Her emotional side, however, wasn't doing as well. On the one hand, everyone had been supportive, especially Dylan. He'd stayed when she'd expected him to flee from her secrets that had now come to rest between them, even if he hadn't realized it yet. Secrets she still couldn't remember but knew were true.

On the other hand, she now knew that she'd been pregnant and no longer was. She felt cheated of the experience, of feeling the baby move inside her, of giving birth, maybe even of losing him or her. Was that what had made her leave her life and forget? She couldn't believe she was the type of woman to walk out on a baby—her baby. So why had she?

Every time she allowed this thought to come through, she experienced occasional flashes of another life—mostly the beautiful woman in the mirror and a man in white with a blurred face. These were quickly accompanied by a heavy numbness that spread through her chest. The numbness made it possible to shower and dress and even to think about Dylan. She didn't want to leave him or Forgotten.

She was brushing her hair to go downstairs to the café when a knock came on her door. "It's me," Maggie called.

Hailey went to let her in, but the door opened before she reached it.

"Oh, you're up. Good. It's past noon." Maggie lifted a tray. "I've been checking in on you. That's why the door's unlocked. Doctor's orders, though Dylan took the night shift."

Hailey blushed a little at that. Having him curled up next to her, annoying her by checking her breathing so often, had been the only thing besides the numbness that had helped her stave off the emotions surrounding the mysterious pregnancy.

Hailey followed Maggie to the desk, where she set the tray of food. "Thank you."

"How are you feeling?" Maggie's face was sympathetic.

"Good."

Maggie shook her head. "Try again."

Hailey slumped into the chair. "I thought I could make a new life for myself here, but I can't now. I have to know."

"Aw, sweetie." Maggie rubbed her shoulder. "I'm sorry."

"I'm so afraid that I was a terrible person . . . before . . ." *Before* because Hailey was determined that whatever she'd been, she wasn't the same person now.

"You mean the kind who would abandon a baby?" Maggie's voice was soft and sad. "There are many reasons things like that happen, and they don't all mean you're a terrible person."

"What if I sold the baby?" There, Hailey dared say the words aloud. The money under her mattress seemed too small for such a devasting idea, but maybe she'd been desperate.

"No. You would remember something like that."

"I'm going to the police," Hailey countered. "They should be able to find out who I am, right?"

Maggie studied her for a moment. "Maybe. I think it's a good idea. But let's wait until Friday when our chief of police is back. The other officers mean well, but they could put all of their experience in one of Caleb McColl's pinky fingers."

Why did waiting sound so good? Hailey nodded, biting down on her lip and trying not to cry. "It's too bad I can't get back on the bus and retrace my life." She managed a mirthless laugh with these words, which elicited a smile from Maggie.

"No, but the driver might remember where he picked you up, and they usually have surveillance at bus stations, so the ticket and credit card might be traced. Caleb will know what to do."

Thinking of the stash of bills, Hailey wasn't so sure. But that wasn't what haunted her the most. "Wh-what if there's a baby out there who needs me? Oh!" She gasped as the reality hit her again, and she hid her face in her hands. In that instant, she was swept up in a longing so huge there wasn't enough space in her heart—or even in the vastness of the universe—to hold it.

Maggie leaned over, her arms going around Hailey and anchoring her to the here and now, away from that terrible vastness. "It's not like that. Charlotte says you don't seem to be making milk, so whatever happened, it's been longer than a few weeks, I'd say. That means if there is a baby, someone is taking care of him."

Hailey hadn't considered the lack of milk, but then she'd never given birth before—or at least not that she remembered. "I don't know," she muttered.

"I do." Maggie gently pulled Hailey's hands from her face. "Everything will work out. Come down after you eat, though, okay? Charlotte's here, and she'd like to take you back to the doctor's office for some more bloodwork, as a precaution."

"How much is this all going to cost?" Hailey couldn't help the thought.

"Let's not worry about that right now. Charlotte's a friend, and Doc owes me for taking meals to his shut-ins. Besides, you might find that once you remember, you're fully insured. And if not, we'll call in the favors." She smiled encouragingly. "You think you can make it down the stairs?"

Hailey pursed her lips. "Truthfully? I feel better than I have since I got here, and I'm not taking any painkillers."

"That says a lot about what you've been enduring." Maggie swung her head back and forth in a wide arc. "You were in pretty bad shape."

Maybe she deserved it. But Hailey didn't say that aloud. No. The woman she was becoming was going to face her fears . . . and remember. Because she had to know. She wouldn't be able to stay in Forgotten without knowing.

What about Dylan? The thought almost made her cry again, but she'd face him too. She wouldn't lie to him again. Whatever happened between them, she wouldn't be like the woman who'd broken his heart.

Using the napkin Maggie had brought, she wiped her tears away and picked up her fork. Her stomach growled in anticipation. Funny how the body still went on. How it still responded . . . and still desired, as she had for Dylan last night.

"That's it." Maggie turned to leave.

"I think I might love him," Hailey whispered to Maggie's retreating back. "Could that be possible already?"

Maggie turned in the doorway, her smile bright. "I once fell in love with a man in a single, wonderful, marvelous night. So yes, I'd say it was possible." She turned around again, but Hailey had to know.

"What happened to him?"

This time Maggie was slower to turn. "We were young. I didn't know what I'd found. I walked away, and I've regretted it ever since. I guess sometimes it only comes around once." She rounded the door and disappeared.

Hailey stared after her. If she left Forgotten to pursue the truth, would she feel that way forever about Dylan?

CHAPTER 18

ylan stared up at the big house on Lincoln, wishing he could turn his Tahoe around and go back to Forgotten. But that would be retreat, and he wasn't retreating until he found answers—answers that were probably inside this monstrous house.

He'd been at the clinic until two-thirty and then stopped by the café with the hope of seeing Hailey, but Maggie told him Charlotte had taken her for blood tests. While he waited for a bag of food to take with him, Maggie had also told him that Hailey was planning to talk to Caleb when he got back in town.

"She wants to put it behind her," Maggie had said. "I think that's a good sign. I'll let her know you were here. It'll mean a lot to her."

These thoughts from Maggie gave Dylan the courage to continue with his plan to drive over the Kansas-Nebraska border to Lincoln. The traffic once in town had been horrendous, and he was reminded once again of the relief he'd felt at leaving New York. Not only the city and the crowds, but the memories of Bristol and of the person he'd been. He'd thought to leave behind the gullible fool who'd given up his future plans for a woman who didn't love him, but maybe in going back to Forgotten and finally meeting Hailey, he'd actually rediscovered that man. Because when he'd left New York, he never wanted to love a woman again. Now he wanted nothing but to love one particular woman, even if it meant giving up a part of himself. That was okay with him. If love couldn't change you, maybe it didn't mean enough.

The house loomed over the street. Was this city Hailey's home? Was this mansion where she slept at night? These and more questions assailed him, and he knew there would be no way to find answers here in the SUV.

The comparatively short stretch of grass and flowerbeds looked cared for. Did Hailey do that? Or her twin?

Even knowing it was an impossibility, he still hoped there was a twin.

He jabbed at the doorbell, checking the time on his phone. Would the senator be home? He'd recently experienced a personal tragedy, but did that mean he'd taken time off to be with his wife? And what was Dylan going to do if a woman who was a twin to Hailey opened the door? Maybe he should have gone to see the father instead.

Too late. Steps were already approaching. Senator Brice Granville opened the door himself, casually dressed in black lounge pants and a white polo. As his pictures had shown, he had black hair, blue eyes, a slender face, and thin lips. At thirty-eight, he was already going gray at the temples, which Dylan supposed made him distinguished. Despite the senator's thinness, the polo didn't do as well as his customary suits at hiding the beginnings of a paunch. He might work out, but if he did, it wasn't strenuous. Nothing like wrestling a two-thousand-pound bull or even like chasing down drug runners.

Dylan pulled his thoughts away from that. It wasn't as if he'd come here to challenge the man for Hailey's hand.

"Hello, may I help you?" Brice Granville asked, his gaze going over Dylan's head as if fearing—or hoping?—to see a news van parked in the street.

"I need to ask you a few questions," Dylan said.

"I'm sorry. I've already spoken to the press. I'm not giving more interviews."

"I'm not a reporter. I'm here about your wife."

The response was immediate. "What do you know about my wife?"

Something wasn't right. The man looked ready to slam the door in his face at even the mention of Hannah Granville.

"My name is Dr. Dylan Morgan," Dylan said, gambling with the words. "I was with her last night." If it turned out Hailey wasn't connected with this family, the senator might call the police, but for now he sensed the man was hiding something, and he was going to push.

With a scowl, Brice looked up and down the street before motioning him inside the huge entryway. "What do you mean?" he said, but only once the door was closed. "My wife is here, of course."

Not in sight, she wasn't. A sweeping staircase ran up the right side of the entry, leading to a second floor, and there was clearly a sitting room of some kind to the left. Dylan could also see a slice of a second sitting room at the other side of the entry, past a set of clear double doors. No sign of anyone but the senator. Pictures filled the walls of the entry, one of them a large wedding photo. The way the new Mrs. Granville tilted her head was pure Hailey. His gut lurched with the knowledge.

"Well?" demanded Brice. "This better not be a trick to get an interview. Are you wired?"

"Why would I be wired?" Dylan pulled out the neck of the button-up shirt he wore, a deliberate invitation for the senator to check him for a communication device.

Brice ignored him. "You're really a doctor then?"

Before Dylan could reply, a woman in a fluttering silk robe and dangerously high heels came through the double glass doors opposite him, an open bottle of wine in her hands. She had long blond hair, full lips, and heavily but expertly applied makeup, and underneath the robe, she wore only the tiniest black bikini he'd ever seen, which she filled out to advantage. She was definitely not Hailey's twin or the senator's wife.

"What's taking you?" she said, as she bent gracefully to lick something off the lip of the bottle. "I've got the wine ready and—" Her words cut off as she saw Dylan.

"Go back to the deck," Brice ordered.

"I'm sorry, Ma'am," Dylan said, putting on his best bedside manner. "It's my fault. I'm Dr. Morgan. I'm here about Mrs. Granville."

The woman folded her arms and shifted her weight to her back leg, her front bent as if she were posing. "Did you find her then?" she asked.

"Jacquie," Brice said. "This is none of your business. Go back outside and wait for me."

"Why?" Jacquie tossed her head, hurt radiating from her dark eyes. "Are you afraid she'll find out about us? It's always Hannah, Hannah, Hannah. I'm sick of hearing about Hannah. She should be hearing about me. About us. About what you've promised. Instead, it's Hannah this and Hannah that. Well, you know what? I'm sick to death of Hannah. The baby is no longer an issue, and I've done everything you've asked. You need to tell her about us, or it's over."

She swiveled on her heels, teetering perilously, and started back the way she'd come. "I'll see myself out, but I'm taking this." She lifted the bottle of wine. Before reaching the glass doors, she turned and disappeared down what must have been another hallway. Seconds later, a groan of an automatic garage door reached their ears.

Dylan couldn't help feeling sorry for the woman, even knowing she was seeing a married man. "You can go after her," he said to Brice. "I can wait." It wasn't all kindness. If the man chose Jacquie, he wouldn't be around Hannah.

Brice snorted. "No need. She's not going far—just to the apartment I pay for. I know where to find her. Now, tell me, why are you here?"

"It's about Hannah."

"Do you know where she is?"

Dylan arched a brow. "You *don't* know where she is?"

"If you're a reporter, I'm calling the police." Brice reached in his pants pocket and came out with a cell phone.

"As I already told you, I'm not a reporter." For a senator, the guy was exceptionally dense. "And if Hannah isn't here, then I *was* with her last night."

"Where is she!" Brice ground out, flushing red with anger. "The idiot woman isn't in her right mind. She ran away from the hospital a week ago. She's a danger to herself and others. She needs mental help." He jabbed his finger against his temple.

In his mind, Dylan was shoving the jerk into the wall, hand on his throat, lifting him high until his own weight choked him, his other fist pummeling the cheating scum until he stopped talking so disrespectfully about a woman he should have cared for with his life. This man should have been the one to hold Hailey last night, not a man she'd barely met. That thought made Dylan want to hit him even more.

"She doesn't want you to know where she is," Dylan said through gritted teeth. "But she will be okay. No thanks to you."

"Why, you . . ." Brice came at him, his face furious, but stopped short of hitting Dylan with his clenched fists.

"Do it," Dylan taunted. His own muscles were bunched and ready. He wanted nothing more than to lay into this jerk with everything he had.

"It wasn't my fault," Brice muttered. "It wasn't!"

That was interesting. Whatever Brice thought wasn't his fault, Dylan was fairly certain it was.

"Then what happened?" Dylan remembered the reddened ring around Hailey's wrist. "Did you tie her to the hospital bed?"

Brice blinked. "Is that what she said? Look, you have to understand, she was crazy out of her mind. I had to make sure she wouldn't hurt herself."

The fury Dylan had held in check burst from him. "And you didn't think that holding her would help? You didn't think being faithful to her would help? She lost *your* baby. She was devastated. Were you even around when it happened?"

Dylan must have hit on some kernel of truth because all the fight went out of Brice Granville. His shoulders slumped. "If you have a message from Hannah, tell me," he said dully. "Or get out."

Dylan took a step back toward the door, not willing to turn his back on the man. But there was one more thing. "The woman leaving the hospital in the picture? It wasn't Hannah. Who was it?"

"We had to do something for the media. Coming here was the only way to cover up the fact that she ran away from the hospital."

It wasn't exactly an answer, but it told Dylan all he needed to know. "Well, it worked. I hear you're up in the polls and that a run for the governorship is inevitable. I hope it was worth it." Pulling open the front door, Dylan strode over the threshold and down the walk.

He was opening the door to his Tahoe when Brice Granville shot out of the house and ran down the walk, where he suddenly stopped and stood staring.

"Is she okay?" he asked raggedly. "Just tell me if she's really okay."

He didn't deserve to know, but there was real anguish in his face. On some level, the man worried about Hailey—Hannah— even if it was only because of his career.

"She's fine," Dylan said, and he hoped it was true.

"Is she coming back?"

Dylan's heart hurt with the question. "I don't know."

Dylan's feet dragged as he rode the elevator up to Frank Waterford's office. It was nearly six o'clock now, and he hoped Waterford was like the typical TV attorney, working late hours. He wasn't looking forward to meeting another man from Hailey's life. The first hadn't been much to speak of, and the father might not be much better if Hailey had chosen to run rather than to confide in him.

Run? No, it was worse than running. She'd purposefully blocked them all out. And what about the baby? What had happened? The news was full of the loss but not the cause. What had made Hailey run?

A too-thin receptionist wearing a white blouse and an incredibly tight, knee-length skirt looked up from the counter where she'd already put her purse. "I'm sorry," she said, tucking a length of brown hair behind a tiny ear. "We're closed. Unless you're meeting one of the attorneys and no one put it on my calendar?"

He shook his head. "I need to see Frank Waterford. It's a matter of urgency. About his daughter."

Her widened gaze went toward the right where the hallway intersected the reception room as if she expected Frank to appear there. Pulling her gaze back to him, she said. "Are you with the private investigator? They're still together now."

"No." Dylan made his voice hard. "I'm here because I know where Hannah is."

If possible, her eyes widened even more. "Right. Um, let me call him." She picked up a phone. It seemed to ring a long time before the other line was picked up. "Mr. Waterford? Sorry to bother you, but there's a man here. A—" She looked at Dylan.

"Dr. Morgan," Dylan supplied. The title had gotten him in with the senator, so no reason to change it now.

"A Dr. Morgan. He says he knows where Hannah is." She listened for a few seconds before hanging up the phone. "He'll be right here." She picked up her purse, glanced toward the door, then set the purse down again and busied herself with some paperwork at the desk. Evidently, her curiosity was more powerful than her desire to leave work.

Frank Morgan came into the room with a powerful stride.

"If that son-in-law is trying to commit my daughter to a mental hospital, I won't stand for it. I have a copy of the divorce papers he was supposed to sign over three weeks ago. He'll sign it, or I'll have him in court!"

"No." Dylan held up a hand, warding off the big man. "I'm not a medical doctor. I'm a veterinarian, and I'm here because I'm Hailey's—Hannah's friend."

Frank's brow creased, and his eyes glared suspiciously. "How do I know this is true? Is she here with you?"

"She doesn't know I'm here, but look"—he pulled out his phone and clicked the photo gallery—"this is from last night. We had pizza." He shoved the phone in front of Frank.

The man's face softened when he saw the first picture. He took the phone and scrolled through the pictures, the anger seeping from his face. "She looks so happy. Pizza? I don't think I've ever seen her eat pizza—not since she was a teen." He sucked in a breath when he reached the picture of Hailey in the dress shop, wearing the pink dress.

Frank's gaze met his briefly before shifting to the receptionist. "Will you please go to the small conference room and tell the gentleman there that I no longer require his services? I will, of course, pay his current charges." Waiting only for her nod, Frank clasped a hand on Dylan's shoulder. "Come on. Let's talk in my office."

The office was at the end of the hallway, furnished with dark wood furniture and even a brown leather couch. It was to this that Frank motioned him.

"How long has she been missing?" Dylan asked, sinking into the comfortable depths of the couch.

"I haven't seen her in a week," Frank said. "After she lost the baby, she was upset, understandably so, and I wanted to take her home, but Brice thought she needed the doctors and medicine. I think he was really trying to keep her from leaving him. They had a huge fight right before it happened."

"Before what happened?"

"Before she lost the baby." Frank walked over to the desk and picked up a manila envelope. "Six months ago, I drew up these divorce papers for my daughter. She had separated from Brice after finding out about his most recent affair. But less than a week later, she found out she was expecting and decided to hold off on giving him the papers to see if they could make it work." He frowned. "Actually, I think it was Brice who convinced her. He hadn't wanted a child, but his advisors said it would be good for his eventual run at the governorship, and he got on board fast enough after he learned she was pregnant."

"She was happy about the baby?" Dylan asked, his mouth dry.

"Over the moon." Frank's paused, pursing his lips as if overcome by emotion. "She'd wanted one from the first moment they married. And even though she didn't believe in Brice anymore, she wanted to be the mother she never had."

"Never had?"

Frank nodded, still standing over Dylan with the manila envelope in his hands. "My wife died in childbirth when Hannah was only eight and her brother, Alex, was five. Ellie was pregnant with our second little girl."

"I'm so sorry."

Frank shrugged in the resigned manner of a man who had long ago come to terms with his loss. "We made it through. I probably worked too much, but my kids turned out well. Hannah's a teacher—or was before she married Brice. She quit to help him win his senate seat. She managed his entire campaign and still entertains all the right people." He gave Dylan a wistful smile. "She makes the best bread in Lincoln with a recipe from her mother that she perfected. Everyone at her parties talks about it. Anyway, Brice had a real shot at the governorship, but I don't know that he'll make it without her. And my son, Alex, well, he married a girl from South Africa and now works for a computer company there. We've only visited once. He took us on a nice safari."

A safari—one more connection with Hailey's make-believe family. *She was trying to remember,* Dylan realized. Maybe her memories weren't all that far away. His chest tightened at the thought, even though remembering was what she needed most.

Frank set the envelope beside Dylan and thumbed over his shoulder. "Would you like a drink? I've got scotch."

"Some water would be nice. I've got a long drive ahead of me."

"Right." Frank put ice in two glasses and retrieved a large plastic bottle from a mini fridge. He filled the glasses and handed one to Dylan.

"So what happened with the baby?" Dylan asked. He remembered Hailey's lost expression last night, and the memory tugged on him.

Frank swirled his water around in his glass. "Three weeks ago, Hannah came here for a copy of the papers to finally give to Brice. I don't know what happened between them, but she'd decided she was going through with the divorce." Frank took a long drink and shook his head. "I'm afraid I wasn't very supportive. I told her she should stay with him, and that I'd convince him to go into anger management. The next thing I know, she's calling me from the hospital, crying that Brice had done something, and she was losing the baby. That's all I know.

By the time I got there, it was all over, and she was sedated. Brice had already left." His nostrils flared. "For two weeks, I went to see her every day, but she was never awake. I even brought her a shirt I bought in Africa so she could have something besides that hospital gown while she was there."

"When you went to see her, was she tied to the bed?"

Red seeped into Frank's face, and he sank onto the other end of the couch as if his legs would no longer hold him. "Not at first, but the last couple times I went, yes. A single restrain on her right wrist—and it was chafing her skin, which told me she was pulling on it. I finally raised a fuss and demanded the doctors take the restraint off and let her come home with me, and they did take it off, but they called Brice. He had me removed from the hospital. The next day, he called to tell me Hannah had been moved for her own safety and wouldn't tell me where. That's when I hired the private investigator."

Dylan clenched his glass. "A week ago?" Hailey had gotten off the bus in Forgotten on Wednesday, which would fit the timeline if she'd gathered what she could and left.

"Right. He found out she'd left the hospital on her own. Walked right out, apparently wearing nothing but the T-shirt I'd left for her. At first, I thought she'd go to a friend's or even to my house. Losing the baby was a terrible blow, but she's a strong girl, my Hannah. But she never showed up, and we couldn't find her. She didn't have her phone or her purse or clothes or anything except her wedding ring." Frank's voice had taken on an agonized note. "She didn't come to me for help, and I don't blame her. I let her down. I should have offered to go with her to give Brice the papers, not tell her to stay with him. I should have made them release her to me right at the beginning."

"According to the news, she left the hospital on Saturday," Dylan said.

Frank snorted. "My son-in-law has more fake news created than most politicians, and that's saying a lot. When I saw that article, I thought Hannah had come home, and Brice was breaking the news about the baby belatedly to keep face or whatever."

"The newspapers didn't already know?"

"No. And that's puzzling in and of itself. I'm not sure why Brice kept that a secret. Because it certainly has people feeling sorry for him. Probably because of Hannah wanting to leave him."

Remembering what Brice had said about it not being his fault, Dylan asked, "You think he had something to do with her losing that baby?"

Frank stared at him. "I don't know. Brice has a mean temper, but physically he's as cowardly as they come. Brice said she simply went into labor. I don't know if that's true." He paused before rushing on, "So where is she? Are you going to take me to her?"

That wasn't exactly the way Dylan had thought this trip would work out. He'd wanted to gather information before presenting it to Hailey so she could decide. But here was a father who obviously cared about his daughter, even if he'd let her down.

"She's in Forgotten," Dylan said reluctantly. "Across the border in Kansas."

Breath whooshed out of Frank in one long sigh. "Forgotten?" Eyes fixed on something only he could see, Frank reached over to set his glass down on the side table. "Oh, of course."

"You know the town?"

Frank dragged his eyes back to Dylan. "My wife's originally

from Forgotten. She moved to Lincoln with her parents as a teen, but when the kids were little, we used to go down with them every year to the Spring Planting Dance." He looked away again, staring into the distance. "We were always going to buy land and build a cabin near the lake, so we could spend holidays there, but her folks died, and then . . . well, we ran out of time."

Dylan had the same feeling. He'd run out of time. His search for the truth had led him here, and now there was only one thing left. "You can come back with me," he offered. "But there's something else you should know."

Frank jumped to his feet. "What? She's not mad at me, is she? But I can fix that. Before she married that weasel, we had a good relationship."

"It's not that." Dylan wondered how he would tell the man that his daughter had no memories of him or her life before she'd shown up in Forgotten. There wasn't a way to soften the blow. "You'd better sit down again while I explain."

CHAPTER 19

When she went to the doctor's office with Charlotte, Doc Sayer—whose first name was David, though no one actually called him that—had set aside time to discuss her memory loss. Hailey was glad Charlotte stayed with her as she confided about the woman she'd seen in the mirror and the other flashes of what had to be memories.

"I think there's more," she said, tapping her fingers on the armrest of the chair where she sat in front of the doctor's desk. "I'll suddenly have a déjà vu feeling, you know. But when I try to look at it closer, it vanishes. Am I crazy?"

Doc Sayer leaned back in his chair and tented his hands on his chest. "It's not my field of study, though of course I did take a psychiatric course in med school. Memory loss can happen for many reasons that don't necessarily signal a debilitating psychotic break. Physical and emotional trauma and medication are the top contenders, all of which you likely experienced recently, especially if you lost a child."

She put her hand on her stomach. "When you say that, I feel . . . so sad."

"I'm guessing on some level, you remember what happened, but it's still too painful to deal with. The mind is a fascinating thing."

"But will I ever remember?"

"Conditions similar to yours are very rare, so it's hard to say, but generally, yes, it comes back. Even then, you may miss pieces of your memory forever, particularly the precipitating event. But the very fact that you are aware of your memory loss is already a big step. Some people like you who wake up one day and don't remember their past life aren't even aware that something is wrong. Only when faced with issues of getting ID and living as a new person do they realize something's wrong and seek help."

That made perfect sense to her. "There were times right when I first got here that I almost started to believe I was Hailey Waters. But"—she grimaced—"Dylan kept pushing me for information, and it was like I couldn't quite fit into this new person . . . or something." She shook her head. "It sounds crazy, though, because I feel like me."

"It sounds like you had a trauma," Charlotte corrected from the chair beside her, giving Hailey a gentle smile. "Not that you're crazy."

"That's right," the doctor said. "And now that you know, you can begin to process it."

"How?" Hailey wanted to know.

Doc Sayer studied her without speaking for a long moment before leaning forward to rest his hands on his desk. "To be honest, I really don't know. But to start with, you can explore how you feel about what you do know. If you brought anything with you, examining it might jog memories as well. Sometimes memories come back suddenly while other times they're slower to return."

"Or maybe they never come back?"

"It is possible." The reluctance in his voice was clear. "I was reading an article only this morning about a man who remembered after thirty years."

A flutter of panic rose in her at that idea. How could she build a life like that?

"Don't worry too much," Doc said. "There are psychiatric methods you can pursue, but I really think it'll come back when you're ready. Being physically well is a great first step."

"I feel ready now." It wasn't quite true.

He smiled and said kindly, "Maybe you need a stimulus, something to jolt you back. The police might be able to locate someone from your former life."

You mean like my baby? Hailey wanted to say but didn't. That wasn't fair to these people who had been so kind to a stranger. She also didn't say it because if her voice had somehow managed to form the words, she was almost certain she'd break down and cry.

"I did have some things with me when I came to town," she said instead. "In a backpack."

"There you go." Doc Sayer glanced at the wall clock, but he didn't excuse himself. "You should examine those for clues. Maybe you'll remember something."

"I'll try." Hailey had already been over the backpack, but maybe now that she knew part of the truth, she could view everything with new eyes. Or was it possible her mind had purposefully overlooked something to protect herself? From what the doctor had explained, it seemed possible.

"Meanwhile, your tests look perfect," Doc continued. "And there's no reason you can't return to all your regular activities within a day or two. But take it easy until then."

"That means no working in the café," Charlotte clarified. "So don't even think about it."

Hailey had been considering that. "Okay, but I do feel much better."

Doc smiled. "Then you can take short walks. Sit up and watch TV. Easy stuff. But don't tire yourself out. Sleep as much as you can, and eat well. Let us know immediately if your cramps worsen or you develop a fever." He glanced again at the clock. "Do you have any other questions?"

It was kind of him to ask when he so obviously had a paying customer waiting to see him. "No. But thank you so much. You saved my life."

"Oh, no. Maggie and Charlotte are the ones you should thank. I was doing my job. They went above and beyond."

Hailey nodded. "They did." She'd already thanked Charlotte profusely on the way, but the midwife had been every bit as willing to pass the credit to Maggie and the doctor. Hailey was beginning to feel like a town project, but in a comforting way. Almost as if she belonged.

"Come on," Charlotte said. "I'll get you back to the café."

A short time later, Hailey waved goodbye to Charlotte and made her way to the back door of the café. She didn't feel like going upstairs. Instead, she found herself longing for a little company. Normal company. Her thoughts strayed to Dylan. He'd said he'd check in on her when he could, but there was nothing she could do to hurry that up. She could show up at

Dylan's clinic on the pretense of visiting Sable, but the idea of walking there was too daunting. She'd felt energetic when she woke, but she was quickly flagging. She really needed to get a phone.

Of course, she probably had a phone somewhere with all her other personal belongings. That made her smile. Yeah, she had one. But where?

Considering this, she walked up to the bar to find Maggie cleaning the coffee machine. Besides one table of customers that Keisha was helping, the Butter Cake was nearly deserted.

"How'd it go?" Maggie set down her rag and came to lean on the counter opposite her.

"My numbers are good." Hailey pulled herself up on a barstool across from Maggie. "I'm dragging a little right now, but I'm okay. Thanks to you."

Maggie laughed. "You're welcome. Oh, I have something for you." She spun around and retrieved a tray with a wrapped sandwich, a bowl of fruit pieces, a slice of gooey butter cake, and a steaming cup of tea. "It's herbal tea. So you can still take a nap after. And I've wrapped the sandwich for later, in case you're still too full from lunch to eat it now."

"But how did you know I'd be back now?"

"Charlotte texted me before you left the doctor's office. I was going to take it up to you, but since you're here . . ."

"Thanks." Hailey speared a slice of strawberry. "I'm sorry I let you down. I can pay for this week, though. I have a little money."

Maggie waved it aside. "I'm not worried about you taking a few days. You'll be right as rain in no time, and I'll have my new employee back. I'm planning to take a few afternoons off after that." She smiled. "Besides, I'm a firm believer in what goes around comes around, so even if you don't end up staying in town, I'm okay with that. I'm your friend."

Emotion rose in Hailey's heart, sparking tears, which she tried to swallow with her strawberry. "I plan to stay, but I . . ." She shrugged. "I don't know what I'm going to remember."

"I know." Maggie touched her hand. "You're welcome to sit here or take it upstairs. I left a few DVDs outside your door, and in case you didn't know, I have two online streaming channels you can choose from."

"That sounds great." With all the pressure today, Hailey thought maybe a good love story was exactly what she needed, the sappier the better. As long as it had a happy ending.

"Want me to carry it up for you?" Maggie asked.

"No. I got it." Hailey stood and pulled the tray toward her.

"Oh, I almost forgot. Dylan came by while you were gone. Said he was heading out of town and wanted to stop and say hi. He'll be gone awhile, but he'll stop by when he gets back if it's not too late."

Hailey felt both excited and embarrassed at the prospect of seeing him. "How late is too late, do you think?"

Maggie shrugged. "If you go to bed and don't want to be disturbed, let me know and I'll make sure he gets the message."

Hailey hesitated. "So, does he know? About why I needed surgery?"

"Not exactly, I don't think. But he's not a dummy. You should tell him the truth."

Hailey nodded. She only wished she knew the whole truth herself.

Hailey sat at one of the outside tables on the side of Maggie's café, staring at her backpack. It was after eight, and the sun was low in the horizon as twilight crept over Forgotten. The café was closed, and the only noise she'd heard when leaving her room was the television from Maggie's suite.

Hailey hadn't meant to sleep the rest of the day, but she had, and now it was time to start figuring things out. One by one, she removed the items from her backpack and laid them out on the table, from the oversized black T-shirt to the toiletries. She also set out the hundred-dollar bills and the tan money belt.

She wished Dylan were here to go over the items with her, but maybe it was better this way in case she had a sudden memory flash. After setting everything out, she checked all the pockets and zippers and the lining of the backpack. Nothing there, and no seams that looked unusual.

Slowly, one at a time so she wouldn't miss anything, she picked up each item. The toiletries meant nothing to her, but now that she looked at them more closely, she realized they were generic and probably inexpensive. *Like sample sizes they might give to patients at a hospital.* She felt a pang at the thought, but it made sense since she'd likely gone to a hospital because of the baby.

Even if the toiletries had come from a hospital, she wouldn't know which hospital, so she set those aside. Next, she examined the lion T-shirt. It was ridiculously big for her, and she'd never wear it except for something to sleep in—or for midwifing puppies—but she felt a reluctance to throw it away.

This is important then, she thought.

The world stuttered, and for a bright second, she looked out over a tundra at a pride of lions. The flash happened so quickly, she couldn't see it clearly, but it made her remember the story she'd made up about her father with Dylan. She smiled and held the shirt to her face, breathing in the scent. No memories in that, but she'd washed it here.

The shiny red gym shorts, though her size, were a complete mystery and a fashion mistake. The plastic water bottle held no clues and could probably be purchased in thousands of different stores. The yellow summer dress, while bright, was obviously cheap and hadn't held up well to being washed in Maggie's machine. She could have bought that anywhere. The remaining cash from the pocket in the backpack also wasn't hiding any clues. That left only the money belt with the ten thousand dollars.

Maybe something was hidden between the bills. She counted the money from the belt slowly, making sure the stiff bills weren't sticking together. Nothing. She tried the second zipper of the money belt that appeared to be large enough for a driver's license or other small ID. Still nothing. Her fingers crumpled the material, getting ready to throw it in frustration . . . and then she saw something else. It was another slot, running the entire length of the material but without a zipper. Just a very tight pocket behind the one with bills. And it rattled slightly.

Hands shaking with excitement, she pulled out a thin, folded paper. Unfolding it, she stared. A ticket, not for a bus, but from a jewelry shop. *Item sold,* it read. *One diamond wedding ring.* The price tag was ten thousand and five hundred dollars.

She drew in a breath as the face of a suited man with a huge belly and a kind smile fractured her current reality. "I'll keep it for a month," he said, leaning toward her, "before I resell it. But you know it's worth ten times this, so it's better that you come back. There are better ways to get rid of a wedding ring you no longer need."

The memory vanished, and Hailey laughed out loud. "I didn't steal it!"

The next thought made her gasp. *Wedding ring?*

But she was too excited to remain depressed for long. The address was in Lincoln, Nebraska. That wasn't far. Now she had a place to start. And enough money that was really hers to help her retrace her steps.

Her throat suddenly felt dry. Was she ready?

She considered everything she'd gone through, especially finding out that she'd had a child. The ache in her chest told her it hadn't ended well. Could she deal with it?

Yes.

And then what? She didn't want to leave Forgotten. Not Maggie or Charlotte, or the cranky old customers at the café who flirted with her and left her big tips. And especially not Dylan. She wanted to wear her new dress to the Spring Planting Dance. She sat there thinking and staring at the paper as the sun dipped beneath the horizon.

She heard the vehicle before she saw the lights, and as she recognized Dylan's Tahoe pulling into the back parking lot, a flutter of excitement and also a little sadness zipped through her.

He waved as he stepped from the vehicle, hurrying toward her. "Hey."

"Hey." She wanted to throw herself in his arms, but she felt suddenly shy as she stood to meet him.

He put both hands on her shoulders, squeezing softly as he stared down into her face. "How are you feeling?"

"Great." A tiny laugh escaped her as she shoved the receipt at him. "Look, I didn't steal the money. And it's a clue. I think I might be from Lincoln."

Was that a shadow passing over his face? He released her to take the paper, but he didn't look at it. "I think so too." His dark eyes held hers, asking a question she couldn't answer because she didn't know what it meant.

He swallowed hard and started speaking again. "I have a friend who did a little digging for me. You know that picture I took of you at Joni's Dress Shop? Well, I sent him that, and he . . ."

Hailey stopped listening as a figure came from the parking lot behind him. Why hadn't she noticed the other car pulling up next to Dylan's? If it had been there this whole time, the man inside it hadn't chosen to come out until now.

Dylan stopped talking and turned to see the man. He gave a grunt of frustration and raised his voice to say, "I told you to wait until—"

"Dad?" the word shot from Hailey. Memories flooded her. This man was her father. Her father, who had gone with her to visit her brother in Africa and bought the black T-shirt. The heartbroken man who had held their hands so tightly at their mother's graveside so long ago.

She gasped, pulling away from Dylan to run toward him. "Dad!"

He enveloped her in a hug. "Hannah, baby. I'm so sorry."

"It's okay. I'm okay." And she was. She didn't remember all of it. The hospital was hazy, but the fight with Brice was vivid. As was her fear of him and what had happened next.

"Did Brice hurt you?" her dad demanded. "So help me, I'll kill him."

She tilted her head, searching the new flood of memories. "I gave him the papers at his office. We fought. He said horrible things, and I threatened to tell the media about his affairs. He followed me outside, tried to stop me from leaving. He grabbed my arm hard. I pulled away and stumbled into the road. There was an SUV coming toward me. I jumped back and it went by. I was safe. But there was a man on a bicycle coming fast. I didn't see him—until it was too late." A sob escaped her throat, raw and aching. "Dad, I lost my baby."

Her father held her tightly, his hand rubbing her head as he had when she'd been a child, pressing her tearstained face into his chest. "I know. You don't have to say any more."

So she didn't. She could handle what had happened now, but that didn't mean she had to talk about it. Not yet, not here. She drew away, and her father let her go. He bent over to scoop up a manila envelope from the ground.

"We stopped and got these signed," he said. "Brice agreed to everything. I told him I'd go to the media if he didn't. All I have to do is file the papers. I should have done it for you before." Tears skidded down his cheeks. "Will you forgive me?"

"If you'll forgive me for running away."

Her dad looked around them. "Forgotten. Of all places."

"Mom's place." She nodded, a fresh batch of tears spilling from her eyes.

"Can I take you home now?"

She thought about that. "I don't want to leave."

"There are things you need to do."

"I know."

She turned and saw Dylan watching them, the lion T-shirt in his hands. She took her dad's hand and pulled him over to the table. "It's my dad," she said.

"We already met." His tone was teasing, but his smile didn't quite reach his eyes that glittered with unshed tears.

"I know, but now *I* remember." She stared into his face, wishing she could kiss the sadness from it. "Thanks to you."

He lifted one shoulder in a shrug. "You're leaving, aren't you?"

She nodded, tears skidding down her face. "For a while." She grabbed his hands, holding them through the black T-shirt. "Why don't you keep this for me until I come back?"

And then she did kiss him, wishing it would never end.

But it did.

CHAPTER 20

ntil I come back. The words Hailey—no, he had to remember that she was Hannah now—had spoken had reverberated in Dylan's head hourly since she'd left Tuesday night. He'd chatted over text with her in the three and a half days since. They'd talked about Sable and adopting one of the pups, the work on his house, the café, and even the weather, but nothing about when she was coming back.

If she was coming back.

Dylan knew she might have changed her mind about filing the divorce papers. Or that now with her returned memories, her life in Lincoln might be far more appealing than a small, backwater town. She had a father to think about, and there were probably friends as well. The possibilities haunted him. What if she never came back?

"I think it's time to make the announcement," Maggie said, touching his elbow. She handed him a piece of paper. "Here's the Singles Mix winners' list. The Ladies Auxiliary just closed the bidding."

Dylan nodded, glancing briefly at the first of the two pages. There were three columns, one with the number and the title of the baked good, followed by the man who had bid the most for the item, and then the name of the woman who'd brought it. The men, of course, had bid on the baked goods without knowing the identity of the woman behind the food, and the reveal was always something he'd looked forward to in the past. Now he regretted volunteering. He didn't want to be here at the Spring Planting Dance. He wanted to be in Lincoln.

His gaze swung toward the raised dance floor that he and the other men had spent most of the morning erecting. On a connected stage, Mayor Campbell was reminding everyone to use the trash cans that had been conveniently set up around the fairgrounds. They were only an hour into the dance, so they'd hear that announcement at least five more times before midnight.

"If I win your bread, you're not going to make me dance, are you?" His question for Maggie was more of a growl. At her urging, Dylan had bid for a loaf of bread that had still been steaming at the beginning of the dance. He loved her bread and was happy to do it, but he didn't feel like dancing.

She smiled. "Oh, you won, and that loaf of bread was worth every penny, but I'll leave the dancing decision up to you."

She was about to walk off when he said, "What if she doesn't come back?" He hadn't meant to ask, but the words somehow slipped out.

Maggie put both hands on her hips. "Well, her dad paid me for two weeks rent, but I suppose if she doesn't come back, I'll have to hire a new employee." She smirked at him. "It's kind of your fault, you know."

"I did it for her. Besides, it was only a matter of time until she remembered."

"I know. Still, you should try to have fun tonight."

The comment worsened his mood. "I'd go home now if I didn't have to help clean up." He tapped the paper with the fingers of his other hand. "Or read this."

She smiled. "It'd be a shame not to dance at least once. You'll change your mind."

He probably would. He'd owe her two dances because of the bread, and he wasn't the kind to leave a woman hanging. Last year, he'd danced with a sixty-something widow, and they'd had fun. He was glad it was Maggie, at least, so she'd understand why he wasn't quite himself.

"Fine," he muttered. "I'll dance." Turning on his heel, he strode to the dance floor.

The mayor saw him coming and said, "It looks like the hour of bidding is over. Dylan Morgan, our own veterinarian and fourth great-grandson of Forgotten's founding couple, will now read the results of the Singles Mix."

Dylan climbed onto the stage and took the microphone. "Thank you," he said, forcing a joviality he didn't feel. "Is everyone having fun?" Cheers resounded from the audience. "Now I know the bidding for the Singles Mix has been hot and heavy over the last hour—well, actually a good hour or so before as well, while we finished setting up. As you know, there weren't only cakes this year, and we had a lot more entrants. I've heard that some of our single ladies submitted several entries. And that's okay because some of our single men out there have won more than one item. That gives them all more chances to find the right match—though maybe it says something special if the same man buys two items from the same woman!" More laughter accompanied this comment. "Along with the other charitable events here tonight, the proceeds, of course, will go toward paying for next year's dance. So thank you!"

Preliminaries out of the way, he glanced down at the paper in his left hand. "Okay, our first entrant is Very Berry Pie. The winner of that is Jeremy Wilson." Everyone clapped. "Don't eat that all in one sitting, Jeremy," Dylan quipped. "And the lovely lady who made that pie is Ayleen Jenkins. Jeremy, you can pick up your pie any time tonight at the Singles Mix booth, and we hope you two enjoy your dances." More clapping, accompanied by a few hoots and hollers.

"Next we have Traditional Chocolate Cake . . ."

He'd read through the first page before he found the bread he'd bid on at the top of the second page that had only a few remaining winners. "The next item is Hot Stuff Bread, and believe me, this bread was steaming when I bid for it, that's for sure. And it looks like I won!" He grinned at the audience, who rewarded him with whistles and catcalls. "And the very lucky woman who is going to dance with me is . . ." A few good-natured jeers accompanied this quip.

When he glanced down at the paper to finish his sentence, Dylan expected to see Maggie's name. But the name that jumped out at him was Hailey Waters. He stared, unable to believe what he was seeing. His eyes jumped from the paper to the crowd on the dance floor below him, searching. He saw Maggie's mocking stare and Jeremy's smirk as he obviously expected Dylan to say the name of a widow in town or maybe a preteen girl. Dylan ignored all of them.

There she was, dressed in the gauzy pink dress with capped sleeves from Joni's Dress Shop. The full skirt whished as she walked toward the stage, angling around the people separating them. Of all the amazing clothes she must own as the hope-fully former wife of a state senator, she'd chosen the dress she'd bought with him. Did that mean something?

His heart thudded wildly as he pushed the microphone and papers into the hands of the confused mayor before jumping off the stage. He strode forward, hurrying to meet her, and the crowd parted in front of him, curious now at what he was up to. He stopped about a foot away from her, wanting to sweep her up in his arms but not knowing how she might react. Brice Granville was a snake and a liar, but he knew how to charm a woman—and they shared a past Dylan couldn't touch. Had she gone back to him? Was she here only to say goodbye?

"Hi," she said, lowering her eyes shyly, then blinking up at him in an amazingly seductive way that made him want to kiss her. She extended a hand. "I'm Hannah. Hannah Waterford."

Her maiden name, he thought, hope shooting through him. He took her hand, and her flesh felt so good, so right against his.

"Hi, Hannah. I'm Dylan." He closed the space between them and pulled her up into his arms, right in front of the entire town, spinning her around and burying his face in her sweet-smelling hair. Whistles, catcalls, and clapping filled the air.

"Well, that's an incredibly happy result," the mayor's voice boomed over the microphone. "See how great the Singles Mix is for our singles? But let's go on. We have only two more winners to announce. Come on, all eyes up here." People shifted their attention back to the stage.

Dylan had eyes only for Hannah. He put her down and took her hand, leading her to the edge of the dance floor, where long benches, bolted to the floor itself, were set up so people could sit and watch the dancers. It was only slightly less noisy, but it would have to do.

"When did you get back?" he asked, pulling her down with him onto a bench.

"This afternoon. I was going to surprise you earlier, but then Maggie and I came up with the bread idea."

"She'd said I'd dance."

Hannah laughed. "I think she enjoyed this as much as I did. I was also late getting here because I had a little issue unhooking my car from the moving van."

"Moving van?" Dared he hope?

"I figured it out, but I ended up walking half the way here with the bread because by then I was sure there wasn't a parking space left. Luckily, Maggie came to see what was taking me so long and gave me a ride. She had orange cones saving her space."

"Smart woman." He waited a breath before adding, "So, how are you?"

"I'm good."

"And your memory?" Their knees were touching, and it felt so right.

Her smile was wistful. "I remember everything except large sections of the days I spent in the hospital. Probably because of the sedation. Even the memory of leaving it is foggy. Though I apparently bought my yellow dress and some red shorts in their gift shop on my way out. But I'm okay, really. I'll be seeing a therapist in Lincoln for a while, but it's mostly so my dad's happy. He wants to be sure I'll visit."

That had to mean she was staying here! Dylan was sure his grin was obscenely wide, but he didn't care.

"Looks like I won your bread," he said, standing up from the bench and extending his hand to help her up. "Do you want to dance?"

Her grin widened. "There's no music."

"No? Because I'm definitely hearing music." He was trying to be flirtatious and hoped she didn't notice the catch in his voice.

She twisted her body side to side, swishing her dress. "Well, according to Joni's, this is the perfect dance dress. I'd hate for it to go to waste. So yes, let's dance."

She stepped into his arms as the music began again with a soft ballad. Though it was likely intended for all the Singles Mix participants, Dylan felt as if the music was only for them.

Dylan's reaction was all Hannah had hoped for, and she gave herself up to the dancing. She'd had a busy week, filing her divorce, claiming her wedding ring and putting it up for a proper sale, and moving all her things from Brice's house. She took her car, the furniture she'd chosen, and the nice settlement her dad had suggested instead of alimony for the five years she'd worked on Brice's career. Brice, of course, had tried to dissuade her, but she'd already learned the hard way that he would never be faithful and that waiting would only cause them both more heartache. She no longer cared about his career or believed he wanted to help anyone except himself. Standing up to him hadn't been a problem, especially with her father at her side.

Now, she was finally back in Forgotten, dancing with a man she was almost sure she loved. No one had ever looked at her the way he was looking at her now.

They danced five times before taking a break to buy snacks. Dylan won her a stuffed bear at a carnival booth, and Hannah managed to douse a laughing Keisha, who was taking a stint in a dunking booth. Together, Hannah and Dylan manned the community food booth for half an hour, where they shared two pieces of Ronica's Kansas dirt cake.

The night was magical, more so now because Hannah had the memories of being here with her parents and her brother. "We have to eat cotton candy!" she said, pulling Dylan to the long line waiting for the treat.

When they returned to the dance floor, darkness had already fallen. Dylan was a marvelous dancer, and it felt as though their bodies were made for each other. But he hadn't kissed her yet, so she wasn't sure. Maybe she was reading him all wrong.

A tapping on her shoulder made her turn. A big, sixty-something, red-faced man in jeans and a flannel shirt stood there grinning at her. At first Hannah thought he was trying to cut in, but a diminutive blond woman next to him nixed that idea.

"Hello," the man said. "I'm Chief Caleb McColl, and this is my wife Natalie. We hear you were midwife to Sable and our puppies."

Hannah laughed and shook his hand. "Oh, I only assisted. Dylan here did most of what needed to be done."

"Well, we're so happy it all went well," Natalie said, smiling. "We're saving little Pebbles for you like Dylan asked, if you're sure you want her."

"I do!" There was no reason at all Hannah should cry about that, but tears sprang to her eyes nonetheless.

"Then she's yours," said Chief McColl. "We can't keep all of them." He gave his wife a stare.

"Yeah, but I get two." Natalie punched her husband with a playful blow. "And all the others have been claimed as well, so we're good. My, but that dress looks great on you."

"Thank you," Hannah said.

"I don't know if I told you that she owns Joni's Dress Shop," Dylan put in, squeezing her hand.

"That's right, and you probably don't know this either, but my younger daughter designed your dress. I did the actual sewing."

"I love it." Hannah released Dylan's hand to spin for them. "It's perfect for dancing. I hope to buy many more at your shop."

"You're staying in town then?" Natalie asked, her smile widening. "Because we have a lot of folks who only come in for the dance."

Hannah had been one of those folks once. No longer. "I'm here to stay." She didn't know for how long, but she needed this town, and she hoped Dylan would become a permanent part of that. Did he feel the same way about her?

The song ended and another began. Dylan nodded at the McColls and pulled her away into the middle of the dancers. "Don't look now, but Jeremy Wilson is coming this way."

"I promised him a dance," she said.

"Maybe so, but not this one."

She laughed. "What's so special about this one?"

He glanced at his watch. "You'll know in a minute." He swung her around—even further away from Jeremy Wilson.

The world melted away until there were only the two of them. This, Hannah knew, was right where she belonged—in Forgotten and especially in Dylan's arms.

"Almost time, folks," whispered a soft voice into the microphone, barely above the music. Hannah wasn't sure she'd actually heard the voice until Dylan slowed and tightened his arms around her.

"Ten, nine, eight . . ." the voice continued, accompanied now by people in the audience.

"I love you, Hannah Waterford," Dylan said as the count-down continued. "With all that I am."

He leaned over and kissed her. It was a soul-binding, earth-shattering, mind-healing kiss that answered all her questions and promised so much more. At that moment, she heard a clock somewhere in the town strike midnight.

The town legend, she thought.

She was laughing and crying all at once. "I love you too, Dylan Morgan." She wrapped her arms around his neck as he kissed her again.

They didn't stop kissing for a very long time.

achel Branton has worked in publishing for over thirty years. She loves writing women's fiction and traveling, and she hopes to write and travel a lot more. As a mother of six great kids and with a growing number of grandchildren, it's not easy to find time to write, but the semi-ordered chaos of her life gives her a constant source of writing material. She's been known to wear pajamas all day when working on a deadline, and is often distracted enough to burn dinner—well, when she remembers to cook it. She lives in central Florida and loves going to the beach with her husband, hanging out with her grandchildren, and riding very tall rollercoasters.

Under the name Rachel Branton, she writes romance, romantic suspense, and women's fiction. Rachel also writes urban fantasy, paranormal romance, and science fiction under the name Teyla Branton. For more information or to sign up to hear about new releases, please visit www.RachelBranton.com